Dragons of

Dwakka

Umbrillo

Abruq

Silver Batal and the Water Dragon Races

Silver Batal and the Water Dragon Races

K. D. HALBROOK

HENRY HOLT AND COMPANY
NEW YORK

Henry Holt and Company, *Publishers since 1866*
Henry Holt® is a registered trademark of Macmillan Publishing Group, LLC
175 Fifth Avenue, New York, NY 10010 • mackids.com

Library of Congress Cataloging-in-Publication Data
Names: Halbrook, Kristin, author.
Title: Silver Batal and the water dragon races / K. D. Halbrook.
Description: First edition. | New York : Henry Holt and Company, 2019. | Series: Silver Batal | Summary: Silver Batal, a young desert-dweller, dreams of becoming a water dragon racer, and when she befriends a rare dragon that can swim and fly, she may just get her chance.
Identifiers: LCCN 2018038287 | ISBN 978-1-250-18107-7 (hardcover) | ISBN 978-1-250-18108-4 (eBook)
Subjects: | CYAC: Dragons—Fiction. | Adventure and adventurers—Fiction. | Family life—Fiction. | Fantasy.
Classification: LCC PZ7.H12837 Sill 2019 | DDC [Fic]—dc23
LC record available at https://lccn.loc.gov/2018038287

First edition, 2019 / Designed by Liz Dresner
Printed in the United States of America by LSC Communications, Harrisonburg, Virginia
10 9 8 7 6 5 4 3 2 1

Silver Batal and the Water Dragon Races

One

When the dust in the cliff-hewn city of Jaspaton got too thick and the wind too whipping, even the most ancient and stalwart of the yarns-ladies would leave their colorful silk tents and go indoors. And when they went indoors, so did everyone else.

Everyone sensible, at least.

On such a day, Silver Batal raced down one flight of stone stairs, and then another and another, refusing to let the trader on the desert floor out of her sight.

"Don't go yet," Silver shouted, spitting strands of hair from her mouth. The winds carried her words in the wrong direction.

The trader rolled the side flaps of his wagon down and struggled against the weather to secure them. He shook his fist angrily at the sky, but Silver laughed. His struggles bought her more time to catch him.

"Silver!" At the communal bread oven, her cousin Brajon called her name.

"Can't stop!" Silver leaped over a chicken flapping its wings furiously to keep from blowing away. The leather bag holding Silver's letter bounced against her hip.

"I have news for you," Brajon said. "About you-know-who!"

At that, Silver hesitated, and her ankles twisted in different directions. She lurched forward, catching herself just before she would have hurtled down another set of stairs headfirst. But her bag continued swinging forward, spilling its contents down one level of Jaspaton.

"I'll get it," Brajon said. He ran, grabbing the chicken and clutching it to his chest along the way, and gracefully dashed down the steps.

"Ba*wack*!" the chicken squawked in protest.

Brajon scooped up the jewelers' tools, the paper-wrapped candies, and the coins Silver kept in her bag. Someone else, though, reached the letter first.

Nebekker, one of the most ancient of the yarnsladies—and certainly the most mysterious—slowly picked up the parchment and scanned it.

Silver tapped down the stairs in her soft boots and held out her hand. "Thank you," she said.

Nebekker kept reading, and Silver ground her toe into the dusty step impatiently. In Jaspaton, everyone treated the elderly with reverence, but Silver hated the way the old woman was casually reading the letter. No respect for privacy!

As she waited for Nebekker to finish snooping, Silver moved to one of the stone overlooks and leaned against the copper railing, peering down. The trader's flaps were secured, and now he was trying to calm his herd animals. And for good reason—no Jaspatonian would ever be caught out in the vast desert in such a storm.

Brajon appeared next to Silver and dumped her belongings

back into her bag, plus a good fistful of dust. "I think that's everything."

"Almost everything." Silver motioned to Nebekker.

"Is that a letter to—"

Silver nodded quickly.

To Sagittaria Wonder, the best and most brilliant Desert Nations water dragon racer in the whole world. Silver's hero.

Brajon shrugged and shifted the chicken, who was trying to stick its head down his tunic. "You can tell her everything in person when she comes to Jaspaton in two weeks."

Silver's heart thumped so hard she was sure it could be heard over the whole desert.

"She's coming *here*? Why?" Silver glanced over her shoulder. The trader was climbing into his wagon and pulling his scarf over his face.

"You know that really thick seam of gold we discovered a week ago?"

Silver rolled her eyes. Brajon said *we* as though he were already a full-fledged miner, not an ele-miner. "Yes, of course," she said, "but what does that have to do with Sagittaria?"

"Just today, Sormy Mohan said"—Brajon cleared his throat and lowered his voice to mimic the grizzly old head miner—"'the queen's coming from Calidia to look at our gold. She's bringing that dragon racer, too. They need a design for some kind of racing cup.'"

Silver clutched her cousin's shoulders. "You mean Sagittaria Wonder is really coming?"

"That's what I heard." Brajon wriggled out of Silver's grip.

Silver pulled a stick of charcoal from her bag. Her breath came fast. Sagittaria Wonder was the champion, the legend, the *best ever*. "If I could just get my letter back from Nebekker,

I could add one more line . . . tell her I'm desperate to meet her."

The water dragon racer coming to her old, dusty city—it seemed impossible. After all, there wasn't a single body of surface water near Jaspaton, not even one measly stream. But she *was* coming, and it could be Silver's opportunity to seize her dream. What if Silver could somehow convince her parents to let her see Sagittaria? And Silver could convince Sagittaria to take a certain hopeful racer back to the city of Calidia? She would do anything to learn from the greatest water dragon racer in the world. Feed Sagittaria's dragons. Shine their scales. Sweep the floors. Shovel dragon dung, smiling the whole time. She would be the most obedient squire ever.

And then, someday, *she* would become the new greatest water dragon racer the world had ever known.

Down on the desert floor, a wagon flap had come loose, and the trader was shouting at the winds. Silver's heartbeat quickened. There was still time. "Nebekker, please. My letter."

The old woman startled, as though she'd fallen asleep while reading.

"How often do you write these fan letters?" Nebekker said, sounding disgruntled.

"Whenever there's a trader headed to Calidia," Silver said. Like *now*, she wanted to say. But she kept her mouth shut. Not even urgency could make her be rude to an elder.

"For the past two years," Brajon piped up.

"Gawp glop," the chicken added.

"And how many times have you told her about"—Nebekker pointed to a line—"'the strange old yarnslady from no one knows where'?"

"Never! I mean, only this once." Silver's face flushed. "I've already told her about everyone else I know, so that's . . . you're . . . all that was left."

Nebekker looked at Silver for a long time. The old woman's eyes were green. Opaque, like jade. Different from the glittering brown quartz eyes that most people in Jaspaton had. When Nebekker's stare became too uncomfortable to hold, Silver dropped her gaze.

"I'm sorry I called you strange," Silver whispered.

Brajon couldn't keep back a snort. Silver nudged him hard and peeked up through her lashes, but even Nebekker's eyes flashed with amusement before growing solemn again.

"I know a way you could get Sagittaria Wonder's attention," Nebekker said. "And it's not with these silly fan letters." Without waiting for a response, the old woman swept down the road.

A delicious chill raced down Silver's back. A strong wind whipped her clothing and sent spirals of dust into the air. Without thinking, she raced after the old yarnslady. "What do you mean?" she asked breathlessly as she caught up.

"Come see me this evening, after the last lantern is lit. I'll teach you what you need to know. I'll show you how to make a water dragon racing suit to impress even the great Sagittaria Wonder."

Silver's mouth dropped open. "You know how to make riding suits?"

"Soon you will, too." Nebekker disappeared up a shadowy staircase.

There was a victorious cry from the desert floor. The trader was finally on his way, but Silver no longer cared. She dropped her letter in the dirt and spun in a circle, her grin as big as the whole desert. The chicken, finally free from Brajon's clutches, dove past her into an alley.

"Did you hear that, cousin? I might soon be on my way to Calidia!"

"You think? Nebekker's not exactly a cuddly old grandma helping everyone out of the goodness of her heart." Brajon wiggled his fingers at Silver. "Ooo, maybe she's secretly a magical crone who's going to—"

"Imprison me and force me to weave for her forever?" Silver laughed. That was the plot of an ancient desert fable. But Nebekker wasn't an old mystic, and this was real life, not a story.

Silver went to the overlook again and curled her hands around the railing. In the vast desert, the storm began to settle and a new landscape of dunes took shape. Somewhere, far on the other side of those golden hills, the water dragons that swam in the Royal Pools of Calidia waited for Silver Batal.

Two

That evening, Silver snuck out while the stars still dotted the desert sky, creeping down roads that were empty save for a desert beetle scuttling across the toes of her boots.

When she reached Nebekker's house, she hesitated, hand raised. Brajon's remark clouded her thoughts. Could the old woman really help Silver impress Sagittaria Wonder?

Nebekker was from far away, but where, exactly, no one seemed to know. She had simply shown up in Jaspaton one day, many years before Silver was born, emerging from the desert with only a walking stick and a small pack on her back. Some said she'd been raised by nomads in the far reaches of the vast desert, while others claimed she was from Calidia. If that were true, Silver couldn't understand why she'd leave the excitement of the royal city to come here. Either way, Silver had never seen evidence that Nebekker knew anything about water dragon racing.

Before Silver could make up her mind to either turn back or knock, the door was flung open.

"I thought I heard someone out there," Nebekker said. "Don't just stand there gaping. You're letting dust in."

Nebekker ushered Silver inside. The house was small and shadowy, for there was only one candle burning on the low table in the center of the main room. Shelves lined the walls. They were covered with oiled wood boxes and milky marble bowls. Sparkling glass canisters and beaded clay urns.

Exotic smells that reminded Silver of the traders from afar hit her nose. Floral scents, like the perfumes the yarnsladies sometimes accepted in exchange for their blankets and rugs. Damp smells, like in the inks they imported to dye the wool yarns.

Silver gasped when she caught sight of a wooden jug inlaid with a mother-of-pearl water dragon. Her fingers itched to pick up the container and explore its contents.

"Sit." Nebekker pointed to the cushions around the table. She pulled a pitcher down from a shelf, and Silver strained her eyes in the dark to see what strange and foreign concoction it contained. But when Nebekker poured a glass and set it in front of her, she discovered it was only plain, cold succulent tea.

Nebekker sat across from her. "So, you love water dragons, hmm? They are very interesting creatures."

"You love them, too?" It felt like dune beetles were scurrying inside Silver's belly.

"Ah. Hmm." Nebekker peered through the dim circle of candlelight at Silver. "You seem surprised. You young ones always forget that we old ones were young once, too. We had parents who disapproved. We had hopes. We were rebellious." She laughed. "Maybe you're right to distrust us. Too many of us old ones forget what it's like to be young. To have dreams!"

Someone who understood! Silver wanted to tell Nebekker everything. How important it was that her hero was coming to town. How her parents—and everyone in Jaspaton, really—couldn't comprehend her. How she would give anything to race a water dragon.

Silver swallowed thickly so all her secrets wouldn't come tumbling out at once.

"You said that you would teach me how to weave a racing suit," she said.

"I did." Nebekker nodded. She pushed her tea away and took up a bit of wool. "But now I'm not so sure. I've seen you around. You're headstrong. You rush things. Your thoughts are too far away to focus. You have no patience and little respect."

"That's not true," Silver cried, then quickly lowered her voice.

"It is, and the whole city knows it, ele-jeweler."

Silver winced at the traditional Jaspatonian diminutive—*ele,* meaning "one who belongs to a trade."

"I'll do anything. I'll be patient and work hard and—"

"What do you know about water dragons?" Nebekker said.

"Everything! The Shorsa is the breed with the most wins, but Sagittaria Wonder races on a Dwakka and hasn't lost in two years, except for the World Cup, which the Island Nations have held for the past five years and—"

"So you know something about the races, but I asked about water dragons."

Silver lowered her eyes. The walls in her room were covered with charcoal drawings on parchment of water dragons and their riders. The dragons were brought from hundreds and thousands of miles away, by traveling traders and scouts, for the royal families and wealthy merchants across the desert and beyond. Articles about the great water dragon races—who attended, who won, who perished—surrounded the pictures. Silver's own writing was also on the wall. She'd created diagrams and fact sheets about every type of water dragon she'd ever heard about. The fat, bubblelike Floatillion, whose green skin was as smooth as stretched fabric. The two-headed Dwakka, with one always-smiling face and one sinister face. The tiny Shorsa, almost too small and upright to be ridden, but as fast as a desert wind.

"I know so many things," Silver said, her gaze drifting to the water dragon jug. "But I want to learn *everything*."

"Then Calidia is a good place for you." Nebekker gave her a shrewd look, then sighed deeply. Silver fought a smile. It seemed that she had convinced the grouchy elder.

"Did you know that this wool, when worked tightly with thin strands, is light but also water-repellent?" Nebekker said. "Both admirable qualities for a water dragon racing suit."

Silver touched the wool. "How do you know all this?"

"I, too, once wanted to learn everything. But there isn't time to talk about that. We have to work quickly. We'll use you as the model."

Nebekker told Silver to stand, then took her measurements. She lay parchment on the table, and Silver watched, mesmerized, as Nebekker brainstormed a pattern, made up of hundreds of individual scales pieced together. As night shifted to morning, Nebekker showed Silver a way to work the wool that was different from the traditional Jaspatonian methods. A way that created lighter fabric with tighter, smaller stitches that would lie flat and point downward against the body.

For the next ten days, Silver snuck out every night to work

on the suit. Most of the time, they worked quietly. Sometimes, Silver attempted conversation.

"So you were a weaver in your old town? Where *did* you come from?"

"From far away" was all Nebekker said.

Silver fell silent. She knew it had been rude to ask. Jaspatonians never asked personal questions, because they didn't have to. There were few secrets in a place where everyone had known everyone else their whole lives.

But Silver's curiosity was too fierce, and soon more questions bubbled up.

"How did you get those scars on your hands?"

"From hard work," Nebekker said.

"Everyone says you just appeared outside Herd Valley one day. No one with you, not even a herd animal. Is that true?"

"Might be."

"But you couldn't have traveled here alone. It's too dangerous."

"So I've heard."

"Why won't you answer my questions?"

"I will when you ask the right ones."

One time, Silver said, "Are you going to tell anyone? Please don't. Especially not my father." Her words had spilled out too forcefully to be stopped. She snuck a glance at Nebekker.

"I don't plan on telling anyone." Nebekker sniffed and looked down her long nose at Silver.

And she didn't. Instead, she taught Silver what she needed to know until there was just one lesson left before Sagittaria Wonder's visit: how to join the scales into a racing suit so remarkable it would ensure that Silver's dreams came true.

Three

Another autumnal storm built over the vast desert, coloring the midday sky slate gray. Silver sat across from Nebekker, frowning and squinting at her stitches. There were only two more days until Sagittaria Wonder arrived in Jaspaton, and Silver was hurrying to finish in time. Her chest was as heavy as the dark clouds. She hoped the weather wouldn't delay Queen Imea's traveling group.

"I hope anyone out in the dunes stays safe," Nebekker said.

Nebekker didn't look up from her work. Her fingers sped across the stitches perfectly. With a groan, Silver ripped out her last five stitches for being too loose.

"No desert folk would go out in such a storm," Silver said. "Only coastal people get lost."

Silver paused her work and glanced out the window as lightning cut the horizon in half. "Except Sagittaria Wonder. She could find her way with her eyes closed. Like that time she raced her Dwakka through not one but two whirlpools!"

That was during the Desert Nations Autumn Festival races two years ago, the first time the finals course had whirlpools.

How Silver wished she could've been there! She bent over her stitches eagerly. If everything went according to plan, she would be cheering on Sagittaria at this year's races.

"You don't even know what a whirlpool looks like," Nebekker grumbled. Silver hid a smile. Nebekker always got a bit grouchy when Silver started rambling about Sagittaria Wonder.

"It's a shame your cousin's birthday will be so stormy," Nebekker said, peering out the window.

"Maybe there won't be so many people at his party, then," Silver muttered.

Nebekker gave her a long look, and a drumbeat of emotion pounded in her belly. Silver didn't mean that, really. Her cousin Brajon was her favorite person in the desert—or anywhere—and she wanted his birthday to be spectacular. It wasn't his fault that he was beloved by all in Jaspaton and that hundreds of people would come to wish him well. Or that his mother, Silver's aunt Yidla, was likely at that very moment putting the finishing touches on a birthday feast that would rival what Queen Imea enjoyed in her fine palace. And it certainly wasn't his fault that he was going to receive a coveted dune board this year: It was the traditional thirteenth-year present.

Silver made a low sound in her throat. She'd messed up another two stitches. *Be patient, find rhythm, respect the craft.* Nebekker had repeated these words often over the two weeks they had been weaving together, but Silver didn't have time to be patient. There was a plan for a spectacular riding suit tucked safely in one of Nebekker's pots, and an even bigger plan rooted in Silver's head. *If* she finished in time.

"Fly, fingers, fly," Silver whispered under her breath.

The front door flew open. She glanced up, expecting a gust of wind. When she saw who it was, she stashed her work under the folds of her tunic, her heart racing.

"Silver, I—" Brajon was shouldered aside before he could finish speaking.

"So this is where you're hiding!" Silver's father squeezed into the room, his voice triumphant. The wind slammed the door shut behind him, and his scarf whipped around his black hair before settling on his shoulders. The low light emphasized the sharpness of Rami Batal's cheekbones and jawline, flashing against the thin circlet of gold around his forehead and softening the myriad metalworking scars on his hands.

"Ele-jeweler, you are supposed to be in class on the lower levels." Rami frowned as he looked at them, seated on floor cushions. "What are you doing in here?"

Silver shot a nervous glance at Nebekker.

"She asked me to help her with a project. Something to impress her mother," Nebekker said, lying smoothly.

"Exactly," Silver blurted out. It wasn't the whole truth, but it didn't have to be a lie, either. Someday, she did want to impress her mother. But on her own terms.

Rami hesitated, choosing his words to the elderly woman carefully. "You are kind to help her."

Silver watched her father looking around Nebekker's small home. She could see the wheels turning in his head, wondering what on earth his daughter was doing with the strange old yarnslady. His gaze paused at the jug decorated with the water dragon.

Silver swallowed, forcing her scurrying pulse to slow, and tucked the racing suit even farther under her tunic. She couldn't have her father asking questions.

"I'm almost finished, Father. How did you know where to find me?" Silver narrowed her eyes at Brajon, who hunched over guiltily.

Brajon was half a year younger than her but almost two heads taller and a whole lot heavier. He had new muscles since he started going into the mines on his twelfth birthday, following in his father's footsteps. He was an ele-miner. Not that anyone ever called him that. He was always simply Brajon. Silver wished she could simply be called her own name, instead of always *ele-jeweler*. There were hundreds of miners for Brajon to blend in with, but there was only one Batal family. Silver's path in life—and her shortcomings on that path—had nowhere to hide.

"You have responsibilities, Silver," Rami Batal said. "You missed your morning classes."

"I know! I just—" Silver hated that tinge of disappointment in her father's voice, but she couldn't explain herself.

Her father sighed impatiently. "I saw the marks on your last exam, and you can't afford to be missing any lessons. You will make them up tomorrow. Go home and get ready for the party. You should be glad I'm still letting you go."

Rami Batal pointed to the door. Silver scrambled to her feet.

"Nebekker," he said more gently, "Silver should not be bothering you."

"She isn't bothering me. I invited her," Nebekker said, her fingers still flying over her work. "But I never did invite *you* in."

Not even stern Rami Batal could keep his lips from turning up slightly at the old woman's saucy tone.

"Then I'll be on my way," he said, bowing his head slightly.

"But, Silver, there will be no more visits until your marks improve. Go home now. I must return to the workshop."

As her father left the house, Silver's heart dropped and her cheeks burned. How would she finish the riding suit if she was banned from Nebekker's house? She avoided looking at Nebekker or Brajon as she gathered her things.

"Thanks for telling him where I was," Silver hissed as she brushed by her cousin before darting down the road.

"See you at my party," Brajon called after her cheerfully.

◊ ◊ ◊

SILVER RUSHED HOME and slipped into her bedroom. Directly across from the entrance was a fact sheet for the Aquinder, the most fabled of all water dragons. She walked over and brushed the corners of the paper with her fingertips. It was mostly blank, except for a scribble of what she thought it would look like based on the stories the traders told. Long and muscled, with fins and fur around its head and, most important, the only water dragon with wings to allow it to swim *and* fly.

Under the drawing, there was only one sentence: *Does it really exist?*

Silver rubbed her thumb over her sketch. According to Jaspatonians, a desert girl obsessed with water dragons also couldn't exist. But as Silver closed her eyes, she could feel a spray of seawater on the back of her neck, the warmth of water dragon skin beneath her palms, the thrill of crossing a finish line in first place. She could even feel the weightless sensation that would come when she and her Aquinder lifted off into the sapphire-blue sky. Tears prickled her eyes. They were impossible creatures, she and the Aquinder.

"You're supposed to be getting ready for my party." Brajon had come into Silver's room so quietly that she hadn't heard him part the curtains that hung between her room and the hallway. His words pulled her out of her dreams and back onto solid ground.

"Don't you know how to announce yourself?" It was good manners in Jaspaton to clear one's throat or speak to let others know you were coming. Silver quickly turned away from her cousin and wiped her sleeve across her face. She knew the muslin would leave a muddy streak on her cheeks, but she didn't care. "Besides, you should be back at your house waiting for all your adoring fans to arrive."

Brajon ran his hand through his hair, a shimmering gold wrist cuff catching the light. Silver recognized her father's fine handiwork. An early birthday gift.

"I came to apologize about Nebekker's. Uncle Rami kept asking where you were, and I couldn't lie to him. If you're not careful, your father will pull you out of school."

"I *was* careful. Until someone spilled my secret." Silver frowned. Brajon finally had the decency to turn pink and look away. "It would help if he did take me out of jewelers' classes so I could finish the suit. Ele-jeweler," she said bitterly.

Brajon shrugged. "Have it your way. You'd be such a pretty ele-yarnslady, and you and Nebekker could sit around being weird together all day long."

"Nebekker's more interesting than anyone else in boring Jaspaton." Silver grabbed a scarf from her floor and hurled it at Brajon's head. Her cousin laughed and ducked into the hallway.

Silver knew her father would never banish her from his trade. After her grandfather nearly drove the family business to ruin, Rami had worked tirelessly to make the Batal name once again synonymous with the best jewelers in all the desert. His final hurdle was to impress Queen Imea. Both Silver and her father had been eagerly awaiting her arrival, although for very different reasons. Her father, to secure his family legacy, and Silver, to escape it.

Brajon poked his head back in and sighed. His long black hair fell across his eyes. "Come on, Silver. You can't be all sulky in here. There's going to be an epic feast."

On cue, Silver's belly rumbled. Both cousins laughed.

"I'm coming," she said to Brajon's retreating back.

She picked up her favorite scarf and draped it across her neck, then changed her mind and tucked it into the bag she had hidden under a pile of cushions. She grinned, and what felt like desert hawks soared in her belly as she raced to catch up with her cousin.

In two days, she would take that bag with her as she departed Jaspaton with the great Sagittaria Wonder.

Four

Silver dragged her feet behind her parents as the Batals escorted Brajon back to his home for the party. Her mother peeked back a few times to make sure Silver was keeping up, but her father surged forward, his hand on Brajon's shoulder.

"Thirteen years old," he said. "Your path is chosen. Your future is secure. Comfort. Certainty. It's a nice way to be."

"Sure is, Uncle Rami." Brajon peered over his shoulder and winked at Silver.

Silver stayed silent as they descended the staircases carved into the face of the Jaspaton cliffs toward Brajon's house.

"Ah, there's my missing birthday boy," Aunt Yidla exclaimed, greeting them at the front door. She was swathed in her usual apron, but her dark hair was tucked under a festive, glittering wrap. She pulled Brajon into a hug, squishing his face into her neck. In the past year, he'd grown taller than her, too. "Come in, come in. Everyone's here. Oh, aren't those pretty!"

Their grandparents were there, aunts and uncles and

cousins, some of Brajon's friends from school, and some old family friends. Even Nebekker had come, silently tucked into a shadowy corner. Brajon held up his new gold cuffs for everyone in the house to see. They all fawned over the impeccable design and execution. Rami nodded modestly, but his face flushed with pride. He glanced at Silver as if to say, *See the admiration that is waiting for you?*

Silver bit back a groan and melted into the crowd.

Aunt Yidla had pulled her finest crystal goblets out and filled them with a syrupy berry cordial, ruby red in the slowly fading afternoon light. Silver took a glass. The cordial was from Calidia, but it had been made in lands whose names she had seen only on maps. She loved studying maps, imagining where she might live someday. Settlements in the mountains to the north and south of the desert . . . cities in the Island Nations. Places where the landscapes were green and lush, and where rain and water were plenty. Places where, she imagined, there were hundreds of happy water dragons. She was determined to see them all.

"Silver," her grandfather said, interrupting her thoughts. "Tell me about your studies. Are you also presenting a piece to Queen Imea, like your father?"

"I don't think so," Silver said quietly. "My skills need a lot of work."

Last year, she and Brajon and everyone their age had graduated from the standard curriculum: reading and writing and math, but also useful desert skills like basic wool working, cooking, herding, and sky watching. Now, students studied their family trades alongside their other studies. Considering Rami's reputation, Silver should have been excelling in jewelry making and metalwork. Instead, the other ele-jewelers outclassed her. And laughed at her. She had no friends among them.

"So humble!" her grandfather said.

"No, she's not," Brajon said, teasing. "She's just as daft as a desert fox."

"And you're as useful as a jelly pickax," Silver shot back. Their grandfather chuckled at the cousins' banter.

"Ah, desert foxes are incredibly clever!" Nebekker called from across the room. "To survive the desert requires great intelligence and capability."

The buzzing activity in the room quieted for a moment, but when Nebekker sipped from her glass again and said no more, the fun continued. Aunt Yidla brought over Brajon's birthday gift from her and Uncle Saad.

The present was large and heavy, bundled in a big piece of emerald-green fabric. Silver moved closer to her cousin as he took the gift in his lap and pulled the wrapping away. The dune board was deep brown, inlaid with a smooth white-shell border. As Brajon ran his hand over the waxed surface, Silver's own fingers itched to touch the wood. Painted in the center was a Decodro, the ten-armed water dragon. In a different world—one in which Silver had her own dune board—she would make a joke about how the Decodro represented Brajon's ten fingers, always getting into the treats in his mother's kitchen.

Instead, a knot formed in her chest and pulled itself taut.

"It's nice," she croaked. It was better than nice. It was the best dune board she'd ever seen.

Brajon's smile faded. He looked at the board for a long time. Then he looked up at his cousin. "You want to take the first ride?"

"No way! It's your present."

"I wouldn't mind."

"I would." Silver's father came up behind them. "You know Silver's not allowed to ride dune boards. I don't want her hurting herself right before . . ." Rami shifted his gaze. "Well, it's a secret."

Silver looked up at her father in surprise. *A secret?*

"Aw, Uncle Rami. It's easy enough. And if you fall, the sand is soft."

"Silver would find a way to break a finger. A jeweler's hands are her most precious tools."

Silver's face burned, any curiosity about the secret lost in her embarrassment. "Can I at least go out to the dunes and watch Brajon ride?"

"I see no harm in letting her go," Nebekker said. She had crept up to Silver's side. "She's a clever desert fox, after all."

She nodded to Brajon as she set her empty glass on a table and turned to leave. "May your year be as sweet as desert-bloom jellies."

Rami Batal huffed at the old woman's retreating back, then turned to his daughter. "No point in standing around while everyone else is riding," he said as he walked away to sample treats from the tables groaning with food.

Silver let out a long sigh. Dune boards were traditional thirteenth-birthday presents. The wood was precious, brought all the way from Calidia. The dragons painted on them were supposed to represent the recipient. The Decodro on Brajon's had most likely been chosen because of his love for finding and reaching for all the shiny things in the mines. But for Silver's thirteenth birthday?

A jeweler's kit.

Brajon gave Silver's shoulder a sympathetic squeeze. She forced a smile and joined in as Aunt Yidla led the crowd in the traditional birthday song: ". . . years of health, friendship, and joy . . ."

When they got to the part about success and wealth, everyone put up their hands like they were throwing gold coins at Brajon. During the next lines about staying humble and grounded, everyone flipped their wrists so their palms seemed to press against the floor.

Everyone except Silver.

She let her hands float at her waist. She didn't want to stay grounded. She wanted to soar.

◊ ◊ ◊

AS THE WINDS died down, the party picked up. Etched copper platters of glistening meats in rich sauces were devoured and refilled. Glasses were topped off with cordial and wines. Towers of sparkling fruit jellies and custard-filled cakes iced in pastel colors slowly disappeared. The older family members broke out into traditional folk songs, at the tops of their voices, while the younger people danced, spilling out into the streets with merriment.

It was too much for Silver. Her head ached from the noise and the berry cordial, but mostly she was anxious to return to Nebekker and her racing suit. Would anyone notice if she left? Silver looked around at all the familiar faces celebrating her cousin, many of whom hadn't bothered coming to her thirteenth-birthday celebration half a year earlier. Of course they wouldn't notice the ele-jeweler slipping away.

Ducking her head, she pushed her way through the crowds and into the cool desert night. Without looking back, she quickly went up the first flight of stone steps to the Jaspaton midlevels.

It was Brajon's voice that stopped her.

"Hey, cousin! Where are you . . . Wait, what's wrong? You look as sad as a beetle lost in a sandstorm. Aren't you enjoying yourself?"

Silver tucked loose strands of hair behind her ears. "The party is wonderful. All those people, and all that delicious food, but I just don't belong here."

"Silver . . ." Brajon tucked his dune board under his arm.

"I'm sorry I left." Silver took a deep breath. "I didn't think you'd notice I was gone."

"Sure, I noticed. I don't want you to go." Brajon's voice went low, and Silver knew that he wasn't just talking about the party.

In her mind, her reply was clear: *What if I'm already gone?*

But those weren't words she could say to her cousin. He was her best friend, but even he would never understand.

"Listen," he said. "There's a bunch of us going to the dunes. Come with us. Let's take my board out for its first ride."

"I can't, Brajon! My father's already suspicious after Nebekker's today. I need him to bring me along to meet Sagittaria Wonder, and he won't do that if I get in more trouble."

"He'll say yes. Who could refuse this adorable desert-fox face?" Brajon reached out to pinch Silver's cheek, but she swatted his hand away with a laugh. "What you need," he said, "is to clear your head. Come on, cousin. Come race with me."

"Are you sure he won't find out?" Silver's stomach fluttered.

Brajon pushed his face close to hers. "Dune racing is our

version of water dragon racing, and you know that's the real reason Uncle Rami won't ever let you do it. I say, do it this once. Show him what you're capable of. You never know—he might pack your bags for Calidia himself once he sees your talent."

Silver nibbled on her bottom lip. Brajon grinned, knowing he'd convinced her. Her laughter bubbled over.

"Run, Silver," Brajon said.

And they ran, darting down stairs and beneath stone archways. They picked up even more speed as soon as they left the city borders, where loose ground and stunted, gnarled trees created a line between civilization and the desert wilds.

Silver's heart beat so fast she thought it might fly away into the fading twilight. But then she tripped over her own feet and went rolling in the sandy gravel and sage of the lower desert. She lay on her back, laughing up at the ink-blue sky.

Brajon came back and helped her up. "Don't break something before we even start racing!"

They were off again, sprinting to catch up to another group of kids. The farther they went down the trail to the vast deserts, the more barren the landscape became.

Brajon paused. Before them, the smooth caramel-colored dunes rose into the sky.

"Race you up!"

Silver started several paces ahead of Brajon, but her party slippers sank into the sand. In no time her legs were burning with the strain of climbing the dune. She gasped for breath and used her hands to help her up to the top.

"How . . . do you do this . . . over and over . . . again?" she asked Brajon, who panted beside her.

He laughed and flexed his biceps. "You get strong!"

Silver rolled her eyes and pushed herself with another burst of energy. Soon enough she reached the summit where several kids were waiting for them. They took a moment to compare the dragon breeds painted on their boards, then lined up as though it were a real race.

Brajon set his dune board on the sand and arranged the tip of it to face straight down the dune. "Climb on," he told Silver.

A tiny squeal stopped her from getting on the dune board. She looked over her shoulder. One of the kids—a boy Brajon knew from the mines—had somehow grabbed a desert fox by the ruff and was swinging it in a circle.

"Stop that," Silver said, sprinting over to him. "Let the fox go."

"They're rodents," the boy said. He dangled the little animal away from his body as it yelped.

Silver didn't stop to think. She dove at the boy.

As the boy kicked, one of his legs caught her across the chest. Silver grunted and fell to the sand. The fox, dropped in the tussle, paused to sniff her once, then ran and disappeared into the desert.

"See?" the boy said. "The rodent couldn't even chirp a thanks for saving its life."

Silver got to her hands and knees and caught her breath. Brajon came over and shoved the boy in the chest.

"Leave my cousin alone," he said.

"Don't hurt foxes," Silver rasped. Brajon helped her to her feet and walked with her back to his dune board.

"Forget about that two-faced scorpion. No wonder there's a Dwakka painted on his board," Brajon said. "Let's just ride."

Silver nodded. But the excitement she'd felt as she'd

climbed the dune had faded, and nerves had taken its place. The dunes seemed as high as the top of the Jaspaton cliffs, level with the clouds.

Still, she placed her feet on the dune board, hip width apart. The silver threads decorating her tunic flashed like moonbeams.

"Bend your knees a little," Brajon said. "And hold your arms out for balance, like this. Everyone will count, and when they say go, I'll give you a push. Ready?"

"Ready as I'll ever be."

"One . . . two . . ." Brajon didn't let the other kids get to three. With a shout, he shoved Silver in the side and sent her down the dune.

"Cheater," she yelled as the nose of the dune board tipped down. It took her less than a second to tighten her muscles and find her balance. And once she did, she soared.

Her braid whipped behind her, her scarf trailing long. She narrowed her eyes to keep the stinging sand out of them. She flew and flew down the dune. Within moments, she was turning the board left and right, making snake tracks across the sand. Whoops and hollers came from above. She looked to see several of the kids chasing after her. Brajon remained at the top, his hands pumping the air as he cheered.

All the clumsiness Silver displayed when she was on her own feet disappeared. A thrilling thought flicked through her mind: *This must be what it's like to ride water dragons.*

When she reached the bottom, the dune board slid to a stop. Silver pitched forward, her arms flailing, and toppled off. She lay still in the sand, catching her breath, reveling in the moment.

"Decodro wins," Brajon shouted from the top.

"Fun, huh?" Mohad, one of the politicians' sons, said, peering over at her.

"The most amazing thing I've ever done," Silver said.

She grinned, grabbed the board, and ran up the dune again.

They spent the hours leading to dawn riding down the dunes, then staggering back up them. Brajon and Silver took turns with his board. With each ride, Silver grew more and more confident. Her snake tracks got wider, she spun in circles, and she squatted low and dragged her hand in the sand as she flew down the slope. She felt weightless, strong, and fast. She wanted to feel that way forever.

Silver set the board in the sand, ready for her last run. She looked all around, from the pale cliffs of Jaspaton before her, dotted with homes carved into the stone facade, to the vast reaches of deep desert behind. Just past the desert, she imagined she could see the sea, even if it was just the watery expanse of horizon, colored pale blue by a setting full moon.

Silver sighed. Sometimes, she loved her home. In the morning, the light was golden through her window, and in the evenings, the city sparkled with the jeweled colors of thousands of gemstone lanterns hanging on every level.

But she was ready to leave it all behind.

"Ready?" Brajon climbed on behind her. They would ride together this last time, so that no one was left stranded at the top. He kicked off, and they shot down the dune. The descent was faster this time, with their combined weight, and Silver loved the pressure of the wind on her cheeks.

She was meant for speed.

The kids waiting at the bottom walked back to the city

with Silver and Brajon. They all talked and laughed and recounted their rides.

"I've never seen someone get so good so fast," Mohad said.

Silver beamed. "Thanks."

They entered the city, sending pebbles skittering around with their dragging feet. "The way you cut back and forth across the dune"—Brajon nodded in admiration—"no wonder your father never let you ride. If he knew how good you'd be . . . I can't believe that was your first ride!"

"Do you think riding water dragons—"

"Your first ride?" Silver started at the sound of her father's voice. "Certainly your last." Rami Batal walked out of the shadows, his eyes flashing with anger.

Silver's stomach flipped. She had been so caught up in the excitement that she hadn't seen her father standing at the city entrance. She wondered how long he had been waiting for them to return. She hastily lifted her trailing scarf off the ground, but all that did was display the ragged, fraying edges, front and center. There was no way she was going to convince her father that she had only stood at the bottom of the dune and watched. Even if he hadn't heard Brajon talking. Without another word, he took Silver by the elbow and hauled her home.

Five

The next morning, the fire in the ele-jewelers' workshop roared with life, pushing the metallic tang of molten metal into every corner. Concentrating students surrounded tables littered with drawings, tools, and uncut gems. Queen Imea and Sagittaria Wonder were due to arrive in Jaspaton the next day, and everyone was in a frenzy.

Silver hammered a warm slab of gold, intending to make a cup. Her hands moved automatically, but her mind skipped far, far away. *What does the palace look like? What are the water dragon training grounds like? A desert city on the sea . . . There must be hundreds of dragons there for me to ride.*

"Batal!"

A sharp, painful rap on the back of Silver's hand brought her out of her reverie. The metalwork teacher, Gama, stood over her with an expression as dark as desert storm clouds. He would have always hated Silver, simply for being Rami's daughter—Gama's family had once tried and failed to take over the Batal workshop—but his dislike intensified with every clumsy project she presented him.

The six other students in the room snickered. Phila, Gama's daughter and the eldest in the class, shook her head slowly. *Failure,* she mouthed.

Silver looked down. She'd hammered her goblet into an unidentifiable mess.

"And finally," Gama said, "understanding dawns on the ele-jeweler's face."

Under her breath, Silver said, "Someday—"

"Someday, you'll live up to the Batal name? Unlikely." Gama still held his jeweler's loupe, ready to rap her knuckles once more. Silver winced in anticipation.

"Gama," Rami Batal boomed as he entered the room with more materials for the students. "What inspired work is this daughter of mine doing today?"

Gama whirled around, a smile creeping like a dung beetle up one side of his face. "She—"

"I'm really close to getting it right," Silver said, thrusting forward the mess.

Her father came closer, bowing over the lump of gold. He frowned, but only for a moment. No one else saw it but Silver.

"Good, good!" he said, straightening up again. "Gama, I need to borrow my ele-jeweler now. I have a special project for her."

Gama's lips pursed. "Special project?"

"*Secret* project," Rami Batal said. He winked at Silver.

Her toes curled in her boots as she recalled his mention of a secret at Brajon's party. Probably some sort of secret chore.

"It's almost midday," Silver told her father. "I have a lot to do. I . . ."

She looked from her father to her teacher and back again. If she didn't sneak to Nebekker's house as soon as possible, there was no way she was going to complete her riding suit in time.

"You can't be doing anything as important as what I need," Rami said. "Come along, Silver. A good midday to you, Gama."

"Good midday, Rami—and ele-jeweler."

As soon as Gama's back was turned, Silver made a face. Just *ele-jeweler.* She had a name.

Rami marched out of the teaching workshop. Silver followed, her feet scuffing the stone pathway. There had to be some emergency she could make up. Her thoughts darted around like desert foxes playing on the dunes.

"There is a great hero coming tomorrow," her father said suddenly.

She froze. Other than Brajon and Nebekker, no one knew Silver idolized Sagittaria Wonder. It was safer to keep the racer to herself. Writing fan letters was one thing. But having a hero who wasn't Rami Batal? That felt wrong, somehow.

But then, her father had said *a* hero, not *her* hero.

"Keep walking, Silver. You must come out of your dreamworld and pay more attention to the present." Up ahead, Rami drew his arm wide. "Look at these beautiful lands. An ancient city full of our family's great history, the valley to the north to raise food and wool, an underground river that swells with rushing water in the spring, and all the raw materials a craftsman like me could hope for. Old lore says this land was touched by ancient goddesses. They buried all their treasures under our sand for us to find, bit by bit. My daughter, we have everything we need here."

Her father took her fingers in his. "Even Queen Imea wants to come see our riches. She arrives tomorrow. And with her, the great water dragon racer, Sagittaria Wonder. I have been working on a secret project to impress her. A racing cup for the spring festival."

Silver worried her father would notice that her palms were sweating.

Her father went on. "First this cup, and then my masterpiece for the queen. It has been my life's work to return glory to my family, and it comes to this moment. For all of us . . . For *you* and your future."

"I know," Silver said miserably.

Rami let go of her fingers and continued walking. "I want you to share the moment with me. Let's show the world we are Batals! I want you to add your own special touch to the racing cup."

Silver tried to swallow, but it felt like sand was coating her throat. Her father's smile was wide, though his eyes were cautious. They both knew this was a big step for her . . . and they both knew she could mess it up.

They reached the Batal family workshop. Silver took in a breath of familiar air. She'd grown up in this space: She crawled on the floor covered with thick, colorful rugs; played with her father's jeweler's instruments like they were toys; even took meals in the workshop, sitting on her mother's lap while her father worked late into the night.

Rami Batal led Silver to a table at the back of the workshop, on top of which sat a tall cloth-covered project. Her father pulled the fabric away.

"Here it is. My design for the Island Nations Spring Festival cup."

Silver gasped and felt her chest swell with pride at her father's work. The gold-and-gemstone cup gleamed with a rainbow of marvels and meticulous metalwork. The Island

Nations supplied the cup for the Desert Nations Autumn Festival qualifying races, and the desert royals returned the favor for the Spring Festival final, where the biggest race of the year crowned the world's grand champion. For jewelers, there was no greater honor than having their handiwork selected to represent their homeland.

But even as Silver admired the cup, she didn't see how she could ever enhance its beauty.

Her father beamed and turned the cup so the back—polished gently to reveal all the setting-sun colors of the gold—faced them.

"See here along the bottom? I saved that spot for a very special person. I know you've been working on hammering metal in class. I want you to design a simple pattern here. Perhaps something that would put the viewer in mind of our desert dunes." Rami faced his daughter. "Silver, I want us to present this cup to Queen Imea and Sagittaria Wonder together."

Silver swallowed, hard, and blinked rapidly. She longed to tell her father about her dreams to be a water dragon racer—to bring a new kind of glory to the Batal family. Her chin tipped up and her chest pressed forward and her mouth opened, and the whole workshop began to spin with dizzying light and color and sparkle, but . . .

No words came out.

Silver simply couldn't tell her father the truth. Not when he looked at her like that: like she was his ele-jeweler.

Silver cleared her throat. "I'll try."

Her father gathered materials, then stoked the fire in the depths of the workshop. Rami gave Silver an encouraging smile before brushing through the curtain that separated the workshop from the showroom.

She sighed and warmed the gold around the bottom of the cup, then began. Hammering was a detailed task, but as her *clank, clanks* sounded through the workshop, her thoughts drifted.

Who would want boring dunes on a winner's cup? Silver knew a better option was something that captured the beauty and the power of a water dragon. She closed her eyes and pictured the only real dragon she'd ever seen. It was seven years ago when she'd snuck into a trader's wagon, lured by a gentle and sweet snore.

There, tucked in a wooden cage at the front, was a small sleeping creature, its tail coiled twice around its body. When Silver knocked over a bottle, the little orange dragon's eyes popped open. They were the dazzling blue of sapphires. The dragon yawned but didn't uncurl. It tucked its face deeper into its tail, gazing at Silver the whole time, but the corners of its eyes crinkled, and Silver smiled back. When a giggle escaped from her, the trader called a *Hello?* from outside the wagon. Silver rolled beneath the fabric cover and out the side, then ran for home.

Now, she pulled herself out of her memories and groaned at her work. Uneven dings and dents littered the formerly smooth surface halfway up the sides. She sighed and pushed the ruined part of the cup close to the heat with a pair of long tongs, to soften the metal again.

She'd loved meeting that little dragon on that day so long ago. She wondered what had happ—

She screamed and yanked her hands back. Searing pain ripped through her forearm, and she clenched her teeth as she cradled her wrist to her chest. The cup clanked to the ground.

"Silver!" her father shouted, rushing back into the workshop. "What happened?"

The pain was excruciating, but Silver pushed it down. "The fire popped and caught me," she said.

She tucked her arm behind her back so he couldn't see how badly she was burned. "It's nothing. I'm sorry—I wasn't paying attention."

"Are you sure?" Rami Batal frowned, but as he reached for her arm, he caught sight of the cup on the floor. He bent down and slowly picked it up. Silver's heart sank as she saw the large dent in its side.

"Silver, what have you done? I give you an opportunity to be a part of my proudest moment, and *this* is what you offer? You can't even focus for one minute, daydreaming all day about . . . about . . . *water dragons*." His voice shook, and for a moment, he raised the cup as though he were going to throw it against the workshop wall, but instead he lowered it.

Silver opened her mouth to apologize, but Rami held up his hand and shook his head.

"Enough." Her father wiped his palm across his forehead. "Silver, I need you out of the workshop if I'm to fix your mistake in time."

Silver's eyes filled with tears as her father led her out by the arm, her burn throbbing with the beat of a Jaspaton festival drum.

Six

Not even the breezes of late afternoon swirling lazily through Jaspaton could cool Silver's flushed face as her father took her up two flights of stairs toward the yarnsladies' tents.

When Silver realized where they were going, part of her flashed with relief. The other part of her flared with an emotion she didn't quite understand. Why couldn't her father see what everyone, even Gama, could see? Silver had no talent for metals or jewels, no matter how much Rami wanted her to.

Her father didn't say anything more until they'd reached the upper levels of Jaspaton, where the yarnsladies' tents afforded views far and wide.

"Sit in here," he said. "And don't leave. Not once. I don't care if the greatest sandstorm in history rises up." His words were clipped, but as he turned to leave, his mouth softened. His eyes did, too, in a way that hurt Silver. She'd rather have her father's anger than this disappointment.

Silver dropped her gaze to the ground and didn't look up until she heard Rami leave. She set her jaw. Someday, he would see her for who she really was.

Trying to ignore the pain of the burn, she picked her way through the yarnsladies and the goods scattered about. Baskets, clothing, and scarves for the approaching winter season were the basics, but there were also luxurious rugs threaded with silver and gold; blankets made from the finest fur from the herd animals' underbellies; and felted coats with fluffy collars. Instead of the usual organization of the silk tent, the place was chaotic as the women prepared for the queen's arrival.

"Do you think these buttons will suit the queen's tastes?" one yarnslady asked another, showing some hammered-gold rounds.

"It appeals to *my* tastes," the second woman said.

All the ladies laughed, but Silver suppressed a groan. Hammered gold was the last thing *she* wanted to see.

"She's a high-mountains goat," a third yarnslady said, following Silver with her eyes. "Untamable."

"Wild," another said.

"Smelly," said a tiny ele-yarnslady, sticking her five-year-old nose in the air.

Silver ignored them until she saw a familiar face. She plopped down on a rug. "I don't smell."

"You smell, all right," said Nebekker. "But not bad. A bit salty. I don't mind."

Silver squinted at the old lady. For a yarnslady, her hands were surprisingly rough and scarred. And she kept her hair cropped short, unlike the waist-length waves all the other women had. The project in Nebekker's hands wasn't like the others' work, either. The patterns weren't symmetrical or ordered, as was Jaspaton's tradition. Even the five-year-old ele-yarnslady knew how many lines of red wool to weave before adding turquoise and then an almost imperceptibly thin line of amethyst. But Nebekker's patterns swirled and tumbled.

The other yarnsladies went back to their gossip, working their wool in time to their laughter. Silver scooted closer to Nebekker.

"I couldn't come this morning," Silver said. "Not after getting in trouble last night. But now I have time to finish my suit. Do you have my scales?"

Nebekker leaned forward to collect one of her baskets. As she did, a pendant fell out of her caftan, swaying in the light for a moment before slipping back under the clothes again. Silver had never known the old woman to wear any jewelry. From that glimpse of the pendant, she couldn't make out what kind of stone was encased in the swirl of silver wire. It was blue, but not deep and rich like sapphire. Clear, though, unlike turquoise. Perhaps topaz or aquamarine, except Silver had never seen violet slash through the blue in those stones the way it did through Nebekker's.

Nebekker dumped a pile of wool in Silver's lap. Silver smiled as she quickly got to work, the fight with her father fading into nothingness.

"My father wanted to punish me by sending me here, but it's the best thing he could've done. He's practically escorting me off to Calidia."

Nebekker gave her a sidelong glance.

"Silver, you've hurt yourself." Sersha Batal came up behind her daughter and took her arm to inspect the burn. She rubbed cool cream on the wound. "Does it hurt?"

The cream felt delicious on her skin. "Not anymore," Silver said. She hastily stuffed her scales back into Nebekker's basket with her other hand.

"You must be patient with your father." Sersha sat cross-legged next to Silver. "I know you're frustrated, but your father is trying to do what he thinks is best."

Frustration heated Silver's chest. "Best for him!"

"Best for *us*. You have a rich future here in Jaspaton, if you'll only develop some discipline. You are loved here. That's not a thing to toss dust at."

Silver looked away. Her mother was never angry with her; Sersha simply fell back on her unwavering belief in her daughter. Silver felt both warmed and suffocated by it.

"You and your father are so much alike. Driven in a way that makes you a touch narrow-sighted," her mother said, squeezing Silver close. "Keep heart, my girl. My wild desert fox. You'll find your place soon enough."

After her mother left, Silver looked at the injury on the inside of her wrist for the first time. She gasped. The burn was a raw and angry red that was already beginning to blister. There was a shimmer, though, as if it were gold, not the fire itself that had popped and was embedded in her skin.

But the most interesting thing about the injury—the thing that solidified Silver's knowledge that she was neither meant for the jeweler's workshop nor the yarnsladies' tent—was the shape of the burn.

In the right light, it looked like a coiled water dragon.

◊ ◊ ◊

WHEN NIGHT FELL, all of the town's work ended. Silver stacked the wool in her bag with a renewed sense of determination. Her glance continually flickered to the water dragon–shaped burn, and she smiled.

"The scales are finished," she told Nebekker. "I only need your help joining them. Tomorrow morning I'll have a suit, and then tomorrow evening I'll ride away from Jaspaton in Sagittaria's very own cart. See you before first light."

Before Nebekker could answer, Silver rushed to follow the yarnsladies out of the tent. As they left the shadows, the ladies draped colorful scarves over their heads and dipped their hands into a bucket of cream to keep their skin soft. They crowded the door so that Silver had to shove to get through.

"Rude," that little ele-yarnslady said, rubbing her hands together slowly.

"Silver!" Sersha Batal caught up to her daughter. "I'm staying late. There's still so much to get ready for tomorrow. And your father expects to be in his workshop all night."

"Oh." Silver tried to keep her voice steady, but excitement thumped in her veins. With everyone so busy, no one would notice her finishing her riding suit. She glanced around for Nebekker, but the old woman had slipped away. Good. Nebekker would be waiting for her at her home.

"Go to your aunt and uncle's if you need anything."

"I will."

"And, Silver?" Sersha laced her fingers with her daughter's. "Look at the things these women have accomplished together. Look at the honor we will bring our city when the queen arrives. I am proud of the work I do. So is your father. I want you to be proud of your work, too."

Silver nodded and took her hand back, then left the tents.

If her racing-suit reveal went as planned, she would be proud of her work.

And Sagittaria Wonder would be amazed.

Seven

Silver wrapped herself in layers of brown and white scarves and slipped into the night.

Her cross-body sack, filled with riding-suit scales, slapped against her belly, stuffed full after an evening meal with Brajon's family.

She snuck down the stairs and roads. Pebbles pushed into her soft boots as she darted to Nebekker's house at mid-cliff level. The windows were dark. She raised her hand and knocked quietly.

No answer. The wind shifted, brushing Silver's scarf from her face. She knocked again, shuffling her boots on the dusty stoop. Where was the old woman? Silver looked up and down the road, but all activity was near the workshops and the yarns-ladies' tents.

Maybe Nebekker had gone to help the yarnsladies. Maybe she was sleeping. But Silver *needed* to finish her suit. So where was she?

Silver tapped on the door a little louder and then, finally, banged with the side of her fist.

"Where are you?" Silver whispered. She reached for the door handle, looking over her shoulder and gnawing her bottom lip. One did not enter a home without permission.

She swallowed and turned. The door opened.

Silver slipped in and shut the door behind her. Nebekker's house was still. No sound and no light.

"Nebekker?"

No answer. It felt wrong to snoop. But what if Nebekker was injured—or worse? It wasn't even just about the scales. Silver's heart hurt to think something could be wrong with the old woman . . . with her friend. She tiptoed around, peering into every dark corner, hoping to find Nebekker peacefully snoring away. But the house was empty.

Silver wiped her sweaty hands on her trousers and returned to the main room. She went to the shelf where her racing-suit plans were tucked into a pot, and she stuffed them in her bag. Silver looked around the room one last time, as though she could have missed Nebekker in a tiny crack in the wall. She stepped into the road and closed the door behind her.

If she had any hope of finishing her suit by tomorrow morning, she would have to hole up in her bedroom and work nonstop. She'd just have to figure out her own way to attach the scale pieces together.

◊ ◊ ◊

SILVER RUBBED HER eyes for the hundredth time and looked out the window. It was still deep-mine black outside, but daybreak would come all too soon. Hours of weaving and hooking and knotting, and the scales were still scattered around her floor. Some had partially unraveled after her joining experiments had left them looking tired and limp. Others were still connected but with haphazard knots.

"Flying desert dust, Nebekker! Where are you when I need you?"

She considered going to Nebekker's house again, to see if the old woman had returned in the night, but she couldn't force her legs to move. She was too tired. Her eyes betrayed her. Images of wool were mixing in a fog with huge shadowy blobs that looked like water dragons.

When her curtains *shush*ed open, she didn't even have the energy to hide the scales. Let her father find out. At least then she would be free from this torturous work.

But it was her cousin. Brajon clomped into the room and closed the curtains behind him.

"I was getting a snack and looked up to see lantern light in your window. What are you doing?" He squinted at Silver's mess of yarn.

Silver couldn't hold the emotions back any longer. A hot tear rolled down her cheek. "Look at this! Nebekker was supposed to show me how to join the scales together, but she's missing."

"Then figure it out."

"I'm trying! Do you think I've just been sitting here all night wasting this lantern oil?" Silver glared at her cousin. He watched her carefully for a moment, then went to the window and stared at the night.

"Look at this," he said.

Silver heaved her heavy limbs up and joined him, and Brajon bumped her shoulder gently.

"How many times have we watched our deep-desert sky together?" he said. "As dark as ink. Except over there, where it's purple, like deep amethyst. Soon, that'll turn blue, then orange. Then we'll have brilliant light. Do you think they have the same skies in Calidia?"

Silver gazed up at her cousin. Even if the skies were exactly the same, the company would be different, and that made her ache inside.

"Do you never want to go somewhere?" she asked. "Never want to have adventure? Those colors on the horizon—don't you want to be able to *touch* them?" She sighed and gingerly felt the wound on her wrist. "There's so much more out there than I can find here."

Brajon shrugged. "Jaspaton's my home."

Silver made a low sound in her throat and shoved her wrist under Brajon's nose. "Look at this."

"That looks painful."

"That's not the point. The shape proves I'm meant for water dragons!"

"I know," Brajon said softly. "I don't need a burn to tell me that."

A silence fell over the cousins. It was comfortable, as all their moments together were, but there was something new around the edges. Something that hinted at a change to come. Silver both thirsted for it and mourned it at the same time.

"Look." She pointed to a spot in the sky that was starless.

"Must be a sandstorm out there," Brajon said.

"Maybe." But sandstorms usually blacked out the whole night. This was more like just a strip of stars was missing. Except that the strip was moving, winking out stars across the sky. Silver shivered. "Strange."

"Our desert sky is full of mysteries. How could you want to leave it for the royal city?" Brajon said.

Silver knew he was asking *How could you want to leave* me?—but when she didn't answer, his shoulders slumped.

"Cousin," he said, "I don't know anything about wool working, but I can do lots of different kinds of knots. You could just . . ." He grabbed two scales, lined up the flat sides, and knotted a length of yarn between them. He held up the finished product. "Okay, so it's not perfect. But at least they're holding together without a gap. And you can hardly see the knots."

"Hardly? The only thing bulkier than your knots is your head." Silver laughed and took the knotted scales to examine them. "But they'll have to do. Sagittaria will understand that this is just a prototype."

"I'll help with the rest. Even though you're as ungrateful as that desert fox you saved." Brajon grinned as Silver stuck her tongue out at him. "We have to hurry if you want this done before sunrise," he said.

Silver tugged the suit-design sketch from under her leg and set it in between herself and her cousin. They both got to work. Silver's energy returned. Her fingers flew.

"Thank you for helping me," she said. Her smile couldn't be contained.

"I'll do anything if it means I get rid of you for good," Brajon said. But just as quickly as his smile had appeared, it fled.

"You'll always be my number one reason for coming back to visit," Silver said, taking his hand and giving it a squeeze.

It was dawn when they finally finished connecting the scales. Silver watched her cousin sweep past the curtain to the hallway, then she began packing her suit into her bag with a heavy heart.

Eight

Silver woke with a snort. She wiped a trail of slobber off her chin and sat up. The sun streamed through her window. There was so much noise it sounded like a parade was marching by outside. Running. Shouting. Traditional festival drums pounding.

"Silver!" Brajon barreled in, leaping over her to look out the window. "The Calidia group has been spotted. Sagittaria Wonder will be here any minute."

Sagittaria Wonder! Gifting boring old Jaspaton with her glorious presence. The day had finally arrived, and Silver had almost slept through it.

She ran to the window, but there was so much dust being kicked up she couldn't see the arriving travelers. She grabbed Brajon's arm and pushed him out of her room. "Go. I have to get ready."

"I was just leaving. I have to be out there greeting really important people."

"Ugh!" With one last shove, Silver sent Brajon into the hallway. She pulled off her dirty clothes from the day before and wiggled into the riding suit. The softness was incredible. So was the heat. She tugged at the collar.

She heard voices in the hallway and quickly dove behind some cushions.

"What are you doing out here?" Silver heard her mother say to Brajon.

"Waiting for Silver. She's getting dressed. And taking too long."

"Perfect timing, then. I have something for her to wear."

Silver heard Brajon's huge feet shuffle.

"Uh, you can't go in there," he said. "She wants to surprise you. She's doing her own hair."

In the beat of silence that followed, Silver began to sweat. Everyone knew she couldn't do more than the simplest plait.

"Oh, that's . . ." Sersha's voice trembled. Was she crying? Sersha cleared her throat. "That's new for her." She gave a little laugh. "Silver?" she called.

"I'm almost done," Silver yelled, struggling to untangle her hair. "I wanted to look my best for the queen's visit."

"I can help with that. I'm going to push something under your curtain."

A square of fabric appeared. Silver walked over and unfolded a beautiful ruby-red caftan, embroidered with golden birds. She drew her finger over the gold threads slowly. "It's the prettiest thing I've ever seen."

"Your grandparents brought it back from Calidia for me the very first time they visited the royal city," her mother said. "You're taller than I was back then. But hopefully, this will fit you."

With the riding suit beneath, the caftan squeezed Silver's skin. Once she added her scarves, the heat would be unbearable. But the red silk was so lovely and her mother's voice was so eager that Silver lied and said it fit perfectly.

"Are you ready? Come out so I can see," her mother said.

Silver licked her lips. Her nerves sizzled like desert lightning. Would her mother notice the extra bulk beneath the caftan?

Silver pulled the curtain aside.

Sersha's eyes widened and grew misty. Then she saw Silver's hair. "Hmm. We'll keep working on that."

Her mother worked Silver's thick hair into two reverse braids and secured them with silk ribbon. She pushed gold combs into the tops of the braids. Then she took Silver's hands in hers.

"The world's waiting for you, Silver Batal. I don't know if it's quite ready, but when is it ever ready for a storm? The winds come anyway."

There was a soft pressure on the top of Silver's head as her mother pressed a kiss to it. "I have to go present my wares. Your father is expecting you in his workshop. Scamper over."

Silver took a deep breath. Brajon nodded to her. She took one step. Then another. Then she bolted for the road.

Outside, madness reigned. Silver pushed and shoved for many minutes to get to one of the circular stone overlooks, and from there to the staircase that would take her to the family workshop.

Halfway down one set of stairs, she tripped over a sack someone had left on a step. Her body went weightless, shooting into the air, flying down three steps, then toppling head over heels down seven more before landing in a heap. Hands reached for her, trying to help her to her feet. She batted them away and pushed herself to her knees to inspect the damage. Bruises would blossom on her back and legs by the end of the day, she knew. But what she was most worried about was the tear all the way across the bottom seam of her mother's caftan.

She got to her feet, her bones protesting every move. A slow drumbeat of pain began in the back of her head, matching the rhythm of the celebration drums that were being played on the higher levels.

"I think this is yours?" a man said, holding out one of the gold combs.

"Thank you," Silver said. She tucked it back into her hair. It didn't matter if it was crooked. She had to get to the workshop before Sagittaria Wonder. A cry went up from the crowds spilling out over the perimeter of the city and the deep desert. Queen Imea and her retinue had arrived.

The Batal workshop wasn't far. But not only was the caftan torn; it was covered in dust. The vibrant red now looked flat like jaspers instead of brilliant like rubies.

The crowds began to thin out as people returned to their workshops or storerooms or vendor stalls to put the final touches on their wares. Silver went to another overlook and squinted at the little figures far below. She could make out the white robes of the politicians shaking hands with the visitors. About halfway back in the line of traders and merchants was a vibrant-blue cart, its top and sides curtained with what was no doubt a finer silk than her mother's caftan. At the front of the cart, a silver dragon's-head carving glinted in the high sunlight.

Sagittaria Wonder.

The greatest water dragon racer that had ever lived. Silver

forgot her aches and pains. She rushed into her father's workshop with a thrumming excitement in her chest.

"Silver! Are you all right?" Rami Batal gaped at her. "What happened to you?"

Silver wiped her nose. The back of her hand came away with smears of blood. "The crowds. And the stairs."

"Never mind. There's no time." Her father sighed. "Phila, can you help clean her up? Take this brooch and pin it to her caftan. That should hide the tear."

Phila grumbled but walked over. Silver knew that she must resent that Silver was here at all. Phila was the most gifted of the ele-jewelers and had earned her spot while Silver was just . . . her father's daughter.

Silver had never seen her father so flustered before. He fumbled his words as he gave more directions to the other ele-jewelers.

"Put the gold pieces . . . No, let's group them by gemstone . . . Oh, but the mixed gem pieces. By size. Try that. No, some of the finest are the smaller ones. They'll get lost that way. Go back to separating them by metal . . . I don't like that, either." He faced his daughter again. "Finish getting cleaned up. I need you to model a few things."

"Model?" Silver yelped. "But I thought I'd stay out of the way . . ." She pointed to the dark, safe corner where she was planning to sit and watch, gathering her courage until she could approach Sagittaria Wonder and reveal her suit.

"My work looks best when it's worn. And who better to model it than the future of the Batal jewelers? Silver, you *must* appear graceful. Be still and be silent. Let the jewels speak, not you."

Silence was not going to be difficult. Silver's face burned

with humiliation. It was one thing to observe: There was respect in that. It showed that she was an eager and honored student. But to stand there like a mindless showpiece?

Still, there was no time to argue. Her father turned away, and Phila dragged Silver to a basin of water to make her presentable.

Phila curled her lip as she wiped at the dusty caftan. "My parents would be disgraced if I ran around like a filthy herd animal."

"I'm sure your parents are already disgraced to have a daughter who looks like she's constantly smelling herd-animal dung. Ow!"

Phila had poked the brooch right through the caftan into Silver's shin. Luckily, the tightly woven wool of the riding suit had shielded her. Silver growled.

"Silent, remember?" Phila smirked.

Silver had never hated her more, but she held still as Phila fixed the caftan as best she could. "There," Phila said. "You're not beautiful, but at least you don't look like you slept in the streets last night."

"Much better," Silver's father said when she approached him. He pulled away her scarves. Silver hoped the caftan was still covering the neckline of the suit.

"Gold," he barked to his assistants. "Blue sapphires and those emerald bracelets. To create contrast with the red silk. I'll take these." Rami pulled the combs out of Silver's hair and replaced them with a heavy headpiece dripping with gems and artistically twisted precious metals. After only a few moments, her neck ached with the strain of keeping her chin high under all the weight.

With a heavily beating heart, Silver looked to the workshop

entrance. How much longer until Sagittaria Wonder came through that door?

Thick necklaces went around her collarbone, and thin, delicate chains hung all the way down to her stomach. Every finger was stacked with rings. Her father went to place a bracelet on her wrist but hesitated at the sight of the burn. The whole workshop seemed to pause for a beat as an unspoken understanding passed between father and daughter: No matter what happened today, things were going to change.

Rami slipped the bracelet on and followed it up with more glimmering cuffs and chains.

A thunderous boom sounded outside the door, and Rami pulled Silver through the curtains and to the center of the showroom.

"Places, everyone," he said.

Sagittaria Wonder and the royals had arrived.

And with them, Silver's future.

Nine

Sometimes, when the Jaspatonian night was very clear and the winds were slumbering, Silver would slip out of her house and climb the stairs to the very top of the cliffs, and watch the moon blink down on the world. The orb always seemed so big, so close. Like she could reach out and steal a bit of its shine, or pluck a strand of platinum moonlight and wrap it all around herself, so that she could be as beautiful as the stars.

That was, Silver felt certain, what Queen Imea must have done.

The royal leader of all the deserts swept into Rami Batal's showroom like a moonbeam. She was younger than Silver's mother, having been plucked from the mountainous north by the mysterious soothsayers of Calidia and instated as queen when she was only nineteen, but her hair was gray, glittering down her back to sway at her waist. Her big, dark eyes and luminous, tawny-brown skin were accented by yards and yards of the silver-embroidered purple silk of her caftan. Diamonds glittered across her throat and from her ears.

Queen Imea lifted her caftan to step into the showroom, and Silver saw that she wore soft silk slippers and amethyst-dotted gold chains around her ankles. The queen smiled at everyone as she shook hands with Silver's father and the lowly ele-jewelers.

Her husband, the king regent, followed, nodding but not shaking hands. He was tall and somber-faced and dressed more simply, in a white robe like all the politicians had, and wearing no jewelry.

But Silver strained her eyes to see past the royals and their entourage. They were not the ones that excited her. No, that would be . . . after several traders and servants . . . a few more . . . there! Sagittaria Wonder.

Silver sucked in a quick breath. She would recognize her idol anywhere. The description a trader had once given her wasn't entirely accurate—Sagittaria Wonder's nose was much longer, and her amber eyes were set farther apart—but there was something about the way she walked—no, strode—that drew Silver's gaze to her. She was confident. Slim and taut. She didn't hide her muscles behind layers and layers of clothing. Instead, her leather pants and woven tunic clung to her. She looked ready to saddle up and take a water dragon into a race.

Queen Imea approached Silver. "Hello, child."

Silver tore her eyes from Sagittaria Wonder, straightened her back, and smiled. The queen's face was open and mild—fresh, as though she hadn't just been out in the desert at all. There was a spark in her eye that conveyed interest. Not only in the jewels, but in Silver herself.

Queen Imea reached out to touch a necklace. "Did you make any of these yourself?"

"No." Silver's voice was barely more than a squeak. She wished she could have told the queen yes, that she had helped with the racing cup. Silver tried to clear her throat but managed only to change the squeak to a squawk. "I'm still learning. But my father did."

"Ah, you're his daughter? I'd wager my kingdom that one day you'll have just as much talent as he does." The queen leaned very close and whispered, "Probably more." When Queen Imea straightened up again, she winked.

"I hope so." Silver smiled weakly. The royal obviously didn't love her kingdom enough if she would bet on that.

The queen smiled again, then focused on the jewelry, gently lifting several pieces off Silver and inspecting the work displayed on the tables and velvet cushions in other parts of the showroom. With each piece the queen admired, Rami Batal's chest puffed up bigger and bigger until Silver had to push down a laugh.

Sagittaria Wonder was tucked into the far corner. The racer's arms were folded across her chest as she watched everyone barter and laugh, eat and drink.

Phila came to drape new pieces across Silver's neck while Rami held up a pair of dangling gold earrings and described them in rapturous detail to Queen Imea.

"The queen hasn't noticed my designs yet," Phila said.

"She has good taste, then," Silver said. "She's nice, too."

Silver winced. She was sure that Phila had pinched her skin between the necklace clasp on purpose.

"She'll want to ply you with sweetness so that she gets favorable prices from you," Phila said, shaking her head. "You're too gullible."

Silver's face burned. The queen was treating everyone in

the shop with respect. Wasn't that just how everyone interacted with others? Not Phila, though. Basic kindness was not a thing she would understand. Silver looked over Phila's shoulder. The people in the showroom—all the other ele-jewelers, the queen's people, even Gama—were swarming around Silver like gnats, blocking her view of Sagittaria Wonder.

When the royal group had finally had enough, Queen Imea clapped her hands. "I am delighted at what I've seen."

But still, her eyes roamed the shop, as though hoping for something more. Rami Batal seemed to understand. It was the moment he'd been waiting for. Desert beetles flip-flopped in Silver's chest. Although it wasn't her own dream, she still wanted her father to amaze the queen.

He chuckled and pulled a plain wood box off a table against the wall. "Word reached me that you are in the market for a great masterpiece. Jewels that will come to symbolize your perfect reign." He opened the box, and even Silver felt compelled to take a few steps closer and crane her neck. Inside, the most dazzling loose jewels glittered beside a piece of parchment. "Here is a project I am embarking on. A scepter. I feel it will be the grandest thing I ever create."

"How wonderful!" the queen said. "It never does to show all our secrets right away, now does it?" She leaned in close and winked at Silver's father. "Oh, I love when the final card is played on the table. I play all my games that way, too. Politics is dreadfully boring, otherwise." She stood upright again and clasped her hands. "How long until I can hold this masterpiece?"

"I have found half the jewels I need," Rami said, beaming. "Each one must be a perfect example of what a jewel can be. I hope to have the rest in the next year or two."

Queen Imea dragged a finger over the sketch on the parchment. "That's a shame. In a few days, Calidia hosts the Desert Nations Autumn Festival. Six months later, our desert racers will win glory in the finals at the Island Nations Spring Festival. Wouldn't it be a symbol of our land's prosperity to take this piece with me come spring?"

"Six months? I . . . I've spent half my life finding these jewels," Silver's father stammered.

Queen Imea didn't comment further, but her smile faded. A few of her retinue began moving toward the showroom door. Silver nervously plucked at the neckline of her mother's caftan.

Her father swallowed slowly. "I will scour the lands to make it so. It will be done."

The queen's smile lit up her face. "I will send my guard for my other pieces in two weeks. I will come, myself, three weeks before the Spring Festival so that I may personally carry this scepter with me when I set sail to the Island Nations."

Silver knew there would be many sleepless nights for her father in the weeks to come. But she wouldn't be there for them.

"I believe Sagittaria Wonder would like a word with you," the queen said to Rami. She waved over the dragon rider, then left the showroom flanked by her retinue so that only Sagittaria remained.

Her heart thudding loudly, Silver stepped away from the center of the room, pulling off rings and depositing them on a cushion. Her breath quickened, and the patterns in the thick rugs at her feet began to spin.

Silver's father retrieved the race cup he'd been saving for that moment. All the dents and dings that Silver had put in it were once again smoothed out. Her father must have worked all night to fix her mess. "I saved my finest gold for you—"

"I'll judge that for myself," Sagittaria Wonder said, arching an eyebrow.

She looked around the showroom. Her eyes swept over Silver and kept moving, as though Silver weren't there.

You will *notice me,* Silver thought, carefully lifting the massive headdress from her hair. There were no other empty cushions, so she set the piece on a red-and-black stool.

"I'm not sure gold is the right material for this cup, after all," Sagittaria said. "I have a man in Calidia making me a piece out of crystal. It's beautiful. Turns to rainbows when the light hits it."

Rami looked nervous. "Of course, but there is nothing like the rich warmth of gold. It is the sun itself."

"We get enough sun in the desert."

Silver paused at the bracelet over her burn. She didn't understand why Sagittaria was being so curt. This wasn't how she had imagined the racer.

Silver pressed her thumb to the wound to remind herself to focus. She was so close.

"If you like, we can set any number of gemstones in the metal," Rami said quickly. "Unlike a crystal piece, our rainbow would be permanent. It would shine in even the darkest room."

Sagittaria sighed. She reached into her bag and pulled forth a pouch of coins. A piece of parchment fluttered to the ground at Silver's feet. "Here is a deposit for the cup. I'll have the queen's guard collect it when they come for her pieces."

Rami Batal's lips were pale. Payment matters were handled privately, not in front of everyone in the showroom.

Sagittaria's manners were lacking. A Calidian trait, no doubt, Silver thought. She silently vowed to never let the city change her good breeding.

"It will be ready to astound you," her father said.

Sagittaria Wonder turned away to leave.

This was it. Silver's one chance to impress Sagittaria.

"Wait! Sagittaria Wonder!" Her hands shook as she unbuttoned the caftan.

Sagittaria turned, her gaze sharpening as if seeing Silver for the first time.

"Silver!" her father cried out.

"I have something that will astound you now." She sidestepped her father's grasping hands.

Silver let the silk caftan drift to the floor and tore off the remaining bracelets. They fell with a clang.

She stood there clad in her riding suit. "It's the finest wool you've ever seen. Thin but warm. Water-resistant. The scale pattern decreases wind drag. The glove linings increase grip. The . . ."

As Sagittaria Wonder walked toward her—three, four, five slow steps—Silver forgot the lines she'd rehearsed so many times. The water dragon racer pinched a piece of the shoulder of the suit between her fingers.

"What an interesting pattern," she said in a low voice. Her eyes flashed from their shadowy depths. "Who taught you how to do this?"

"I invented it myself." Silver didn't know why she lied, but there was something about the way Sagittaria's eyes looked through her, instead of at her.

"A girl with great ambition." Sagittaria dropped the wool and stepped back. Her lip curled. "I know an important little bit about fiber arts techniques. And a lot about riding suits. This is a mess. The construction is too unwieldy for riding. There's no padding in the seat. It looks like . . ." She smiled slowly. Cruelly. "Like a child made it."

Silver went cold, as though she'd been wandering all night in a vast desert winter.

"It's just a prototype," she whispered.

"Well, I have no use for it."

Silver looked down. The parchment that Sagittaria had dropped was still at her feet. Silver picked it up and held it out to the water dragon racer, her hands trembling.

"Keep it," Sagittaria said, shaking her head. "It's just an advertisement for the races. Give it to the one who taught you this pattern."

Sagittaria Wonder spun on her heel. The rider disappeared out the door, Silver's dreams following her like the last wisps of a snuffed lantern. Silver stood staring at the empty doorway.

Rami Batal gaped at her, his forehead as red as pickled onions.

"Are you mad?" he whispered. "What were you thinking? Have you forgotten who you are? You are a Batal. You are—were—the heir to this work."

Silver's eyes went wide. Her spine seemed to twist upon itself, as though she could shrink to the size of a beetle and scamper out a small crack in the doorway. She had seen her father angry before—so angry he'd seemed like an unfiltered sun. When Gama had told him about how poorly she was doing in her classes, or when she'd snuck off with her cousin and forgotten to bring the daily bread, or even when he'd found her drawing water dragons in the dust on the windowsill. But this cold and distant Rami Batal was worse.

Silver knew she was lost to him.

Her lower lip trembled. She was a shell of a girl. Not talented. Not graceful. Not impressive. Not worthy of the Batal legacy.

And not on her way to Calidia to ride water dragons.

Slowly, she unhooked the remaining jewelry draping her neck and ears, and set it on the table. She hastily pulled on her mother's caftan and retrieved her shoes. The older ele-jewelers pretended to work on their metals and gems, but they peeked at her as she gathered her things.

"Here," Phila whispered, passing the two golden hair combs to Silver. She opened her mouth as if to say more, but Silver turned away. There was pity in Phila's face, and Silver hated that. She didn't want anyone to feel sorry for her.

She just wanted to disappear.

THE ROADS WERE still crammed. Instead of the usual twenty thousand people, there seemed double that. Ladies-in-waiting and drivers and servants and cooks and animal tenders. Silver couldn't imagine how big Calidia was if all these people were only a tiny piece of that grand city.

Vendors on the Jaspaton roads worked furiously to cook their desert specialties for all the Calidians waiting in line. The air became sweet with the heady smells of succulent tea, meat on spits, and desert-rose jellies softening in the growing warmth of the day. Silver's mouth should have been watering, but it was as dry as a desert wind.

Neighbors still smiled at her. People waved to her from high on the cliff, where they were perched to get a good view of the royal caravan. The tale of what had happened at the showroom must not have traveled to them yet, or else they would be laughing.

As for Silver, she wasn't sure she would ever laugh again.

Her suit had been a failure. Her father was furious. Calidia was farther away than it ever had been. But the worst thing of all was . . .

Sagittaria Wonder.

At first glance, Sagittaria had been everything Silver had imagined. Strong, confident, mysterious. Impossible to miss. Waves of power flowed off her. She was the hero of Silver's dreams. She had even called Silver ambitious!

After that, though, her cruelty was like the bite of a scorpion. Fiercely painful at first touch, then spreading throughout Silver's body until she was overtaken with shame. How could her hero be so awful?

Silver wiped her nose with the back of her hand and crunched up the flight of stairs she'd toppled down earlier in the day. All her aches and bruises were returning, now that there was nothing to take her mind off them.

She slammed the door of her house open, then slammed it closed behind her. In her room, she peeled the suit off and tossed it on the floor. With a cry, she tore the drawings off her walls and threw them down, too.

"Where were you, Nebekker?" she sobbed.

Her mother was still at the yarnsladies' tents and would probably be all night. There would be parties for the Calidians, with delectable finger foods, and musicians pounding drums and plucking strings for dancing. They would celebrate their sales, their friendly relationships, and the very beauty of the harsh but generous desert.

Silver would stay in her room for all of it. She looked out the window the rest of the afternoon, fat tears making tracks down her cheeks.

"You're as dumb as a dung beetle," Silver told herself.

Everything she had done, all the people she had disappointed—it was all for nothing.

In the distance, the sun's colors blurred into a muted yellow, then orange and pink as evening approached. And still the winds blew. The sleepless night and wounded emotions of the day overcame Silver. She sank into a restless sleep.

When she opened her eyes again and went to the window, it was dark out. Very dark.

The moon and stars were hidden. People outside carried the colorful gem lanterns of Jaspaton, or the intricately patterned metal lanterns of Calidia. But the light they gave off was dimmed by all the sand in the air.

Were this a normal night of storms, everyone would be tucked away in their homes. Tonight, though, was for celebration. Partygoers were dressed in their finest, but by the end of the night, Silver knew their most beautiful scarves would be frayed and torn by the sands.

The winds settled briefly and a sliver of moonglow broke through the clouds. A deceptive calm. Everyone hurried to their festivities while there was a respite from the weather.

Silver squinted. Down on the desert floor, a dark figure shadowed by a lantern's soft light began trekking out toward the deep desert. Three more people followed, their backs heavy with packs. Who was ignorant enough to leave the city on a night like this?

She dashed out of her house and crossed the road to get a

better view. The lead traveler was tall and slender. Dressed all in black, with long black hair whipping out of a scarf hastily drawn up. Silver knew that confident walk.

Sagittaria Wonder was heading into the desert. And, when the storm resumed, as it surely would, to her death.

Silver raced to get dressed. The great water dragon racer was right: Silver was ambitious, and she would use this opportunity to convince her that she was worth taking a chance on. Even if it meant risking her life.

She started to put on her trousers, but the desert was frigid at night. Her riding suit would keep her warm and keep the whipping sand from blasting a layer of skin off her body.

She snarled at the suit. The awkward, ugly thing had earned her only Sagittaria Wonder's scorn.

Still, she slipped it on, then added the trousers and a flowing tunic over the suit, boots, and a scarf wrapped around her face and head. Grabbing a lantern, she burst out of the house and raced down the stairs and roads to the lower levels.

Already, Sagittaria was out of sight. But Silver knew what direction she had taken. It was a trail toward the sand dunes where she'd surfed. It shouldn't be hard for her to catch up. Silver knelt and struck flint to light her lantern. When the oil-soaked wick caught, she flew with the speed of a diving hawk disappearing into the dark of vast night.

TEN

"Sagittaria Wonder," Silver called into the night.

The calm was eerie. Electricity zapped through Silver's body as she trotted down the trail to the dunes. She knew the stillness wouldn't last. The sand had settled enough for the moon to be seen again, but the stars were still hidden.

She had underestimated how much of a head start Sagittaria had gotten, but Silver was a deep-desert girl.

What was the dragon rider doing out in such a storm? Even the foxes and scorpions were tucked away in their underground burrows. Sagittaria would get herself hurt, or even killed.

Why should I help her? As soon as the dark thought entered her mind, she pushed it back out again. Silver would never live down the shame she'd felt in the workshop, but that wasn't reason enough to wish Sagittaria harm. Especially not at the hands of a desert storm.

Silver—and probably everyone in Jaspaton—had a deep fear of dying out in the desert. The best option was for hundreds of scorpions to poison you. It would hurt, at first, but then a deep sleep that you'd never awaken from would overcome you. The scavenger birds would find your body eventually and make several meals out of it. But the worst option . . .

Silver shivered. Family members gone missing in a desert storm, their bodies discovered days later after the dunes finished shifting. They'd been buried alive, their ears and eyes and mouth and nose filled with sand. Suffocated.

A blast of wind scraped sand across Silver's lips, and she yelped. The storm was picking up again.

"Sagittaria!"

Silver marched on. Past the dunes, which would look different in the morning as they shifted in the storm. Past the end of the trail. Into the vast desert, where her feet sank into the sand and she had to wade through the dunes with aching legs.

Calidians! They might have great palaces and universities, they might interact with peoples from all across the globe, but when it came to deep-desert smarts, they had none.

"Sagittaria!" Her voice was going hoarse. Sand collected in her nostrils in little balls. She snorted them out. Sound muted as her ears filled with sand, too. Who was she to call the Calidians stupid when she had run into the storm just as unprepared?

Silver dropped to her knees. The lights of Jaspaton were now too far to see. Even the dark, shadowy mounds of the dunes had disappeared. She was farther into the desert than she'd ever been before.

She could go back. She *should* go back. It wasn't her fault Sagittaria thought she could take on a sandstorm. But as Silver looked in a slow circle, she realized she had no idea which way home was. She was lost.

"Don't panic," she whispered. She looked to the sky to guide her way home. "Stars, where are you?" There were no astronomical markers to be seen.

It had been many, many generations since anyone but the most remote of nomadic desert peoples believed in the ancient goddesses, but just then, Silver closed her eyes and imagined the arms of them scooping her up from the desert floor and swifting her to safety back in Jaspaton.

When she opened her eyes, she was in the same place, with the same storm bearing down on her. No one was coming for her. She had to get herself out of this mess.

Okay, Silver. What would a dragon rider do? She wiped her face with her scarf, scratching the delicate skin of her eyelids, and winced. *A dragon rider wouldn't be here in the first place. Nowhere for a dragon to swim.*

She laughed at her own train of thought. When she got home—*if* she got home—she would become the model daughter. She would take up jewelry making with great passion. She would burn all her charts and drawings. She would never get in trouble again.

Silver put one foot in front of the next. She counted.

One. Two. Three. She counted to one hundred, then to one thousand. The dunes never came back into sight. Silver's legs turned to jelly. She didn't dare open her mouth, for fear the sand would fill her entire body.

She fell, letting the soft, cool sand envelop her like a blanket. Her eyes drifted closed.

DREAMS BEFORE DYING were the loveliest things.

In Silver's, she was weightless. Her aching muscles held up hollow bones; her clumsy limbs were tucked in close to her body, as though she were being held and rocked gently. The last time she remembered being rocked was by her mother. Then, Sersha had sung to her ancient ballads of desert lore. In the melody Silver heard in her dream, it was the sand itself that sang, rolling and lifting and fading its melancholy notes into her ears.

Silver hummed along with the desert song.

Moisture trickled down her throat. A succulent tea, but not the same that she'd always known. This one was fruitier. Dozens of layers of flavors and very fragrant. Cool.

She coughed.

Water was everywhere. In her face, her eyes, up her nose. Silver sat, and hacked up the contents of her lungs. How could she be drowning when she was buried alive in the desert? She was scared to take a breath, for fear she'd take in only sand, not air. Her head pounded, and her chest was on fire.

A familiar voice. "Breathe, girl."

"I can't!"

"Breathe."

Silver squeezed her eyes shut even tighter. Her body wouldn't listen to her brain. Without her permission, her lungs sucked in.

Air. Not sand. Sweet, sweet air. Silver took another greedy breath, then another.

She dared to open her eyes, but she couldn't see anything. They stung like they'd been pricked by Flying Black-Eyed Scorpions.

"Here." A hand tipped Silver's head back. A wash of water went over her face, followed by a soft cloth. This was repeated several times, until the sand was flushed from Silver's eyes and nose and mouth and ears.

"Is that better?"

Silver sat up again. Opened her eyes. Saw the sparkle of a pale-blue gemstone before it disappeared behind cloth again. Nebekker. *Nebekker* was out here?

"What are you doing over the dunes?" Silver said.

"I should have left you for the scorpions." The old woman frowned at her. "What kind of common sense have you misplaced? I always thought highly of your parents, but if they let you out wandering in this weather, I'm changing my mind."

"They don't know I'm here." Silver peered at the sky, bright with the first blush of morning. The world had settled. The storm was over. "At least, they *didn't* know. They probably do now. I'm supposed to be in my room."

Suddenly, a roar of anger filled Silver's ears.

"You left!" she said, accusing Nebekker. "When I needed you most." Silver leaped to her feet, swayed, and fell back again. That was when she realized she wasn't in the open desert anymore. Before her, narrow trees rose into the sky. Slivers of blue appeared between their trunks. It was an oasis.

Silver had only heard of them. The air was as salty as ever, but it was damp, too. When she strained her ears, she could hear water—dripping and flowing—from somewhere in the distance.

The marvel of the oasis almost softened Silver's heart, but her anger was too great.

"You disappeared, and I had to finish the suit by myself,"

Silver cried. "Brajon tried to help, but it was a disaster. Sagittaria Wonder *laughed* at me. She said . . . She said . . ." But Silver couldn't bear to repeat what Sagittaria had said to her.

Nebekker's frown deepened. "I'm sorry it didn't go well with Sagittaria. But you weren't the only one who needed me."

Silver bit back tears. "Who needed you more than I did? There's no one else out here."

Nebekker's lips twitched. "It's a bit complicated. There is someone. Two someones, actually. But I'd rather you didn't . . . Oh, too late for that."

Nebekker's gaze focused on something in the sky. Silver followed its direction and saw a black dot in the distance. As she watched, the dot grew larger . . . and longer.

"What is it?" Silver whispered.

"My great secret," Nebekker said. She stood as the thing in the sky approached.

Eleven

What Silver thought at first must have been a very large hawk turned out to be nothing of the sort. It was blue. The blue she'd always imagined the oceans were. Its wings and tail were tipped with white. On a day when fluffy white clouds danced in the sky, the creature would be perfectly camouflaged. When it disappeared in the center of the trees with a splash, Silver got to her feet and began running, forgetting her aches and pains completely.

"Wait," Nebekker called, lifting her flowing trousers and running after Silver.

Did I see . . . ? Is it really . . . ?

Silver burst through the greenery surrounding the lake.

"Hoowawrrrrr!" The roar nearly lifted Silver off her feet. A head almost as big as her bedroom greeted her. Its mouth opened wide to show off a double row of razor-sharp teeth and a long, slithering pink tongue. Its black eyes glinted.

Silver scrambled backward. The creature shook its head, spraying water everywhere. It stepped forward, its sinewy muscles rolling under scaled skin. It licked its lips. Opened its mouth to roar again.

"Kirja," Nebekker said sternly. "Knock that off!"

The creature—Kirja—immediately rolled to its back. Its tongue lolled out the side of its mouth, and it panted.

Silver's jaw fell nearly to her feet. She could hardly breathe. Blood rushed to her ears, and her hands shook.

Nebekker put her palms on the creature's belly and rubbed quickly. Kirja's stubby legs shook happily in all directions.

"You're too much a baby to be a—" Nebekker looked at Silver sharply. "Never mind. Kirja, this is Silver. She's all right. You don't have to eat her. Silver, this is Kirja. My Aquinder."

Silver reached out an arm, then pulled it back again.

Belief. It was a hard thing to find. In some tiny corner of her heart, Silver had always known Aquinder were real. But seeing one shocked her.

She thought back to looking at the night sky with Brajon and seeing a moving thing that blocked strips of stars. Could it have been . . . ?

In that moment, everything felt like an impossibility. An Aquinder, living in the vast desert, belonging to an old woman. Maybe Silver *had* died. Maybe this was all just a dream.

Then again, the Aquinder's breath had been pretty stinky. It would have had nicer breath if this were all her dream.

"You can touch her," Nebekker said, beckoning Silver closer. "She won't hurt you."

"Are you sure? I mean . . ."

In every legend Silver had heard, Aquinder had been hunted to extinction hundreds of years ago, after the great wars, because they were dangerous. Deadly.

Kirja wriggled back and forth as Nebekker tickled her underbelly.

Deadly? Silver giggled. More like ridiculously playful.

Kirja's upside-down face sported a dopey grin. A series of snorts that sounded suspiciously like laughter came from her big, round nostrils. Nebekker paused, and Kirja opened her eyes. Her tongue lolled out of her mouth again.

"Come over here. Kirja's going to think you don't like her. Nothing upsets an Aquinder more."

"But I thought—"

"They were only a children's story? Or that they were ferocious beasts?" Nebekker shook her head. "They're neither. Aquinder crave love and attention. And when people learn that, well, they take advantage of that and force them to do terrible things."

Silver edged closer to the water dragon. Kirja's dark eyes followed her movements, and the closer Silver got, the more Kirja wriggled with delight. When Silver finally put her hand on the water dragon's belly, Kirja relaxed, and sighed contentedly.

"It's furry," Silver exclaimed. Her hands sank into the lush coat of silver fur on Kirja's belly, and when Silver pulled away, iridescent strands clung to her fingers.

"Just on her tummy. She's shedding, too. Her winter coat will grow in even thicker. You should see how much hair's in the cave. Aquinder are a pain to take care of." Nebekker's voice sounded stern, but she gave Kirja a look of such deep love and affection that Silver knew the old woman would do anything to keep her water dragon happy.

"Where did she come from?" Silver asked as she went back to rubbing Kirja's belly.

"All the other water dragons came from the depths of the earth through the Black Hole, of course, but no one quite knows where Aquinder came from. The old legends say they were birthed in the stars and bred in the clouds and raised in the seas, but who knows."

"But Kirja . . . How did *you* find her?"

"This urchin found me. It was a long, long time ago. In a life I lived before I came to the deep desert."

Kirja stiffened, and her finlike ears perked up. Nebekker dropped her voice to a whisper. "Come on. No time for tales right now. There's someone out there."

Silver snapped her head up.

"Sagittaria Wonder," she whispered. Silver felt a chill. She didn't want to think about what the racer might do if she discovered Kirja.

Nebekker glanced around the trees nervously. They did a good job hiding the oasis from view, but they also hid the desert. Anything could be out there.

"The cave's this way. Follow close to me."

"What about Kirja?"

"She's been hiding from humans for seventy years. She knows what to do."

Nebekker began walking briskly, but Silver hesitated. She wanted to make sure Kirja was going to be okay.

She needn't have worried. As soon as Nebekker disappeared through the palms, Kirja backed into the oasis lake, until only her head stuck out like a rock. The Aquinder watched Silver, and, if the creature could have talked, Silver was certain she would have told her to hurry.

Silver ran for the palms.

She never made it out of the oasis.

Twelve

"Ah! You're a familiar face. Aren't you that ridiculous child from the jeweler's shop?"

Sagittaria Wonder emerged from the sands like a mirage. Her companions joined her, standing on either side, with their hulking arms crossed over their chests. "Grab her!"

Silver darted in the opposite direction. She pushed through the pebbles on the edge of the lake, splashing water up her legs as she ran for the ring of trees. A palm frond whipped into her forehead, slicing across her brow. Before she could make it to the desert sands, hands grabbed her shoulders, yanking her off-balance. One of Sagittaria's men had caught her, and now tossed her over his shoulder.

"Let me go!" Silver kicked and pounded her fists against his back.

"Hang on to her." Sagittaria laughed. Silver had come to hate that sound more than anything in the world. "Her father will want her returned."

"He'll never pay a ransom to you," Silver screamed.

"Who said anything about a ransom?" Sagittaria said. "I don't want your father's jewels." She put her fingers under Silver's chin and forced their eyes to meet. Silver hated that she still admired the fierceness in the racer's eyes. "But you should believe that he would give his entire workshop for your return," Sagittaria said.

"You don't know my father very well," Silver said.

"No, I—" Sagittaria looked past Silver, and her eyes went wide. "It's here. I *knew* it. All these years . . . all these rumors . . . and it's here. Finally." The water dragon racer took in a deep breath and let it out slowly. "The Aquinder."

"No!" Silver craned her neck.

Kirja rose slowly from the oasis water, her enormous head looming over them all. Water dripped slowly from her scales. Her mouth opened to reveal her teeth, and her black eyes sparked with anger.

"Go back, Kirja!" Silver's heart thudded painfully.

Kirja spread her wings, and Silver's eyes widened. The wings were massive, dark and rippling. Kirja, who only moments before had seemed as harmless as a herd animal, shadowed them all with her size.

"Fly away," Silver shouted. She would find a way to distract Sagittaria. She had to.

"Let her go," Nebekker yelled. She rushed onto the scene, brandishing a huge palm frond.

She slammed the frond into the stomach of one of Sagittaria's men. With a surprised groan, he buckled and fell to the ground. Without a second glance, Nebekker came for the man holding Silver. Her weapon crashed against the back of his knees. He shuddered and fell forward.

Silver rolled to the side to avoid being crushed. A great

whoosh of air flipped her scarf. It was Kirja flying at them, her mouth wide.

"Hrrggaauwnnn!" Her roar shook the ground.

"Aaaahhhh!" Silver pressed her hands over her ears.

Kirja grabbed one of the men and lifted him from the ground. He screamed, his limbs flailing. The Aquinder tossed her head, throwing him out of the oasis to land somewhere in the vast desert.

Sagittaria strode to Nebekker, seemingly undisturbed by the dragon swooping overhead. "I've been looking for you, old woman," the racer said. "Came all the way to Jaspaton because some rumors placed you in the deep desert. The same rumors that said you'd lead me to the Aquinder."

She turned to Silver.

Nebekker raised the frond high and aimed for Sagittaria's head. But just as she was about to bring the heavy branch down, one of the men sprang up and tackled her around the waist.

"Nebekker!" Silver heard the sickening snap of a bone.

Kirja roared again. Her body rolled, and she dove for the ground, her fins and ears flattened against the side of her head, and her wings tucked in, a streak of silver blue. Her speed took Silver's breath away.

But Sagittaria was fast, too. She dropped to the ground beside Nebekker and yanked the old woman's arms behind her back.

"Stop," Sagittaria called out to Kirja. "Or I'll hurt her!"

"No," Silver screamed. One of the two men left shoved her to the ground.

Kirja widened her fins and wings, slowing until she was merely floating above them. Watching. Nervous. She mewled.

"Call her down," Sagittaria said to Nebekker.

"You could threaten to kill me, and I still wouldn't."

Sagittaria Wonder sighed. "Don't be so dramatic," she said. "That's unnecessary."

A glimmer of blue caught Silver's attention as Sagittaria reached for the gemstone pendant peeking out of Nebekker's tunic.

"But this *is* necessary."

Her palm closed, and she ripped the chain off Nebekker's neck. At the same time, Silver flung herself at Sagittaria. The dragon racer looked up in time to throw an arm out as she stumbled backward, knocking Silver to the ground. The pendant flew through the air and landed under a tree.

One man was lying still on the ground and the other hovered to the side, sizing up Kirja. The water dragon didn't pay any attention to them. She watched only Nebekker.

"Tell her to land," Sagittaria Wonder said.

"I can't force her to do anything," Nebekker said. "Not after—"

"Don't lie to me. I've been around dragons all my life. I know their ways."

Nebekker tightened her lips but then nodded toward Kirja. The dragon touched down at the edge of the water and stretched her nose toward Nebekker.

As the man near the lake tiptoed closer to Kirja, Silver got to her feet. Half-formed plans flooded her brain. Leap on the man? Try to rescue Nebekker? Her body froze with indecision.

The man on the ground groaned. He pulled himself up, but he was clearly in pain, and Silver realized that the bone-snapping sound she'd heard hadn't been Nebekker's. It was his.

Sagittaria loosened her grip on Nebekker long enough to wave at the men to close in on the dragon. Silver saw her chance and took it. She dove. At the same time, the men jumped on Kirja, jamming their hands into the tender joints where her wings met her body. Kirja screamed.

So did Silver. "Aaaiiieee!"

Sagittaria toppled back in surprise. Kirja reared, throwing off one man. The other managed to get a rope around one wing. Silver pulled Nebekker to her feet while Kirja swung her head and lashed out at the man with the rope, knocking him into the center of the oasis pool.

Sagittaria ran for the dragon, pulling on the rope until the other man got a rope around Kirja's other wing. Silver threw her body toward the water dragon, but Nebekker caught her.

"No." The old woman shoved Silver in the opposite direction. "Run. Now."

"I won't go without Kirja!" Silver fell at the roots of the trees, refusing to move.

"You *will*. We both will."

Nebekker shoved her again, and Silver got up. They pushed the greenery aside and dove for the sands on the other side. Nebekker grabbed Silver's hand.

"This way!"

They cut left and circled the outer oasis until Silver found herself at a cave entrance.

"Get inside. They won't find us here."

"A cave," Silver said, panting. "In the desert. They'll find us."

"Trust me." Nebekker shoved her inside and pulled on a rope hanging at the entrance. A tapestry perfectly mimicking the landscape of the desert fell into place, obscuring the cave opening.

Nebekker took Silver's elbow and marched them toward the back of the cave. "Keep walking."

"There's nowhere to go." They were headed for a wall. What did Nebekker want her to do—walk through it?

But then Nebekker led them slightly to the right, and Silver realized that the cave continued, in a sharp slope down into darkness. There were myriad smells: stone and soil, water, and something else. Something lush and vegetal. Her ears picked up the sound of water, too. Dripping, somewhere close by. And, not too far away, rushing, like a stream.

Silver had so many questions. "How could you just let them—"

"Keep walking," Nebekker repeated.

Silver scowled. She was finding it hard to trust the old woman. As they stepped deeper and deeper into the cave, flashes of Kirja's expressions flitted through Silver's mind: the Aquinder's uncertainty, her anger, her need to make sure Nebekker was all right.

The water dragon was devoted. Too bad the same couldn't be said of Nebekker.

Silver's boots flew out from under her. She landed hard on her backside, sliding down the slick passageway and coming to a stop in the midst of something thick and wet. She got to her feet as fast as she could.

"Ew." She wiped her hands on her trousers. The water was freezing. She knew she should be freezing, too, but the riding suit beneath her clothes was keeping her warm. "What's down here?"

"Moss," Nebekker said. "And perhaps a few slugs."

"What are slugs?"

Nebekker snorted. "Desert girls," she said. "Imagine a small, slithering animal made of jelly."

"Gross."

Silver's ears tightened with pressure. How far underground had they gone? A chill ran up her spine. She didn't like the way the walls seemed to close in on her from both sides and she really hated how close the ceiling was to her head. She barely had room to stand up straight.

"It's too cramped," she said.

Nebekker guided her with a gentle touch on her back. Silver turned left, then right. Then she turned another corner, and the underground opened up before them.

Thirteen

The cavern was massive, falling so deep into the ground that it was like standing on top of the Jaspaton cliffs, except that instead of the vast desert in the foreground, it was thick layers of moss and, cutting through the middle of it all, a swiftly flowing river. Above the river, stalactites like dragon's teeth hung from the ceiling, dripping water in a pattern that filled the cavern with an otherworldly song.

Nebekker pushed past Silver so she could take the lead. The path to the riverbank descended rapidly down crudely cut steps in the cavern walls. Silver squinted to see each stair in the low light that came from an opening to the right. The glow gave the cavern an eerie quality; the light moved across the walls like sloshing waves.

Nebekker pointed. "The river runs through the oasis lagoon on that side. The lagoon undercurrent is strong. It pushes some water up to the surface."

"Does the river go all the way to Calidia?" Silver said.

"To, and beyond."

At the bottom of the trail, the riverbank was wide, as

though the river had once been mightier and had carved space for itself. Nebekker made her way toward an overhang, where there was a stack of fuel for fires; baskets of preserved foods; piles of blankets; and a variety of tools, like knives and lanterns. She picked up one of the lanterns and lit the wick. It smoked for a moment, then burned clean and clear.

The light opened up the cavern even more, bringing its multicolored rock structures into view. It was the most beautiful place Silver had ever seen.

"You've been here before," she said.

"I've been here often," Nebekker said. She nodded in the opposite direction from the lagoon. "The river flows from Jaspaton in that direction."

"Jaspaton?"

"Yes, Jaspaton," Nebekker said. "Where you'll be heading soon. I don't need you hanging around here longer than necessary."

Silver frowned. "I'm staying here until you get Kirja back."

How could Silver even think about going home now that she knew Aquinder were real?

Nebekker chuckled. "I never invited you to stay."

"You don't own this cavern." Silver crossed her arms and sat down. Right in a puddle. The water was freezing cold, and she gritted her teeth to keep them from rattling.

Nebekker built a small fire, ignoring Silver. From one basket, she pulled out a pot and set it over the fire to boil; from another, a package wrapped in paper. She walked to the river and stood there with the package in her hands, looking toward some stalagmites.

She whistled. "Come on out, pretty one," Nebekker called. "My turn to be your mama for a little while."

Silver waited, pretending not to be watching. Who in the desert was Nebekker talking to? Surely there couldn't be children down here.

Nebekker whistled again. Then her teeth flashed as she grinned. Silver followed her gaze across the river. There was something moving among the stalagmites. Crouched or . . . even slithering. Something that matched the blue light and pale silver of the cavern.

The thing across the river purred.

Purred?

The sound touched Silver to her very core. She got to her feet and ran toward the river without thinking, as though a string tied to her middle were pulling her. There was no staying away if she'd wanted to. Her need to meet the creature was far too great. She stepped into the river.

The ice-cold water over her boots slowed her down for only a moment. But that was long enough for Nebekker to grab her arm and hold her in place. She was surprisingly strong.

"Of *course* this would happen." Nebekker sighed wearily.

"Let me go!" Silver had to get to the other side of the river.

"Stay right here. He'll come to you. The stars know, it'll affect the both of you."

In the back of her mind, Silver wondered what the old woman meant, but she didn't ask, because the pull to cross the river was still so powerful.

She struggled to free herself. "I have to—"

Splash.

Just then, a shadow slipped into the river and made its way to Silver and Nebekker. Silver knelt into the water, waiting.

She didn't know what for or if she was in danger. She knew only that she had to open her arms and greet it.

When the creature finally burst from the water, it bowled Silver over. She landed on her back, hard, rocks digging into her spine. Soaking in the river water, her arms and chest became even colder than before. But she didn't care. She was awash in euphoria.

Within seconds, the warmth of the creature bled into her skin. Its happy heartbeat thudded in time with her own. It purred again and licked her face until the smell of fish and river weeds overwhelmed her nostrils.

Silver laughed and opened her eyes. A pair of obsidian-dark eyes looked back down at her from a sky-blue face ringed with white.

"Another Aquinder," Silver said, marveling. "A little one!"

"If your definition of 'little' is 'the size of a house.'" Nebekker stood with her hands on her hips. She didn't seem particularly happy. "Kirja's son. Another troublemaker, if you ask me."

"No, he's perfect." Silver's heart had swelled to nearly bursting. "And I won't have you calling him names, or else."

Nebekker snorted. "Or else what?"

"I don't know what. But I'll think of something. I'd do anything for . . . for . . . What's his name?"

The water dragon licked Silver some more, then rolled over and let his tongue loll out to the side, just like Kirja had. Silver rubbed his belly.

Nebekker tilted her head back and spoke to the ceiling of the cavern. "It's not how I'd have wanted it, Kirja. He should have bonded with someone with more experience. But it's out of my hands, as you know. We never ask for these things."

Silver rested her cheek on the dragon's belly. "Never ask for what? How could you keep this secret from me? A mom and baby!"

"Never ask to be bonded!" Nebekker stood over them. "You think this water lizard is cute? Of course you would. You don't know a thing about the real world. Neither of you do."

Nebekker retrieved the paper-wrapped package and walked back to her fire. Her sigh filled the cavern. "Come here. Both of you. I have a tale to tell."

Silver got to her feet, and the Aquinder followed suit, swaying a bit before he got full control of his balance. Silver stifled a giggle. The Aquinder grinned. When Silver took a step forward, so did the water dragon. When she took another and then another, he matched her step by step.

"He does everything I do," Silver said.

"Yes, he does," Nebekker said. "What did you expect with your bond?"

"Our bond?"

Nebekker sighed again and waved them over. She unwrapped the paper. Inside was a selection of dried meats. She placed a small handful in the boiling water, then put the rest on the ground. She whistled, but the water dragon hesitated and looked at Silver.

"You have to tell him it's okay to come eat," Nebekker said.

"He doesn't need my permission." But Silver nudged the Aquinder and pointed to the food. He leaped forward, tripped over his own front feet, flipped tail to head, and landed in a heap next to his dinner. Without untangling himself, he lapped sideways at the food with his long tongue.

Nebekker ladled some of the stew from the pot into a ceramic bowl. "Sit down and eat, and I'll tell you some things."

Silver picked up the bowl, but she didn't eat. How could she when so much had happened? Kirja's kidnapping, the underground river, the baby Aquinder, the stories Nebekker had yet to tell. Still, her stomach rumbled at the scent of broth, so she dug into the stew as voraciously as the dragon did.

Nebekker chewed her food for a moment, then set the mug on the ground. "This all started well before I met Kirja. Some five hundred years ago. No . . . long before that. I don't have time to explain the Wakening of Breathing Creatures to you. But you've learned about the Land and Sea Wars, right?"

Silver nodded. "We studied it in history class last year."

"So you say, but I know kids these days get a mangled version of the truth." Nebekker shook her head. "It doesn't do to deceive our children by rewriting history."

Silver glanced at the baby water dragon next to her. He had finished his meal and was now napping, with his stubby legs pointing into the air. His soft snores shook his silver whiskers. Silver wanted to curl up next to him.

Instead, she said, "My teachers always said Aquinder were a myth."

Nebekker clicked her tongue against the roof of her mouth. "I'd like to shock all those vainglorious teachers with a peek at the creature in front of you. What *did* they teach you about the Land and Sea Wars?"

"Just that the water dragons destroyed the coastal cities, then started moving inland. But a great army arose out of the deep-desert cities, and the vast desert nomadic tribes fought back. They—"

"A desert army, was it?" Nebekker shook her head. "Without fail, humans will rearrange history to fit their own ideas of heroes and glory. Let me tell you some real truth.

Aquinder exist and have always existed. Long before the Land and Sea Wars, the dragons gifted humans with bonds after humans helped them send Lava Dragons back into the Black Hole."

Silver's eyes widened. "The Black *what*?"

Nebekker waved her words away. "But as humans began using dragons in their selfish war, they were punished. Bonds were taken away. But then came a young desert boy named Gulad Nakim."

"Gulad Nakim," Silver repeated.

"The first dragon rider. Before Gulad, the desert armies thought there was no way to train the desire to kill out of the Aquinder. But Gulad's Aquinder was as gentle as a desert beetle. He could hand-feed it. When Gulad was ordered to train his Aquinder to be a killer, he refused, and they fled to the vast desert." Nebekker sipped more stew and watched the baby Aquinder sleep, coiled up next to Silver. "The desert was nearly crushed in the war, but just when all hope had been lost, Gulad Nakim returned with his water dragon. Instead of walking side by side, rider and dragon flew in, together. It was then the whole world discovered that humans could ride dragons."

"How had no one realized that before?" Silver said, her hand absently patting the baby water dragon's side.

"Because when bonds were taken away, dragons became temperamental. They were chained to ships . . . beaten until they frothed with rage . . . and then released into cities. Gulad knew that there could be love and respect between humans and dragons. His heart was pure, his intentions only to care for his dragon. And so for the first time in many years, a dragon bonded with a human."

Nebekker suddenly put her hand over her heart and winced. Her breathing got heavy.

Silver leaned forward. "Are you all right?"

"I'll be fine." Nebekker sat silent for a few moments, catching her breath. "Let me finish my story. Gulad and his Aquinder rode into battle and changed the tide of the wars. Soon enough, more humans were able to ride Aquinder, but still no other bonds were known.

"With so much of the earth laid to waste, the island king and desert king finally agreed to end the war. They signed a treaty to unify their people, so that all island royalty would be partnered to landed royalty, and vice versa."

"What about Gulad? And his dragon?" Silver whispered.

"Part of the treaty required that all Aquinder be slaughtered," Nebekker said darkly. "They were considered too dangerous to be near humans."

"They could have just released them back to the seas," Silver cried.

"For the next warmongering king to seek and capture?" Nebekker pierced Silver with a look from her jade eyes. "They killed them all. But they missed several eggs left in nests in the vast desert, and I believe Kirja is the offspring of one of those. Gulad had to have been doing something when he was in the desert. But for all his pains, they killed him, too, hoping bonds would die with him. Kings and queens did not like the idea of anyone other than themselves being able to control dragons."

"But it's not control," Silver said, a lump forming in her throat. She lay a protective hand over the sleeping water dragon.

"No." Nebekker smiled. "But they didn't have the capability

to see it that way, the way it really is. But you will, now that you're bonded."

"What does it mean to be bonded?" Silver asked.

"Your lifeblood pumps at the same rate. You breathe in and out together. You stay by each other's side forever. You would do anything the other needs. Even die for each other. And when that day of death comes for one, the other cannot live," Nebekker said fiercely. "To be bonded is the most beautiful experience a dragon-loving human can have. I was only a girl about your age when Kirja found me, but when I saw her, well, it felt like my body had been torn in half and stitched back together with her blood in me."

"Oh." It was a strange way to describe meeting a water dragon for the first time. And yet . . .

Silver put her hand to her chest, making sure she, too, hadn't been torn in half.

"When I saw Kirja, I knew exactly what she was," Nebekker said sadly. "Like you, I was stunned to discover that Aquinder still lived. Barely . . . she had been injured. Attacked by another dragon, perhaps. I went to her every single day and nursed her back to health. Kirja lived in a cave at the shore for several years. I went to her every single day. I weaved a harness and rode her over the waves. Until a girl in my village saw us. I knew we had to run. If people knew Aquinder were still alive—"

"But Sagittaria knows now," Silver exclaimed, jumping to her feet. "She can't bring Kirja back to Calidia."

"Sagittaria Wonder will be halfway across the vast desert by now. She has trained her whole life for the moment she could mount an Aquinder and soar through the skies."

"But they're not bonded," Silver cried.

"Do you think all the other Aquinder that were ridden into battle were bonded with their humans? Of course not. Dragons can be trained to take any rider, using the right methods. Or coerced, as I'm sure my Kirja will be."

"If they kill Kirja"—Silver's heart pounded—"what will happen to you?"

"They won't do that. She's far too valuable to them."

"She wants to race Kirja," Silver said, suddenly remembering the parchment Sagittaria Wonder had dropped in her father's shop. "Sagittaria left me this flyer." She pulled it from the sleeve of her riding suit. Across the top, the flyer featured a drawing of Sagittaria Wonder sitting in the saddle of her favorite racing dragon, Riptide.

Silver read out loud: "'The Desert Nations Autumn Festival World Water Dragon Racing Qualifiers and Semifinals. Registration on-site for established and claimant dragons.'"

A cool, blunt water dragon nose nudged the flyer from Silver's hand. The Aquinder grinned at Silver and waved its tail side to side.

"Playtime, is it?" Silver grinned, and so did the Aquinder. The water dragon splashed into the river. When Silver didn't follow, he poked his head back out and mewled.

"Sorry," she said, "I can't swim."

Nebekker shook her head. "Can't swim, but you think you can race water dragons." She lifted the fallen parchment with a toe.

"I'll learn!" Silver grabbed the flyer. "What it says here . . . 'Claimant dragons' . . . what's that all about?"

"All desert-based water dragons are by default owned by

Queen Imea, unless registered. Then, the rider or the rider's sponsor owns them. Racing is one way to register them. It's protection for the dragon and its owner."

"But that means if Sagittaria races Kirja in the Autumn Festival, you'll lose her forever."

"Their law is not my law. Kirja and I will always belong to each other. They don't understand bonds, but when Kirja stops obeying them they'll come for me to force her to do what they say. They'll—"

Suddenly, Silver understood. "Use you. Imprison you. Harm you when Kirja won't do what they tell her to do. I won't let that happen!"

Nebekker snorted. "What are you going to do about it? You can hardly walk in a straight line without falling over."

"I'll think of something. I know I will." A fire flared to life in Silver's chest.

"Right now you should focus on thinking up a name for that baby dragon."

Silver pointed to herself. "Me?"

As though he knew they were talking about him, the Aquinder came back to Silver, forcing his head under her arm and giving her a reproachful look when she didn't immediately start petting him.

"You're his bonded human, not me." Nebekker stood and stretched her arms above her head. She turned away, trembling, and wrapped a few blankets around her shoulders. She began to hum and work her hands, but Silver couldn't see what she was doing. Silver's hand absentmindedly patted the Aquinder by her side.

Her Aquinder.

"Nebekker, does our bond mean that from now on . . . forevermore . . . I have to live in hiding?"

"Once, there was a woman who tried to hide her Aquinder from the world. She came to a city in the deep desert where no one, she thought, spent time thinking about water dragons. Then she met a meddling girl who thought of nothing but water dragons. The woman taught the girl a special craft, meant to help the girl find her way out of the city so that the city would remain safe for the woman and the dragon she hid."

Nebekker opened her mouth, as if to say something more, but she hesitated as she looked at Silver. Warmth blossomed on her face slowly, like a desert flower opening at sunrise.

"The creatures that end up mattering the most to us tend to come into our lives unexpectedly," she finally said. "In the end, no matter what the woman did or how she hid, she began to wonder if perhaps Aquinder were meant to find their way back into the world. Perhaps there is a new chapter to their story. One that pesky girl is going to have to help write."

Fourteen

Silver woke with a start. She rubbed her hand quickly over her eyes. The baby Aquinder sat up, too, startled, and looking at Silver anxiously. She'd fallen asleep. Last she remembered, her mind was racing—she was bonded to a water dragon!—but soon enough, her breathing had matched her water dragon's, which at the time was slow and steady, and she nodded off.

But now she was wide awake. Nebekker was missing, and there were voices by the path to the entrance of the cave.

"All you Jaspaton kids have herd dung for brains."

That was Nebekker's voice.

"It's not my fault! Everyone's worried."

Silver blinked. She knew that voice, too. *Brajon.*

"And you thought you'd be some kind of hero? You were more likely to get yourself killed out in the vast desert."

"But I didn't. *And* I found you and Silver. I *am* a hero. Feels pretty good, too."

Nebekker grunted, as if to hide her laughter.

Silver stood. The baby Aquinder stretched himself tall, too. "You have to hide," Silver told him.

The water dragon quickly tromped along the river's edge and dipped into the water. He gracefully swam to the other side, got out, and disappeared into the stalagmites. For about two seconds. As soon as he realized Silver wasn't following him, he stuck his head out and mewled.

"Shh!" Silver waved him back behind the cavern formations. But instead of moving out of sight, he mewled louder. He *howled* for Silver.

"Mer*yaaahhllllll!*"

"Stop that," Silver hissed.

"What's that sound? A monster?" Brajon said. His voice rose. "Silver? Are you down there?"

"Go!" she told her Aquinder.

He completely ignored her.

"If she's been eaten by a cave beast—"

"She's alive and well," Nebekker said. She and Brajon rounded the corner.

Even in the low light, Silver could see that her cousin's eyes lit up when he saw her.

"Silver!" he cried, rushing toward her. He dropped the dune board he was carrying and grabbed her in his arms, lifting her off the ground in a tight hug.

"Can't breathe," she gasped.

She heard a splash, then a high-pitched roar. In a flash of blue, the baby Aquinder slammed into Brajon's side, sending both him and Silver to the ground. Brajon rolled a few feet away, while the water dragon stood over Silver protectively, hissing at him.

"What is that?" Brajon yelled, raising his fists.

"Quiet," Silver yelled back. "It's my dragon."

That shut Brajon up. He froze and dropped his hands to his side. "What?"

Silver put her arms around her Aquinder and rubbed his sides. Both their hearts raced, but Silver tried to silently convey to her water dragon that Brajon wasn't going to hurt them. As if the dragon understood, he relaxed his big body against her and licked the side of her head in relief.

Brajon sat on the ground, his hands tangled in his hair. "How . . . What . . . ?"

"It's a long story." Silver told him everything, starting from when she looked out her window and saw Sagittaria Wonder heading out into the vast desert. "And now it's just me and Nebekker."

"And the water dragon. The Aquinder. They're real," Brajon breathed. "*Your* Aquinder. What does that even mean?"

"It means they've bonded," said Nebekker. "And *that* means a whole lot of not good things."

"Good things, too," Silver said, but she frowned.

Nebekker had been short of breath when she spoke. And in the low blue light, her face had taken on a slight shade of green. She was sick, and it was because she and Kirja were separated. Bonds were beautiful, but it was clear they were dangerous, too.

Brajon sat back on his heels, slowly shaking his head. He didn't look so well, either. "Sagittaria Wonder. A dragon thief. An Aquinder thief."

"Theft runs rampant before big races," Nebekker remarked offhandedly.

"She's not technically a thief," Silver said, telling Brajon about the registration law.

"So that means this one . . ." Brajon waved his hand at the baby Aquinder. "What are you going to do with it? I don't think your father will let you keep it."

Silver barked out a laugh, which her Aquinder mimicked, thinking it was a game. The honking sound echoed through the cavern.

"It doesn't matter. I'm not going back there," Silver said.

"You have to!" her cousin said. "Everyone's been searching for you. Your mother hasn't slept since you left. And mine hasn't cooked."

Silver felt a pull when Brajon mentioned her mother. She nibbled on her bottom lip.

"Sorry to deprive you of Aunt Yidla's feasts," she said. "But I have to stay here. With my . . ." Silver looked at her Aquinder. His big eyes sparkled back at her. She couldn't keep calling him "my Aquinder" or "my water dragon," like he was just a thing. He needed a name. Letters played over her lips, trying to form themselves into the right name for the dragon. "Mo . . . Tr . . . Vi . . ." She racked her brain to remember the names of the ancient deities. There was one responsible for all the matter surrounding the earth: the blue sky, the white clouds. The things that reminded her of her Aquinder's coloring. "Hiyyan," she finally said.

"Hiyyan? Like from the old stories?" Brajon said. "That's what its mother called it?"

"No," Nebekker said. "Water dragons don't name one another in our language. They use their own. This is the name Silver has given her dragon."

Brajon shook his head. "It's not as though you're going to be able to hide it in your room. Not for long, at least. And what about when it has to go to the bathroom?"

"You're not listening to me." Silver stood and brushed her trousers off. "I'm not going back to Jaspaton. I'm staying here with Hiyyan."

"Says who?" Nebekker said.

Silver looked at Nebekker with surprise.

"I can't leave Hiyyan. And I have to help Kirja. And you need help, too. You're sick!"

"No, you can't leave Hiyyan," Nebekker said. She sighed. "But I never expected to have to account for a couple of children."

"We're not babies," Silver said.

"You act like one sometimes," Brajon teased.

Silver stuck her tongue out at her cousin. Hiyyan followed suit.

"Stop teaching that poor Aquinder your bad manners," Nebekker said. "Now that his mother's gone, *you'll* have to show him how to be a water dragon . . . somehow."

"How will I teach him to race?" Silver asked. "How will I teach him to fly?"

Nebekker shook her head. "I'll show you the way back to Jaspaton. You'll be able to come and go as you please, so long as you never let anyone see you. If our secret is discovered, say good-bye to Hiyyan."

Nebekker picked up her lantern and began walking. Silver took a step toward the old woman. Hiyyan whimpered. He began to follow Silver.

She stopped. "He just lost his mother. And now I'm supposed to leave him?" She shook her head, thinking about that tight feeling she'd had when she'd thought about her own mother. "No. I'm not going back. In fact . . ."

Silver looked in the opposite direction, to where the caves

met the oasis lagoon. She imagined what would be beyond that: miles upon miles of underground twists and turns. Places where pinpricks of light would cut across stone walls. Places where the dark would be so deep that she'd wonder if she'd fallen asleep. Or worse. A shiver danced down her back.

Silver pressed her lips into a hard line and went to Nebekker's supplies to begin filling her sack.

"What are you doing?" Nebekker waved her arms and crept back to Silver.

"Brajon, go back to Jaspaton. Return with more supplies for Nebekker. Keep an eye on her. I'll be back from Calidia as soon as I can."

Her cousin curled his hand around her wrist and gazed down on her with worried eyes. "Why do you have to go? Come back with me. Hiyyan can take Nebekker to Calidia . . ."

The thought of separating from Hiyyan made Silver's head thrum. "I'm going, and you're not going to talk me out of it."

Brajon watched his cousin silently for a few beats. "You can't do this."

"I have to." Silver looked at Hiyyan. The water dragon was miserable. She thought of how much she'd miss her own mother when she was gone, and felt the ache that filled Hiyyan's heart. And then there were Kirja and Nebekker. They needed to be together, and they needed to be well. She couldn't let Sagittaria race the Aquinder. She had to get to Calidia as fast as she could.

"No," Brajon said. "I mean you can't do it like this. Taking Nebekker's supplies. You'll need your own."

As realization dawned on Silver, her mouth fell open.

"You're going to help me?"

"It's probably the stupidest thing I've ever done, but—"

Silver threw her arms around her cousin. "A dash to Jaspaton for supplies, then right back here?"

Brajon nodded.

"As soon as I drop you back home, I'm filling the opening to the caves with stones," Nebekker grumbled as she began walking in the direction of Jaspaton again.

FIFTEEN

To exit the underground river system, Silver had to haul herself up a smooth granite slide with sporadic handholds, then slip through a narrow opening beneath a massive boulder near Herd Valley. She whacked her head on the boulder and sat for a moment, pressing her palm to the rapidly growing bump on her forehead.

Brajon snorted. "And you're supposed to be rescuing a dragon?"

"Oh, go stuff sand in your mouth," Silver said to him. "You get food from the kitchens. I'll get lanterns and"—she swallowed a hard lump in her throat—"money."

Brajon gave her a sidelong glance but didn't ask any questions.

"We'll meet back here when the foxes first appear."

About an hour after full sunset. That was when the little desert creatures popped out of their burrows and began searching for food.

The cousins trudged all the way to Jaspaton proper. Silver

pulled her scarves across her face and kept to the deepening shadows. Normally, her father's workshop would be empty in the evening. But perhaps he would be up, working feverishly on the queen's orders.

She picked her way down the stairs and paused at the workshop door. Voices made her sink back into the shadows.

"Of course he's upset. Losing his daughter . . ." The voice belonged to Phila. Silver's chest warmed. Her father missed her, perhaps was even out looking for her. Could she really leave Jaspaton without saying good-bye?

But then Phila went on: "It's inconvenient. We have so much work to do, and that selfish brat went running off. I'd be furious, too . . ."

Silver went cold again. All her father cared about was his precious masterpiece. But it didn't sound like he was in his workshop now. The voices came closer. Silver slithered around the corner. She heard Phila and another ele-jeweler leave the building, locking the door behind them. She peeked around and glared at their retreating backs, then tiptoed to the window at the back of the workshop—the one she knew had a wonky lock—and pounded her flat hand on the frame once, then twice, until the latch dropped. She opened the window and slipped inside. The workshop was empty.

Silver collected two small lanterns and enough oil-soaked wick to last a week. She rifled through the general jewelry-making supplies, grabbing anything that might be useful. A couple of files with pointed tips. A pair of magnifiers. A blanket and cloak draped over one of the chairs.

There was a sheaf of parchment splattered with ink. Designs for royal masterpieces were sketched all over it. Silver paused, chewing on her lip. Maybe her father cared only about his masterpiece, but her mother might feel differently.

Silver tore a piece of the parchment and scribbled a note on it. She began to leave it on the table but changed her mind. Instead, she folded the note, wrote her mother's name across the center, and tucked it in her pocket.

Then her gaze fell over the locked drawers filled with raw materials. Precious metals. Gemstones. One key was with her father at all times.

But she also knew where there was a copy of the key.

With her heart racing, Silver lifted a corner of one of the rugs. There it was: a tiny, silver key. Her fingers shook as she took it and fitted it in the drawers, one by one. From each drawer, she took a few small things: an unmarked disc of gold, a finished ring, two pairs of earrings. Her hands reached for the plain wooden box that held the most perfect gemstones Rami Batal had ever collected. They were reserved for the queen, but Silver opened the lid and let her fingers hover over the jewels. Blood pounded in her ears. What if she stomped on his dreams the way he had stomped on hers?

"No." She thumped the box shut and pushed it away quickly, before she could be tempted again.

Silver squeezed her eyes shut. She was a thief. "I'll pay you back someday," she said into the empty workshop.

She dashed outside and ran as fast as she could to the yarns-ladies' tents, empty now that the royals had left, where she left the note on her mother's favorite cushion. Never once looking back over her shoulder, Silver sprinted out of Jaspaton and to the boulder near Herd Valley, slipping underground like a raindrop disappearing into sand.

◊ ◊ ◊

SILVER WASTED NO words when Brajon appeared.

"Let's go."

They ran. There were tunnels that branched off here and there, but Silver didn't wonder where they went. Her focus was on getting to Hiyyan. The water dragon met her partway to the lagoon cave. In one moment, Silver was running, and in the next, she was on her back, warm wetness across her face, her entire body covered with Hiyyan's weight.

"Hiyyan! Stop it." Silver laughed.

"Gross," Brajon muttered, still jogging. "Hurry up, you two."

Hiyyan took to the river, the current carrying him along. Silver sped up.

When they reached Nebekker's camp, the old woman heaved a sigh. "I'd hoped you wouldn't come back. But have it your way." She pulled a garment from the bag at her side and held it up. "Come here, girl. Let's see if it fits."

"Oh!" Silver reached out to touch the silvery threads.

Nebekker had been working on a new riding suit. Every single minuscule scale was perfectly woven, impossibly thin, and in perfect proportion to the others. They were connected, not with clumsy bits of wool, like in the suit Silver had made, but with the silkiest threads, each part matched so that there were no holes, stubby parts, or extra edges popping out here and there. It was glistening, and it was magnificent.

And then Silver realized what the suit was made of.

"This is Kirja's fur," she whispered.

"That ridiculous dragon sheds like crazy," Nebekker said.

"Try it on. You're growing at practically the rate of Hiyyan, so it might be too small."

Brajon turned around, and Silver stepped into the suit. It wasn't too small. It fit her exact measurements, running just a touch long in the arms and legs, flowing over her skin like water. She ran her hands over the material. It was light but strong, and just as warm as her old suit. The scale pattern was slick but dense. It would provide protection against water while minimizing wind resistance. And the color meant people would have to look twice to see a human on the back of an Aquinder.

She wondered what Sagittaria might say if she saw her now.

"It's perfect," Silver said. "Thank you."

She reached to hug Nebekker, but the old woman pressed her hand to her chest, let out a sound of dismay, and doubled over.

"You're getting worse," Silver said. "Brajon, help me." She was struggling to hold Nebekker upright.

"I'll be fine," Nebekker said faintly. "I just need to rest."

Together, the cousins moved her so that she could sit with her back against the wall. Her breathing was labored, and all the color had drained from her face. Silver arranged blankets around her.

Watching Nebekker's pained expression, Silver knew that she had to leave for Calidia immediately. If Sagittaria claimed Kirja in the races, Nebekker would never see her water dragon again. She would weaken. And if Silver understood the old woman's words correctly, Nebekker could even die.

Silver watched the light patterns play on the walls of the

cavern as she thought. Hiyyan waddled over and sat beside her.

"It's going to be all right," Silver told him. But she wasn't sure she believed what she'd said.

One girl, one boy, and one baby dragon . . . against all of Calidia? It felt impossible.

Sixteen

Hiyyan rested his big head on Silver's shoulder as she assessed her belongings.

"Ugh, your breath is vicious," she muttered. It smelled like fish.

"It's a good thing," Nebekker said. "Means he's learned to catch his meals himself. There're fish here who don't need light and live in the little underground streams."

The young Aquinder turned his face to meet Silver's and breathed right up her nose.

"Hey!"

He let out one of his snorting dragon laughs and rolled onto his back.

Silver ignored him and pulled the thin but tightly woven wool blanket from her pack, as well as the cloak to double as a second blanket. She would need both to sleep in the chilly underground caverns in the nights to come. Brajon handed her the things he'd collected: a selection of dried foods, packed tightly and neatly into cloth sacks. Soap. A lightweight cup. A comb. Silver raised her eyebrows.

"You know I want to be the fastest dragon racer, not the prettiest?"

Brajon rolled his eyes. "So you'll be presentable when you meet with Queen Imea and ask for Nebekker's dragon back."

"We don't even know if the queen is involved." Silver hoped she wasn't. She was beloved by the whole desert for her generous nature and peaceful policies, and she had been so kind to Silver in the workshop. Unlike Sagittaria Wonder.

"And even if she was involved," Silver said, "we can't just ask for Kirja back. We have to . . ."

"We have to what?" Brajon said.

"I don't know." Silver had hardly thought that far ahead. All this time, she'd been trying to figure out how to get out of Jaspaton. Now that she was, she wasn't certain where to go from there. Only that she had to get to Calidia, and soon. She lowered her voice to barely a whisper. "But I have to come up with a plan quickly. I'm leaving tonight."

"Tonight?"

"Yes, and you can help me by not telling my parents where I am this time." Guilt flickered across Brajon's face, but Silver had no time to worry about her cousin's feelings. Her mind was racing with ideas and questions. She went to Nebekker and crouched beside the old woman.

"Help me, Nebekker. How do I find Kirja?"

Nebekker seemed deep in thought as she slowly sat up, settling her back and hips against the wall until she seemed comfortable. Finally, she spoke.

"I have an old friend who might be able to help you, but I haven't spoken to her in years. Her name is Arkilah. She came to my village from the vast desert to study water dragons. No, not the dragons themselves, but the mythologies and lore surrounding them. Arkilah is also Kirja's friend."

"Someone else knows about Aquinder?"

Nebekker nodded. "Last I heard, Arkilah was reading the stars in Calidia. Look for her in the Maze Market just outside the palace. She will do all she can to lead you to Kirja."

Silver nodded and slung her bag across her back.

"One more thing." Nebekker reached into a basket. "I've been saving money for you. I thought I had many more years to save, to convince your parents to let you go to Calidia." Nebekker paused over her thoughts. "Your letter convinced me you were . . . ready to go. All I can give you besides the pattern I taught you is this."

Silver took the small pouch Nebekker offered. Inside were just enough coins to fit in her palm. It wasn't much, but Silver's chest warmed with gratitude.

"I won't let you down," she said.

"Silver." Brajon leaped to his feet, his eyes wild as he appeared to realize that his cousin meant to leave right then. "You can't just—"

"Come with me," Silver blurted out. She wasn't sure where the words came from, only that she knew the journey would be better with her best friend. Silver had been eager to leave, but now that the moment was here and Hiyyan and Kirja needed her, she felt a bit panicked.

Brajon shook his head slowly. "I can't just leave my family."

"They'll be there when you get back. Don't you want to see what happens to all the beautiful metal and gems you pull out of the ground? What about adventure?"

Brajon folded his arms across his chest and raised his voice. "Adventure? You think that's what this is? This isn't a game!"

"No," Silver said. "If I played games, I might have more friends!"

Brajon sighed.

Silver held out her hand. "Best of luck, cousin. I'll send word when I reach Calidia."

She squared her shoulders and slowly turned toward the southeast. As she took her first steps to Calidia, she felt a pang, but she kept moving.

"We'll," Brajon said. He caught up to her and took her elbow. "*We'll* send word. You're not going alone. Especially when you don't have a plan."

"You'll leave without saying good-bye to your parents?" Nebekker said. When Brajon hesitated, she waved him off. "I'll get word to them. I have my ways."

Silver hid her relieved smile when Brajon nodded.

"Thank you, Brajon. And we do have a plan. Get to Calidia and find Nebekker's friend Arkilah."

That was the start of her plan, at least. Silver glanced at Hiyyan. She knew how much her dragon wanted to be with his mother again. She felt the longing in her bones. But she also knew she needed to protect him, and that meant claiming him.

That meant racing him. She dragged her palm across his back. Her heart gave a happy jolt.

Brajon looked nervously at Hiyyan. "I don't think you're going to find Arkilah with all the commotion you'll make flying that thing into Calidia."

"He's not a *thing*! Besides, we can't fly if we're taking the river tunnels all the way there," Silver said. "I don't want to be seen. If we raise an alarm, they might move Kirja. Hide her somewhere we can't find her."

Silver looked away. She didn't mention that if they didn't find Kirja, Hiyyan might never learn to fly anyway.

"Underground the whole way?" Brajon rubbed his hands. "That sounds more like it."

"Here." Nebekker's voice soared through the cavern. She toppled one of her baskets and rummaged through the objects that fell out. "Take these, and don't cut your hands off using them."

She handed them each a long knife, sheathed safely in hard leather. Silver swallowed hard, her throat dry. What would they need the daggers for?

Nebekker coughed. Then, as though reading her thoughts, she said, "For catching and cutting food."

Silver didn't wholly believe the woman, but she buckled the dagger around her waist.

"Now, just follow the river," Nebekker said. "It'll branch off here and there, but always stick with the largest flow. Don't wander into side caves or follow streams. No matter what."

"Why not?" Silver asked.

"Just do as I say and stop asking questions. Do you think I got to this ripe old age by wandering around like a desert beetle?"

"No." Silver leaned down to kiss Nebekker's soft cheek.

Although Nebekker waved her off, Silver caught a small smile. She blinked back tears as she realized that it might be a long time before she saw Nebekker again. The gruff woman had never been one for affection, but Silver impulsively grabbed her hand. Then Silver reached into her boot and pulled out a small object. When she opened her palm, light hit the blue gemstone so that it glittered madly.

Nebekker sucked in a breath. "My pendant. Where did you find that? I thought Sagittaria took it."

Silver gnawed on the inside of her mouth. Guilt overwhelmed her. "I picked it up the day they took Kirja."

"And you hid it from me all this time?" Nebekker looked wounded with disbelief.

"I didn't know—"

"You kept it for insurance," Nebekker said flatly. "In case I sent you away from me. No, from Kirja . . . from Aquinder. You wanted to be able to force me to—"

"I'm sorry. I didn't trust you. I thought it was a chance to hold on to my dream."

"So this is what you believe a dream is worth." Nebekker sighed and cradled the pendant. "But it's even more valuable than you know."

Silver hung her head. It meant even more now to get Kirja back. To prove to Nebekker that she deserved to be bonded to an Aquinder. And prove that she could be a good friend to the old woman.

As the pendant warmed in Nebekker's hands, Silver saw a hint of violet light glow from its core before fading again.

"What just happened?" Silver said.

"The stone is searching for Kirja." Nebekker reached her arm out, then retracted it. Her brow furrowed, like she was fighting an inward battle. Finally, she groaned, grabbed Silver's hand, and pressed the pendant back into her palm. "Take it. You need it more than I do."

"What does it do?"

"As you get closer to Kirja, the stone will know, pulsing brighter and hotter," Nebekker said.

"How does it know?"

"As with so many things having to do with bonds, the hows and whys are a mystery to me."

"Where did you get it?"

Nebekker shook her head. "It fell into my palm at the conclusion of a sort of journey long ago. But there's not time to explain more. You must go."

Silver was filled with a renewed sense of determination. She tied the pendant around her neck, tucked it beneath her tunic, and straightened up. "We'll be back soon—with Kirja."

Nebekker closed her eyes and nodded. Without the pendant, her body slumped again. Silver bent and hugged the woman.

"Thank you," she whispered.

Nebekker nodded again but didn't reply. She didn't have any more words for Silver and Brajon. No instructions, no guidance, no sarcasm. She was already breathing deeply, sinking into meditation to stretch out her heartbeats until they returned.

"What's next?" Brajon asked Silver as the cousins turned to go.

"To Calidia," Silver said—with more certainty than she felt.

Seventeen

The cousins faced the oasis lake.

"Are we going to have to swim to get past the lake? We don't know how," Brajon said. He put his fists on his hips, then set his jaw. "Not that I couldn't learn or anything. Yeah, let's just go. Jump in. Should be easy."

He rushed headfirst into the water, but Silver grabbed his sleeve. "Hold it! Nebekker said the currents in the bottom of the lake are strong. They'll spit you right back out into the cavern."

"What do you suggest? Wait for Queen Imea to send her royal barge?"

"More like a Droller," Silver said. "They're the dragons that transport people."

Brajon groaned. "Knowing useless water dragon trivia won't help us through that lake."

"I also know that water dragons are great swimmers." Silver motioned to Hiyyan, who had swum down the river to the lake. "And that's very useful knowledge right now."

Hiyyan grinned.

"Oh, absolutely not. I'm not riding Hiyyan." Brajon backed away.

Hiyyan lifted his head in the air, looking greatly offended. He turned his back to Brajon and pouted.

Silver patted his tail and scowled at Brajon. "If this is how you're going to be the whole time, we're not going to make it very far."

Brajon kicked a pebble as he searched the area. Then he brightened and pointed. "Look, I think there's a way to get around the lake if we can reach that ledge. Hiyyan can lift us to it."

"Or, he could just swim us through the lake," Silver said with a sigh.

Brajon scraped his boots a few times against the ground. Silver's heart softened. She might want to soar in the skies, but solid earth was where Brajon was most comfortable. She reminded herself that the idea of being in dark, cramped caves made *her* nervous.

"Look," she said. "I think we can climb those rocks part of the way, then balance on the stalagmites to get us to the ledge. Hiyyan can give us a boost, too. Then he can swim across the lake and meet us on the other side."

Brajon broke into a relieved smile. "We can use Hiyyan's head as a step!"

The Aquinder made a displeased snort but went along with their plan. He hoisted them up to the higher rocks, then walked alongside them as best he could as they balanced across the stalagmites. Brajon reached the ledge first and pulled himself up.

"Perfect!" he said. "This goes all the way past the lake. It's a little low, so we'll have to crouch. At least, I will. A little desert beetle like you should be fine."

Silver was concentrating too hard to shoot back a retort. She placed her foot against the ledge, but her boot hit moss, and she slipped backward, her arms wheeling in the air. Brajon reacted quickly, grasping her wrist. Her body swung swiftly to the side, and her rib cage slammed into the tip of a stalagmite. Silver let out a cry of pain, and Hiyyan whimpered in sympathy.

"Ungh." Silver wriggled like a scorpion in Brajon's grasp, her boots trying to find a grip on the slick wall.

"Stop. Moving. Like. That," Brajon grunted. "Give me your other hand."

"I'm trying!"

"Try harder!"

Silver looked over her shoulder. She had a long way to fall. The cavern, a place of beautiful shadows before, now gaped menacingly at her. She was sure the stalagmites were thirsting to impale her.

Silver stopped squirming and dangled in the air. She closed her eyes. They were supposed to rescue a dragon like this? There had to be a better way.

"Brajon, hold on to me tight. I have an idea."

As her cousin braced himself, Silver swayed to the left, then to the right, then harder and faster. Finally, she had enough momentum to fling her right arm up to Brajon. He caught it and, with one movement, yanked her onto the ledge.

"Thank you," Silver said, then paused to catch her breath.

Brajon's face was a touch pale. "That wouldn't have been a pretty drop."

"Next time, we ride Hiyyan," she said. "I don't care what you say."

Silver worked her way across the ledge, her back to the lake and her eyes trained on the ground, calculating each step before she took it.

On the other side, Hiyyan was there to meet them, his skin glistening with water. When he saw Silver, his grin was massive. Waves of relief passed through both of them.

Silver laughed and jumped on his back to be lowered gently to the ground. Brajon hesitated, still on the ledge.

"You can let Hiyyan help you, or you can leap yourself," Silver said. "But try not to break all your bones when you land. Then you'll definitely be riding Hiyyan the whole way to Calidia."

Brajon grumbled but let the Aquinder help gingerly lower him to the cave floor.

On that side of the oasis, the caves were narrower and much darker. No cavern opening wide enough to let blue light in. Brajon paused to strike his flint and light a lantern. He reached for Silver's lantern, too, but she held it away from him.

"Don't. I don't want to run out of oil before we reach Calidia."

"We can get more."

Silver snorted. "Where? The great underground traders' bazaar? Don't be a beetlebrain."

Brajon looked at Hiyyan. "I bet there's loads of blubber under his skin."

Hiyyan growled.

"Don't even think about it," Silver said. "If you hurt Hiyyan, you hurt me."

"Relax," Brajon said, "I was just joking."

Silver was learning the strength of the emotions she felt when Hiyyan was upset or happy, and how they affected her own moods. Every time she thought about Kirja, for example, sorrow flowed through her, and Sersha's face swam in her vision. How could she make Brajon know what it was like when there was nothing to compare the experience to? Her cousin had never even had a pet.

Brajon shook his head. "If I can't make you laugh, then Sagittaria Wonder has won. That old racer could never drag *my* cousin down."

That got a small smile from Silver. "Never mind. Let's keep walking."

The flowing of the river and the dripping of condensation kept Silver and Brajon company for some time. The way was easy and clear, but Silver shivered when she thought too much about the never-ending darkness around them. Never stopping. Never seeing the light again. The ceilings drip-drip-dripping nonstop and water filling her ears in a rush.

How long had they been walking? A few hours? Not the whole night, surely. The back of her neck prickled, as though something were watching them. Silver shook her head. The caves were already getting to her.

Her ears perked, and she froze.

"Did you hear that?" she whispered.

Brajon looked back over his shoulder. "Just the river and the dripping. And you tripping all over the place." He marched ahead, delighted to be in his element. Underground was a second home to him.

"Hilarious."

Silver turned in a slow circle, examining the walls and as much of the shadowy places as she could see into. There was nothing. Listening hard revealed nothing, either. But there had been something a moment ago. She was sure of it.

"Can we stop and rest?" Silver looked at the ceiling nervously. She longed for the skies. Or maybe she was feeling Hiyyan's longing. Probably, it was both of them.

"How long's it been?" Brajon asked.

"I don't know. I've lost track of time."

"I guess sleeping whenever we're tired makes sense, then," Brajon said.

They unrolled their mats, and Silver picked through the selection of dried food her cousin had taken from the kitchens. "I'm too tired to make a fire," she said.

She wondered how Nebekker could stand living in the caverns for so long. Silver popped a few nuts in her mouth and chewed them slowly. It wasn't just worry over the fuel supply that made her want to avoid a fire. Her neck prickled, and her breathing was shallow. She had heard something in the caverns. A far-off rattling.

Silver caught Hiyyan's eye, and something passed between them, but her mind felt too fuzzy to figure out exactly what. It was as though Hiyyan wanted to tell her something but didn't know how.

Or she was so tired and hungry she was imagining things. Silver grabbed a handful of golden apricots and sugary dates. She couldn't recall, later, if she'd actually eaten any of them. Her exhausted body hit her mat and immediately fell into slumber.

Eighteen

Silver woke up to a pair of eyes watching her. Not Hiyyan's expressive black eyes, because he was still sleeping. Nor Brajon's; he was still sleeping, too. But across the cave, two tiny silver specks shone in the dying light of the lantern.

Silver held as still as possible until her foot began to fall asleep. Slowly, a headache began to thump, thump, thump in her head from the awkward way her head was propped against the rocky cave wall. Or maybe it was from the drip, drip, drip of cave water on her upper back. Had she slept like that the whole time? The ache in her shoulders told her she had.

The silver eyes blinked. They were watching her steadily. And then, to the left, another pair of glimmering eyes appeared.

Silver tried to silently alert Hiyyan, sending waves of fear toward the water dragon. He stubbornly snored on. Clearly, their communication needed work.

Wake up! she thought harder. Hiyyan shifted slightly.

One pair of eyes disappeared. Silver felt choked by panic.

Where did the eyes go? Was the creature coming closer? Had it decided she and Brajon would make a good breakfast? She realized one of her toes was peeking out from the end of her blanket. Silver quickly yanked her knees to her chest.

"Brajon!" she hissed.

Her cousin jerked upright. Hiyyan snorted awake and gave a low growl of warning. The Aquinder began moving closer to Silver, but Brajon put a hand up to stop him.

"Don't move," he whispered. "Something's dripping on you."

"It's just cave water," Silver whispered, swiping at her neck. Then she saw the panic in Brajon's eyes. "Isn't it?"

"Don't move," he repeated.

Silver froze. Every part of her except for her eyes. She saw something dropping slowly from the ceiling over Brajon's head. A pale, iridescent string of something that was reaching down until it was about to touch his neck.

"Um . . . cousin . . ."

That's when Silver realized it wasn't *one* string. There were hundreds, all descending from the ceiling of the cave toward them.

"Brajon," Silver screamed. She jumped to her feet and flung her hands all over her neck, her face, her back. Her feet brushed against something squishy, and pricks of pain shot from her soles up into her ankles.

Silver grabbed at her ankles with a cry, and her hands came away with blood. The things—the stretching, wormlike things—were above them and below them and they had *teeth*. They were sucking her blood from the back of her neck and attaching to the bottom of her feet. Brajon frantically danced next to her, trying to yank the slimy things off.

"They're down my tunic!" he yelped. He flung his top off and clawed at his skin.

"Get them off me!" Silver hopped on her blanket to keep more worms from attaching to her feet, but several were already sucking. Every time she pulled one loose, another took its place. Trickles of blood began running down her skin. The scent and sight sent the worms into a frenzy.

"Hiyyan, help!"

But Hiyyan was already trying, biting with his rows of teeth. He beat his wings at the worms that kept dropping from the ceiling and stomped the ones on the ground with his big, flat feet. His thick scales were impenetrable, but he roared, sharing in her pain.

In his frenzy to reach Silver, Hiyyan knocked Brajon to the ground, where more worms rose up to attach themselves to him.

"Help," Brajon screamed again.

In the chaos, Silver slipped and fell to the ground, banging her cheek against the rock. She bit her tongue, and the salty taste of blood exploded in her mouth. A worm seemed to sense the blood on her tongue and lunged for her face.

"Noooo!"

This is the end, Silver thought, clamping her mouth shut and protecting her face with her hands. *Some destiny. I'm going to be eaten alive by worms before I ever get to race Hiyyan.*

But then a pair of those silvery eyes flashed in the corner of her vision. A small furry creature leaped past her face, taking a worm in its mouth and ripping it to shreds. The torn pieces thrashed before becoming still.

And then, more silver eyes and more furry creatures were flying through the air, landing with their sharp little teeth poised to tear the worms apart. There were dozens . . . maybe hundreds of them, all attacking the slithering worms. Silver was in pain as the slimy jaws were yanked from her body. She frantically felt for any remaining worms, then tore one from her shoulder. She threw it into the water, where a fish gobbled it up.

Slowly, the haziness in Silver's vision faded. All the colorful spots that had appeared and burst went away. She lay on the cave floor until her heart calmed. Her body still tingled, but the bleeding soon stopped. Hiyyan stopped writhing and curled up next to her. A few feet away, she heard Brajon working to catch his breath.

Just inside the glow of their lantern, several pairs of little animal eyes watched them, waiting, as though they wouldn't leave until they were sure Silver and Brajon were all right.

"Desert foxes," Silver whispered.

She reached a tentative hand toward them, but the skittish creatures ran, disappearing into the cave's shadows when she moved.

"Thank you, foxes," Silver whispered. She thought back to how she rescued the fox on the dunes on Brajon's birthday. Could it be that they remembered and were helping her? The dune races felt so long ago. They were different kids in a different world.

"Brajon, are you all right?" she asked, embracing her cousin. His face looked peaked. Silver hoped it was because of fear, and not because he'd lost too much blood.

"Those worms . . ." Brajon shuddered.

Silver shook her head. She refused to think about those creatures. Instead, she pictured the desert foxes, streaming into battle with their fluffy tails rising high behind them.

"I know we're hurt," she said, "but we have to move on."

A vision flitted in her mind. A girl and a boy, proudly astride a magnificent water dragon.

Hiyyan bumped Silver with his nose, and they locked eyes.

"Did you send me that?"

The image came back again. Brighter than before. Hiyyan wrapped a wing around Silver.

Silver gazed at the Aquinder in wonder. There was so much more for her to learn about their bond, but the message seemed clear.

"Brajon, I think Hiyyan wants us to ride him for a while. We need to get out of here in case there are more worms, and this gives us a chance to rest."

Brajon hesitated, but finally, he gave a single, decisive nod. "Okay."

Hiyyan bent his knee at a ninety-degree angle, and Silver climbed up. Next, Brajon clutched the Aquinder's mane in his fists and put his foot on the dragon's leg. With a grunt, Brajon hauled himself behind Silver and splatted himself face-flat on Hiyyan's back. Backward.

"Ow." Silver rubbed her shoulder. Brajon had kicked her when he'd flung his leg over the wrong way. "How did you even do that?"

"I mron nwo." Brajon refused to raise his head. With his eyes squeezed tightly shut, he turned his face slightly so Silver could hear him. "Just go. Let me stay like this for a while. It's fine. I'm fine."

"Fine," Silver said, but she couldn't keep down a giggle. Hiyyan also let out a little amused snort. Brajon grumbled his disapproval, but Silver gave Hiyyan a pat, and the Aquinder raised himself up. Brajon squealed once, then clamped his lips together.

"Oh, hush, Brajon," Silver said. "You sound like a herd animal!"

◊ ◊ ◊

THEY STOPPED TO EAT. Hiyyan went off to fish while Brajon started a fire and Silver looked through their quickly dwindling food supplies. She chewed on her lip thoughtfully.

"Brajon," Silver said. She emptied some dried meat and vegetables into her cup and added some river water, then set the whole thing on the fire to boil. "What do we do after we rescue Kirja? Where do we go?"

"Can't we bring her back to Jaspaton and Nebekker?" Brajon asked as he peered eagerly at the cooking stew. His stomach let out a growl.

"No, that's where Sagittaria would go first to find her again," Silver said. "And we can't tell anyone where Hiyyan is, either, because wherever he goes, they'll follow, hoping to find Kirja. It's not right for him to hide away his whole life, and it's not right to separate him from his mother."

"But we have to go home at some point," Brajon said.

"I'm starting to feel like after all of this *I* won't have a home anymore," Silver said quietly.

At this, her cousin fell silent.

Silver slowly stirred the stew with a spoon, watching the curls of steam rising off the surface. The water lost the clarity it had gained from being filtered by rocks and pebbles for hundreds of miles. It turned murky as the meat and vegetables released their colors. The dried food plumped up, and the stew thickened. Soon enough, little bubbles began to pop along the surface.

She thought about cooking with Aunt Yidla. About working fibers next to her mother. About designing jewelry with the weight of her father's gaze on her. It was true that she didn't want to do any of those things her whole life, but it was also true that those people—her family—weren't just their livelihoods. They were also smiles and support, listening ears, love, and comfort.

She would have Hiyyan and she was determined to have her racing career, but would that be enough? In all the stories she'd been told, Silver couldn't remember ever hearing about Sagittaria Wonder's loved ones.

Silver pulled her cup off the fire and set it aside to cool as she looked for Hiyyan. She suddenly felt impossibly lonely and needed to bury her face in his furry mane.

He was easy to find. He'd taken a small offshoot in the cave system, where a school of fish congregated, but he wasn't very far down that stream.

"Hello," Silver called out to him from the main path, nearby. Her Aquinder looked up, a squirming fish dangling from his mouth. He slurped it all the way in and loped over to her. The fish were too bony for her or Brajon, but Hiyyan swallowed them whole, so all those little bones didn't bother him.

Silver sat with her back against the cave wall, and Hiyyan joined her. She stroked his silky fur. He *was* a comfort to her. "Do you miss your mother?" she said to him.

Hiyyan was so young. She didn't even know how long baby dragons stayed with their mothers. She wished she'd had more time to ask Nebekker questions. Hiyyan was going to need help learning to fly, but she had no idea what else he needed to know. She'd always assumed she would learn everything in Calidia, as she trained beside the greatest dragon racer ever. Water dragon life cycles, how to care for them, their preferred diets. She didn't even know if Hiyyan particularly liked the fish in the underground river. Maybe what he really craved was some nice grass or juicy berries. How she wished she could communicate with him more clearly.

Agitated, Silver gripped Nebekker's pendant, wishing it held the information she sought.

Hiyyan seemed to understand, and she felt warm waves coursing through his body in response.

Silver sat up in excitement. This was new and unexpected. Was his temperature linked to his emotions? She wanted to test it out.

"Do you like the river fish?" Silver asked him. In response, he sent a different kind of signal to her. The waves were shorter and quicker. His body temperature was still warm. "Hmm. That feels like a dance! How about . . . Do you want to fly?"

The waves intensified. And they seemed *rounded*, the best word Silver could think of to describe them. Like the waves were music, twirling at the very end. Hiyyan's body grew so warm that steam rose off his skin.

"Do you like Brajon?" Silver asked with a giggle.

The waves slowed a bit, and Hiyyan's hot skin cooled back into a mild warmth. Silver laughed.

"Okay, so you're mostly neutral on Brajon. I don't think his feelings would be hurt, since he feels the same about you. He thinks you're just an oversized lizard."

The Aquinder swooped his head around to look Silver

square in the face with a grimace. Silver laughed again. Then she narrowed her eyes.

"What do you think about Sagittaria Wonder?"

At her name, Hiyyan's skin turned ice-cold. His waves were erratic, with no discernible pattern. Even his breathing was short and stuttering.

"Okay," Silver said. She rubbed his scales. "It's okay. Me too, Hiyyan."

So heat was good; cold was bad. Long, rolling waves were good; short, erratic ones were bad. But what about . . .

"Show me," Silver whispered, "something in your heart."

Silver closed her eyes and waited. Hiyyan had done it before. He'd planted images in her mind earlier—she knew he had.

There was only darkness behind her lids for a long time. But just as Silver was about to give up, light flickered in the corners of her eyes. The cavern back at the oasis. Hiyyan, the smallest he'd ever been, and Kirja. Her big body was curled around the baby Aquinder, and they both sighed contentedly.

Another figure entered the scene. Nebekker, Silver thought, but no. It was a girl.

It was her.

Silver grinned and rested her head against the curve of Hiyyan's neck.

This time, Silver tried to send a vision of her own. One of a hoped-for future. Her mother, her father, Brajon, and all their family surrounding Silver and Hiyyan. She pictured herself climbing on Hiyyan's back and the Aquinder racing across the Jaspaton cliffs, unfurling his wings and taking flight just as they reached the edge of the city. Silver gasped with delight, then she and Hiyyan bubbled over with giggles. The feeling of soaring filled their hearts near to bursting. To the side, Nebekker rode Kirja. They were free, and they were safe.

Silver smiled and opened her eyes. Hiyyan tucked his head under her arm, and he sent the softest, soothing waves of warmth to her. He'd seen the vision. Silver pressed her palm to her chest. She had never felt so connected to Hiyyan before, and she didn't want it to end.

"I promise I'm going to do everything I can to get your mother back. And then we're going to make my vision come true. Freedom and racing and—"

"Silver!" The sound of Brajon's voice broke the spell.

"I'm here," Silver yelled back. "Come on," she said to Hiyyan. "Let's go. We shouldn't leave Brajon alone for too long."

As they neared Brajon, Silver sniffed the air. It was richer than before, full of not just the scents of the cave but also the scents of food and homes and bodies and travelers from far foreign shores. It was increasingly metallic and animal, layered with perfumes and spices.

Calidia. That must mean they were close!

Silver took another deep breath through her nose, but the scents were gone. She realized she wasn't detecting the smells through her nose but through her mind.

"You can smell the city, can't you?" she said to Hiyyan. "And through you, I can sense them, too. Just like earlier, when I heard the desert foxes rattling in the caves. Does that mean we're getting close to Calidia?"

She was filled with Hiyyan's waves of warmth. Silver felt newly energized knowing they were closing in on Calidia. And newly nervous.

Nineteen

Silver left Hiyyan there to fish the river while she went back to join Brajon and share the good news that they were getting close.

She paced impatiently as she drank her stew, lost in thought. The river roared a few feet away. As they traveled, the river would get wider, then narrower, then wider again. Here, the river was fat and rushing, as though knowing the seas—its final home—were close. Silver thought about the northern mountains where the water originated. Back in Jaspaton, the mountains were just a blur of gray on the far horizon, but the tops were covered in snow all year long and the lower valleys, she was told, were bursting with life. Someday, Silver and Hiyyan would fly to them. Silver would see snow for the first time in her life.

A strange sound reached Silver's ears.

Silver held herself as still and tall as the cliffs of Jaspaton.

Rattle, rattle.

Brajon looked up from his stew, his eyes wary. He had heard it, too.

"The foxes," Silver breathed. But if it was them, why were her hands trembling?

Rattle, rattle.

She tossed the remainder of her stew in the river and tucked her cup in her bag. "Brajon, we have to go. *Now.*"

For once, Brajon didn't question her. Silver swung her pack over her shoulder and felt for the weight of her purse at her hip, as she always did. Still full of jewels. *The stolen jewels,* Silver thought with a pang of guilt.

The cousins began to walk, Silver's neck hairs on end. From Brajon's rushed walking, she could tell he was unsettled, too.

"Hold on. I'm going to call Hiyyan," Silver whispered.

Silver closed her eyes, attempting to send an image to Hiyyan, but she stumbled on a rock and fell to her knees.

Rattle, rattle.

Rattle, rattle.

As Brajon helped her up, the sound came faster.

"Let's run."

"Run? All the way to Calidia?" Brajon got a good look at Silver's face and bit off his words. "Okay, let's go."

As the cousins broke into a jog, Silver sent Hiyyan a feeling of fear and an image of all three of them running.

Hiyyan popped into the main cave, slurped down the fish half dangling from his mouth, and burped. He knelt down without needing further instruction.

"Brajon . . . get on," Silver panted as she scrambled onto her water dragon's back. "Hiyyan, get us to Calidia!"

With a roar, the water dragon ran.

◊ ◊ ◊

BY THE TIME Silver stopped feeling like something terrible was after them, her hair was plastered to her forehead and the caverns had narrowed again.

"Thank you, Hiyyan." She pressed a cheek to his neck, hot from exertion, and stroked his back. "You did well. We can walk now."

"What's gotten into you?" Brajon said. He was out of breath from clinging to the back of the running dragon.

Silver shook her head. "I don't really know. I just heard something."

"Right, the foxes."

"It wasn't the foxes."

Silver pressed her lips into a line, and they walked on. Silver closed her eyes and focused on reading Hiyyan's emotions. She sensed he was tired, but she also noticed an ache—his wing joints hurt. Silver frowned. Did Aquinder *have* to fly, the way humans had to eat or sleep?

Soon, I promise, Silver thought.

Hiyyan grunted and sent her more sensations. The smells from before were stronger. And there were sounds. Muffled sounds she couldn't identify, but different from the never-ending dripping water, and boots shuffling through cave dirt. Silver grinned.

"We're really close," she called back to Brajon.

Hiyyan's big feet splashed in the water. Here, there was no riverbank. The water went all the way to the cave walls and partway up, too. Silver closed her eyes again and took several deep breaths. She was starting to feel caged in. The walls and ceiling were too close, the ragged ceiling like a maw.

Brajon put his hand on her shoulder. "It'll open up again, soon."

"I'm okay." Silver reminded herself of the smells she'd sensed. Spices, perfumes. "We're almost out of this place. Nebekker was right. Just follow the main cave all the way and—*augh*!"

The party of three skidded to a stop. The cave narrowed into an opening, which they could have squeezed through, one by one. Except for the massive boulders that were blocking the way.

"No," Silver whispered. All this way, and now they were trapped.

"A cave-in." Brajon groaned. "That would explain why the river's gotten so high here."

At the cave-in, the level of the river was at Silver's chest. Silver slid from Hiyyan's back. Even here, many feet from the rocks, the water was above her knees.

"Maybe there's an opening in the rocks," she said, "somewhere under the water."

"What do you want to do? Swim down there?" Brajon scoffed. "We would have our bodies pounded against the rock by the current."

"We have our water dragon," Silver said.

"Which would be useful if you could see under there. Look how murky it is near the rocks."

"What's your solution, then?" Silver snapped. Calidia was on the other side of those rocks. They had to get through. They were so close to saving Kirja. So close to the races.

"We have to turn back," Brajon said.

"Huh?"

"Hiyyan's hearing is better than ours. I bet he'll know when we're near the foxes. He can hear fox feet running and scratching. That'll be where their burrows are."

Silver's eyes lit up, and she hugged her cousin. "Brajon, you're a genius! Burrows will have holes to the surface. A way for us to get out!"

"More useful than a jelly pickax, wouldn't you say?" Brajon grinned. "Let's go."

Instead of riding Hiyyan, Silver and Brajon walked. They kept close to the wall, dragging their fingers over it and looking closer whenever there was a small crack or hole.

Silver also kept a lookout for those silvery eyes that had watched her before.

"Not much longer now—I can feel it." She closed her eyes and connected with Hiyyan's senses. "I can hear their paws pitter-patter on the other side of these walls. We just have to find an opening or some way to get to them."

Brajon called, "Foxes . . . foxes, where are you?"

Silver was careful to not pass up a single crevice as she searched the walls with both hands. Finally, farther back the way they'd come, she saw them: silvery eyes.

"Fox! Don't go!" she whispered. The eyes disappeared, but Silver broke into a run. Brajon and Hiyyan kept pace with her, the excitement of her discovery spurring them all on.

Silver stopped and patted the cave wall. "I saw its silver eyes. The foxes were *here*."

"I don't see anything," Brajon said. "There's nothing there."

The walls were almost perfectly flat, unwilling to give up their secrets.

Silver closed her eyes and connected to Hiyyan's senses again. She could hear the foxes' yips and calls louder than before. But how were they getting to the other side of the wall?

She moved to a small, dark cave off to the side. Nebekker

had warned them to stay in the main river cave, but Silver sensed that the burrow was here.

Rattle, rattle.

"Come on," Silver said to Brajon. "I hear something."

Silver ran ahead into the smaller cave, holding her lantern in front of her.

"Fox, fox, where are you?" Silver called.

Rattle, rattle.

"We're close," she called happily over her shoulder to Brajon. They were almost out. She couldn't contain her laughter. "Hurry!"

But when Silver faced forward again, she screamed.

Twenty

At the sound of Silver's scream, the beast whipped its head toward her. The creature was so tall it had to hunch over to move in the cave. Four arms extended from its thorax and two long, spindly legs protruded from its midsection. They were as thin as a desert spider's legs, but at least six or seven feet long.

Rattle, rattle.

With horror, Silver realized the beast was the one that had been making the rattling sound.

She watched the creature put its weight on its four arms, dragging its legs, its claws curled into loose fists, its knuckles dragging on the ground. Spikes jutted out on the backs of its leg and arm joints, and its tail flicked back and forth. There were three more spikes on the tip of the tail.

But just as Silver was about to let out another scream, the beast vanished into thin air.

Silver stood frozen, searching the darkness. She heard something roll across the cavern floor toward her. It hit her foot. A small bone, picked clean.

Silver scrambled backward, her boots sliding against gravel. She heard Brajon calling her name and running toward her, but she was too scared to make a noise. She fell, scraping the skin off her palms, but flung herself up again. There was a massive splash as something enormous jumped into the center of the stream, then began moving in her direction, sloshing water everywhere. The thing was coming closer.

The creature reappeared directly in front of Silver.

"Stay back," Silver shouted.

Trembling, she held up her lantern to get a closer look at the beast, then instantly wished she hadn't.

Its head was massive and made up mostly of a huge jaw filled with teeth. She couldn't see eyes or ears or a nose. Only that long fang-filled mouth. The whole creature was white, like the color of bones that had been bleached by the sun in the vast desert. She felt its hot breath blowing on her face.

Brajon finally caught up to Silver, but he slammed into the back of her. She lurched forward, and her lantern fell to the ground and shattered.

"Don't move," Silver said. Her voice shook.

The cave went deathly silent. Even in the dark, the creature's teeth gleamed eerily.

With some relief, Silver sensed Hiyyan joining them in the darkness. He pushed his body in front of her and Brajon, and gave a low warning growl.

Rattle. Rattle.

The cave monster was shifting. Silver wanted to turn and run, but she knew the burrow entrance was near. Her mind filled with the scent of fresh air and desert sand, just beyond the monster. They had to get past the spidery beast.

Rattle.

The creature was coming closer, its unnaturally glowing teeth looming bigger. The beast moved slowly, and the waiting felt somehow worse than being attacked.

For the first time on her journey, Silver reached for the knife at her belt. The metal made a *scliiick* sound as she pulled it from the leather holder. She touched the point. Was it sharp enough to cut into bone? Blood pounded in her ears. She licked her lips.

"Run past," Brajon said. "I'll fight."

"Against that thing?" Silver whispered. "You don't have a chance. We need to stay as far away as we can. Maybe it just had a full meal and doesn't want to attack us."

But as soon as Silver took a few steps forward, her hopeful words were immediately proven false. The creature opened its massive jaw and let loose a spine-tingling screech.

"Geeeeeeeeeeeyyyyyaaaaaaa!"

Then it started running for her.

"Hiyyan," Silver yelled. She crouched and flung her blade in front of her.

Hiyyan met the creature's screech with his own roar. He lashed his tail out just as the beast reached them. A red welt appeared in its bone-white skin and the cave monster stumbled, crashing jaw-first to the ground.

Hiyyan roared again. Silver had never heard anything like it from him. Deep, angry, and challenging. The Aquinder whipped a wing at the fallen creature, but the creature snapped its teeth and tore a small hole in the edge of the wing.

Hiyyan cried out and buckled. His pain shuddered through Silver. The beast snapped its jaws and began lumbering toward the young dragon.

"No," Silver screamed. She rushed forward, jumped on a rock, and flung herself off it, into the air, knife raised high. She brought the weapon down on one of the creature's arms. Instead of bouncing off, as she worried it would, the sharp metal dug into the monster's flesh and ripped through it. A bioluminescent greenish slime oozed out.

The creature screeched again. It flicked one of its legs at Silver, which slammed against her chest and knocked her to the ground. The creature's face loomed over her. It would only take one chomp to snap her in half.

"We did not get this far . . . to be eaten . . . by you!" Silver yelled, and raised her knife again.

With another roar, Hiyyan barreled into the side of the creature with his whole body, both of them crashing against the cave wall with a loud crunch.

Silver scrambled to her feet. Brajon stood there, staring at the fallen creature, his face almost as white as the monster's. Hiyyan was slower to get to his feet, shaking his head as if to clear away the impact of hitting the wall.

"Brajon, go," Silver yelled to him. "Get past! Find the burrow opening!"

Brajon lunged to get around the creature, but it got up, whip-fast, and shot out a spidery leg. Brajon tripped and landed on his chest in the mud. The creature rattled over to Silver's fallen cousin, teeth bared.

"Leave him alone!" Silver hurtled toward the creature, knife raised.

The creature screeched and whipped its head toward her. From the corner of her eye, Silver saw Brajon scramble to his feet and run past them. She stabbed the knife at the creature's face right as it opened its monstrous jaws. The metal lodged between two teeth. The beast reared its head in pain, ripping the knife from Silver's hand. Her weapon was gone.

She could have darted past the creature, but she wouldn't leave Hiyyan, who had finally shaken off his confusion, to fend for himself. Without waiting for the water dragon to crouch down, she jumped onto his back, grabbing big handfuls of his mane, and hauled herself up.

"Let's do this together!" she cried.

Her shoulders burned. Sweat poured down the sides of her face. A kind of electricity zapped through her body and straight into Hiyyan. They were stronger together. Their renewed energy was something magical, something brought on by the power of their bond.

Silver clung tightly as Hiyyan reared on his hind legs and kicked his heavy feet against the creature's side. The monster flew across the cave and landed against the wall. Silver and Hiyyan followed him. The white monster lashed out with its three remaining good arms. One of its claws scraped against Hiyyan, yanking off a scale, and Silver yelped in shared pain.

The water dragon was bleeding, but he hardly seemed to notice. He snapped his own sharp teeth onto one of the creature's arms and ripped it off. He spit it onto the ground and lunged again.

When they were close enough, Silver reached for her knife, still wedged into the monster's slobbering mouth. She pulled it free while it was distracted, the metal glinting in the light.

Wait . . . light?

Silver turned to see light streaming into the cave behind the monster. Brajon had found the burrow opening.

"Hiyyan," Silver yelled, brandishing her knife high. "Finish this!"

Hiyyan reared high again and bore down on the spidery creature. Their combined roars and screeches echoed through the cave until Silver's head was filled with nothing else.

"Arrrghhh!" she yelled along with them, one with her Aquinder. She leaned forward to jam her knife into the center of the creature's head. The tip slid in smoothly, and the creature fell to the ground. It shuddered, letting out a final rattle.

Then, all was silent.

Twenty-One

Hiyyan sat back on his haunches, breathing heavily. He was wounded. Silver was, too. But the white monster rattled no more. Silver slid off her water dragon's back. She pressed her face to his, waiting for her heart to slow its beating.

"Soon. We'll have rest very soon. I promise."

She went to the beast's head, waiting a moment to make completely sure it was dead. There were bits of fox fur between its teeth. Silver frowned. When the cave monster didn't move, she pulled her knife out of its head. The blade came out as easily as it had gone in. But it was covered with slick green goo. And her hand, where it had brushed against the monster's flesh, was striped with a substance that shimmered like white gold.

"Ew." Silver wrinkled her nose. She wiped her hand on her tunic, and dragged the knife through the mud. A pathetic cleaning, but it would have to do for now. Then she remembered the light and looked up. Brajon was already through the burrow opening, but he called back to her.

"Silver! Tell me you're alive!"

"I'm here," she called back. "And I'm alive. We both are."

Silver and Hiyyan limped slowly toward the light. The brightness hurt her head. She squinted and waited for her eyes to adjust. The opening was tight, too tight for Hiyyan to get through, but she felt the water dragon urging her to go on. Earth clung to her body, but after a few minutes of climbing, a hand reached down and hauled her the rest of the way up. She was struck by how close they had been to the surface all along.

Silver flung herself to the ground on her belly and breathed in the dry warmth of the outside world. Silent sobs racked her chest. Her cheek on the rocky, shrubby sand felt so good.

"Look," Brajon said.

Silver raised her head. Like a mirage rising from the desert, a wonderland of stone and metal grew out of the landscape.

They'd reached Calidia.

"We made it," Silver breathed. She squinted at the city, but Brajon was staring at her clothes.

"Is this . . . ?" He touched a spot where Silver had wiped the cave monster's . . . whatever it was . . .

His fingers came away . . . and vanished.

Silver gaped. "Wait, what happened to your hand?"

Brajon blew on his fingers, and they returned to normal. Then he rubbed the substance between his fingers.

"Camouin," Brajon said. "I can't believe it."

When he squeezed slowly, the substance was soft and malleable, but when he kneaded more quickly, the substance solidified. When he'd built heat from the friction, his fingers disappeared, as though they were replaced by desert sand.

"What's camouin?"

"I guess you wouldn't have heard about it in your classes. Not much use for it in jewelry." Brajon smeared the substance on his trousers. "It's a metal used for camouflage, but it's been illegal for hundreds of years. Anyone who possesses it would be hunted down. It was used extensively in the Land and Sea Wars. After that, it was considered too dangerous for humankind."

"Like Aquinder."

Brajon nodded. "All along, it was hiding under our desert. That creature must have known where to find it."

"It was able to turn it off and on." Silver shuddered.

"Heat activates the camouflage properties. That monster must have been able to adjust its body temperature at will. Amazing."

"Terrifying," Silver said, correcting him.

"Either way, we have to get it off us. If someone sees it, we'll be arrested."

Silver looked to Calidia. She pushed her hair out of her face and nibbled her bottom lip. "It would be really useful, though. Think of what we could do if we were covered in camouin. Get into the city, find Kirja, and get out. I could even race Hiyyan without anyone discovering he's an Aquinder!"

Brajon threw his arms out to his sides. "Cousin! Were you even listening to me? The stuff's banned. It's a death warrant if we get caught!"

"But we won't get caught if they can't see us!"

"No way, Silver." Brajon shook his head. "I'm going down to try to find our bags. Put camouin out of your mind."

Brajon slid back into the burrow. Silver turned her face to the sun and soaked in the warmth, then sent those good feelings to Hiyyan, still in the cave. The Aquinder sent back surges of longing. Silver inspected the hole they'd come up through. It was barely big enough for her and Brajon. How would they get Hiyyan out?

"He's just not going to fit," Silver said to Brajon once he'd returned.

Down below, Hiyyan mewled.

"I know," Silver called down. "I'm working on it."

Silver paced in ever-widening circles. "Maybe there's another opening. A bigger one."

As she looked, the foxes began appearing, as if to help her search. At first, just one, poking its fuzzy black snout above-ground and sniffing the air before scampering out. Its fur closely matched the colors of the desert floor: sand and red clay and bits of white. Then another came out, then another. Pretty soon, Silver was surrounded by what must have been the entire colony.

When she sat down in frustration, all the foxes sat down, too.

Harrumph, one seemed to mutter.

"How do I get him out?" she asked them.

She didn't think they could understand her, of course. But Brajon was still circling several feet away, and Hiyyan was stuck underground. Tiredness washed over Silver. It was hard to think straight.

The foxes faced one another. One began to chirp. Others replied. Soon, all of the foxes were talking over one another. Silver put her hands over her ears at their sharp noises.

But then, they were gone—darting down into the hole Silver and Brajon had come up through.

"Oh, fine, go back to your cozy homes!" Silver gave an exhausted sigh.

The thing was, Silver knew the safest place for Hiyyan was in the cave. If she and Brajon were to go into Calidia first to gather supplies, her Aquinder couldn't go. But Silver also knew he was as desperate to see the sky as she had been. It would be heartless to leave him.

She pulled her knife out of its leather scabbard and rubbed it in the sand to clean off more of the gunk. Her father had always been adamant about properly cleaning tools in his workshop.

A patch of sand hit her square in the face.

"Hey!" she sputtered, and dropped the knife, wiping her eyes and mouth with her tunic sleeve. "What was that for?"

She looked for Brajon, assuming he'd thrown the sand, but he was on his hands and knees by the hole they'd emerged from.

More sand flew toward her, landing in her hair.

She stood and walked to where it was coming from. There was a new hole in the desert floor, growing larger and larger as Silver watched. More holes appeared all around them. Suddenly, she understood what was happening. The ground shook.

"Move back!" she yelled at Brajon, grabbing his shoulder and hauling him away. The ground shuddered again as a gaping chasm fell away. A chorus of chirps rang out into the desert sky, and the foxes swarmed out of the hole. Silver took a tentative step forward and peered down.

There was her Aquinder, grinning up at her. Four or five foxes sat on his head and back, grinning, too.

"You destroyed your own burrow?" Silver said. "To help us?"

She recalled the fur in the white monster's teeth. Maybe she'd done them a favor, and this was how they were expressing their thanks.

"Thank you so much," she said. "Come on, Hiyyan. Climb out."

Hiyyan didn't have to be told twice. He clawed at the walls, but his pace was slow and he slid back down. He let out a mewl.

"It's not working. The walls are too slick for his claws," Brajon said.

Silver tipped her head back and turned her face to the sun. *Think.*

When she opened her eyes, a desert hawk circled overhead. Her heart fluttered. She remembered Nebekker telling her about the hidden Aquinder eggs in the desert. Those babies didn't have parents. But they'd learned to swim, to survive, to *fly*, somehow.

"Look, Hiyyan," she said under her breath. "Do as the hawk does."

Hiyyan gazed at the skies. He watched the hawk pick up air currents and rise, then turn and drop before flapping its wings again. The water dragon narrowed his eyes and spread his wings. First, he shook them out, then batted them up and down a few times, mimicking the hawk. He roared.

The foxes on his head chirped indignantly and rolled down to the ground.

Hiyyan flapped his wings harder.

The Aquinder rose majestically out of the river cave. Then he kept going, disappearing into the blue desert sky for the first time.

A strange, heavy feeling filled Silver and she bit her lip, keeping tears at bay. The next deep breath she took could have been made of helium, the way it made her body seem light enough to lift off the desert floor. Dots of light like festival fireworks burst at the edges of her vision.

"He's flying," she whispered.

Giggles bubbled up her throat, impossible to contain.

"He's *flying*!" Silver clapped and laughed as she watched her Aquinder relish his freedom.

Hiyyan made only one swoop before he returned, landing in a heap, like a pile of sandstone bricks. He rolled over and stayed motionless for a moment. Then he raised his head and grinned, his mane flopping from side to side.

Silver ran to him and threw her arms around his neck.

"You did it. You flew! Terrible landing, but I think Kirja can help with that."

Hiyyan's laughter was a honk. For the first time, Silver noticed how big he'd gotten. As big as Kirja. The cave had hidden his height, since he'd often have to hunch over to get through the tunnels, but now his body spread out to its full size. He was a grand beast.

Together, they could do anything.

Silver looked toward Calidia as Hiyyan took to the skies again. Outside the city, orchards of palm and yucca created a green space. She could just see low sandstone buildings among the trees. They spread out quite a way before meeting with several rows of slightly taller and closer-together sandstone structures. Those structures then connected with what she assumed was the heart of Calidia: tall stone-and-metal buildings, glinting brown and silver and white in the sun. Somewhere in there was the great palace, but it was obscured by everything else. Unlike Jaspaton, which was a vertical city, and so it was easy to see everything, Calidia greedily ate a wide swath of the desert floor.

Silver squinted up at Hiyyan. *You'll have to come down before someone from the city sees you,* she said silently.

He gave one last swoop. This time, his landing was a roll. He breathed heavily from his unfamiliar exertion. He sent Silver a host of new scents, including one that was particularly damp and salty. Hiyyan's longing was strong.

"The sea." It was close by. Perhaps just on the other side of the city. Silver put her hand on Hiyyan's side. "I know I keep saying 'soon.' I know I keep promising things. But I will keep all my promises. You'll see the sea. Soon. Promise."

She picked up her bag and put her arms through the straps. It was lighter than ever before. Empty of supplies. Her stomach screamed at her. She was desperate to get to the city, if just to get something to eat. Something hot, something rich with a sauce, something . . .

Her stomach protested again.

"We have to go into Calidia first. Which means you have to stay here and hide," she said to Hiyyan.

Hiyyan peered over his shoulder to the wide hole in the ground. He knew what Silver was thinking.

Silver dropped to her knees and cradled Hiyyan's head in her arms. "I'm so sorry," she said. Her eyes welled with tears. "But it's important that you stay hidden. Remember what Nebekker said? 'Theft runs rampant before major races.' I'm not losing you."

Hiyyan's mewl was as soft as a fox's. He lay on the ground and let the back half of his body slide back into the hole. Then he looked up at Silver hopefully.

"Okay. Halfway in should be good enough. But if you hear or smell any other humans, you have to go all the way in, all right?"

Silver fought back her tears and prepared to go. But then,

as though pulled to him by a rope, she ran to Hiyyan and pressed her cheek to her Aquinder's face.

Finally, she stood and faced the orchards ringing Calidia.

"Let's go," she told Brajon, and she took her first step toward the great royal city.

Twenty-Two

The walk took longer than Silver had anticipated. A common trick of the desert, to make distances appear shorter than they really were. But she kept her gaze focused forward and spoke little to Brajon, to conserve energy. When they finally emerged from the open desert, they discovered a rough road outlining the orchards. Silver rubbed her hand across her face.

"Follow the road or cut through the trees?" she asked her cousin. "If we take the road, we might get there faster, but we also might be seen."

"On the other hand, we could get lost in the orchards," he said.

"Or we might get found by an angry farmer wondering why we're cutting through his land," Silver said. "We certainly look suspicious."

She raked her eyes over Brajon. His clothes hung on him. His skin was paler than usual, at least what was peeking out from under a layer of river cave muck. He looked hungry enough to eat the contents of Aunt Yidla's entire kitchen. Silver probably didn't look much better.

The cousins agreed that the best option was to follow the road but to keep close to the tree line in case they needed to duck and hide. As the desert heat baked into their bones, Silver looked at the cool shade of the orchard with longing. There was no breeze to kick up their tunics and trousers and keep them cool. They wiped their sweaty faces with their scarves, which were soon the color of mud. Without any water left, they snuck a few leaves from yucca trees and chewed them for moisture, making faces at the bitter flavor.

As city noises built up around them, Silver's stomach went tight with nerves.

"Give me your scarf," Silver said. She wiped Brajon's face even more and tried to tidy his hair. She smacked the dried muck out of his clothes with the side of her scabbard. "That's as good as it's going to get until you have a bath. Now do me."

Brajon cleaned up his cousin, but his fingers caught in her tangled hair. "Your hair's really knotted, and there's . . . monster sludge in here. What happened to the comb I gave you?"

"I forgot about it." Silver reached back to try to braid her hair, but despite pulling and ripping, the matted mess remained. She reached for her knife.

"You'll have to cut it off," Silver said.

"All of it?"

Silver hesitated. She hadn't realized before this how much she loved her long locks. On Jaspaton evenings, she and her mother would sit and watch the sun track across the desert into twilight. There would be neighbors stopping by to chat and the smells of evening meals floating lazily up to them.

Always, there was the rhythm of Silver's mother pulling a brush gently through Silver's long hair.

But Silver knew that short hair would be another layer of disguise. Silver wouldn't be as recognizable, and that would make it easier to find out where Kirja was being kept.

With a steady, sure hand, she passed Brajon her knife.

"Up to my neck, at least," she said. Were there any girls in Calidia with short hair? It was unheard of in Jaspaton. "Do it. Quickly. Before I change my mind."

There was the pressure of Brajon grabbing her hair in his fist, then the sound of the knife slicing through the mess. Her head went weightless. It felt like many pounds of hair fell to the ground. Silver had never realized how heavy it all had been. She rubbed her neck, startled to feel the air against it. There was a new coolness there.

"You look really different," Brajon said.

"Good. Is it even?"

"Mostly."

Silver fought back an impish smile. Her cousin still seemed uncertain, but she felt a new sense of freedom. She pulled out the forgotten comb and untangled the few remaining knots as best she could. The freshly shorn ends were starting to curl around her ears.

"This is as tidy as we're going to get," she said. "Let's go."

The melodic rustling of the trees faded away as soon as they slipped out of the orchards.

"Look." Silver pointed at a great sandstone arch that led into the first ring of the city. Her heart skipped with joy.

Across the top of the arch, tiles read: THE ROYAL CITY OF CALIDIA: GATEWAY TO THE SEA. All down the arch, someone had attached the same flyer that had fallen out of Sagittaria Wonder's bag, back in Silver's father's showroom.

The columns of the arch were inlaid with hundreds of jewels, in every color of the rainbow, all arranged to create mosaics in the shapes of water dragons. Silver reached her fingers out, her eyes sparkling, but Brajon pulled her back quickly.

"Don't." He pointed.

A weatherworn sign featured a drawing of a man prying off a jewel in one panel, followed by a panel of that same man being tossed into the sea, rocks tied to his legs.

"They're serious about their punishments here, aren't they?" Silver said, taking a hasty step backward.

"Ready?" Brajon said.

"Ready." Not even the warning to thieves could keep Silver's blood from racing with excitement.

They stepped through the arch. Suddenly, they saw people of every possible type: young and old, tall and short, stick-thin and column-heavy, with light skin and medium skin and dark skin. They wore an eye-pleasing array of fashions, in fabrics that were familiar and ones Silver had never seen before. Silver even spied one person in the distance wearing a tunic in Jaspaton's special weaving pattern, which made her quickly duck her head.

She put her arm over her face and coughed at the dust being kicked up by all the shuffling feet. But through the haze, she saw hundreds of delights. The buildings themselves were two to three stories tall, and a matching shade of sandstone to one another, but their doors and windows were decorated with intricate tile patterns in many colors. Some patterns seemed purely artistic, while others were more practical, spelling out the name of a shop or of the family that lived in the home above a shop. Rugs and tapestries hung from high balconies, and clotheslines crisscrossed like brightly colored festival streamers above Silver's head.

She wished that Hiyyan could be here to see it. She looked slowly left to right, memorizing every detail. Then she closed her eyes and tried to send him an image. Her fingers warmed with his response, and she grinned. She, too, itched to explore everything.

Everywhere, there were water dragons. In the tile designs, woven into fabrics. Even stone heads and figures jutting out from the tops of the buildings.

Silver's mouth fell open. "I feel like I've entered my dreams . . . and I don't know what to do next."

Her nostrils flared. Somewhere nearby, someone was grilling meat over an open flame. Brajon breathed deeply.

"I know what to do," he said. "Must. Find. Food."

Brajon and Silver wove into the crowds, following the intoxicating scent.

On the ground level, shop doors were flung open, and keepers called out to their friends and neighbors to come in and see their newest displays of goods, especially arrived for the Autumn Festival. There were porcelain, simple metalworks, and clothing shops, and dry goods vendors. Most people walked wherever they were going, but every once in a while, a wheeled contraption would come through. Carts full of produce that were pulled by hand, or buggies that were ridden by the power of a chain system, dragging baskets of fresh fish or piles of dried succulent leaves for tea. Silver kept an eye out for the Maze Market, but they didn't seem to be anywhere near the palace just yet.

Furtively, she peered at Nebekker's pendant, but it lay still and dark. The city, though, was full of brightness and energy. It both revitalized Silver and made her realize just how tired she was. They needed to find food and rest. Quickly.

She pulled her arms close to her sides, so that she was even smaller, but people still elbowed and shoved. In Jaspaton, people walked side by side and often held hands as they strolled, but there you could see for miles into the desert. You felt the air around you and could breathe. Here in Calidia, everyone pressed together, and the buildings blocked sights more than a few paces away. Silver felt insignificant in the crowds.

And maybe that was a good thing. Silver and Brajon didn't want to be noticed.

The weight of Silver's father's jewels dragged down her bag, her feet, and her heart. They likely had enough money from Nebekker for a meal, but Silver was desperate to rid herself of the stolen goods.

She squinted at the signs. "I think this is as close as we're going to get to a jeweler's shop," she said, pointing to a clothing merchant.

"But food," Brajon said.

"This first."

She went straight to the back of the store, where a pinched-faced lady served tea to customers draped in fine silks. The customers looked away in disdain when Silver approached.

"Only customers allowed," the woman said, wrinkling her nose.

"I *am* a customer," Silver shot back. "Do you buy jewelry? I have something of value." She pulled a ring from her purse and held it in her palm.

The woman's mouth dropped open. "Where did you get that?"

"I . . . It's mine. It's . . ."

"No wretch like you would have such a fine piece. Thief! Call the guards!"

"No! I—"

Brajon pulled Silver out of the shop before the woman could shout for the guards again. They ran into the streets, dodged a group of children running and screaming down the road, and darted around a corner.

"There she is," a voice at the entrance of an alley said.

Silver's breath came faster. It was one of the customers from the shop. An older man with white hair and a long lavender tunic. He walked toward them.

"The ring is mine," Silver insisted. She wanted to say she wasn't a thief, but that would have been a lie.

"It is," Brajon said.

"I believe you," the man said, watching the two of them carefully. "Will you hold up the ring again? But quickly! Guards are everywhere in this city."

When Silver hesitated, he leaned in closer. "Don't be afraid. I'm interested in buying it."

Silver shared a look with her cousin. Brajon pressed his lips together and gently shook his head. But what choice did they have? They needed money. Silver showed him the ring.

"Such fine handiwork. Gold and rubies." The man considered, then named his price.

Silver bit back a gasp. He wanted less than a third of what the ring was worth. Rami Batal would have refused. But she wasn't her father, and she didn't have much choice.

Her stomach rumbled, and the old man smiled knowingly.

"I'll sell," Silver said. "For your price."

"And for your silence," Brajon said.

"Is there someone after you?"

They shook their heads.

"No?" The old man shrugged. "Then I care nothing for your troubles. I leave for the southern mountains tomorrow, and this will fetch a fair price there."

Silver took the meager handful of coins and watched the man walk away with the ring.

"Added to Nebekker's money, it should be more than enough for our meals and supplies," Silver said. Even so, she smarted at being taken advantage of.

"You did well," Brajon said.

"So did you. 'And for your silence,'" Silver said, mimicking Brajon's voice.

Brajon laughed. "I felt like a mysterious trader with secrets to keep. I was just trying not to appear nervous. I was worried he was going to bring guards back with him."

The cousins returned to the main road. Silver pointed at a small stall with a stone cauldron in the shape of a dragon's head. Its open mouth was tilted to the sky, breathing flames. Behind the fire, a rotund woman turned sticks heavy with meat, while another woman sat to her side, rolling thin rounds of dough and handing them up to be cooked next to the meat skewers.

The line for the vendor was about a dozen people long. Silver and Brajon joined the end of it, tapping their feet impatiently. Silver sucked on the insides of her mouth. She was so hungry she couldn't think about anything else. Not Kirja, not

Nebekker's friend Arkilah, not Sagittaria Wonder. At least she knew Hiyyan was enjoying plenty of river fish.

When they finally got to the front of the line, Silver pointed. She didn't trust herself to open her mouth; she thought she might swallow the entire cart of food.

"One!" the woman rotating the meats called out.

"Five," Brajon called, countering.

The woman's eyes narrowed, then she shrugged. She pulled five flatbreads off the grate and lined each with a stick of meat. Then she sprinkled some herbs over the top and a dollop of yogurt and passed them to Brajon. He blew on them while Silver dug coins from her bag.

The cousins found a quiet doorway to settle in. The desire to sit and inhale the delicious smells of the food battled with Silver's need to stuff it all in her mouth in one huge bite. Brajon didn't have the same problem. He was already on his second one as Silver took a bite of her first.

"By all the dunes in the desert," Brajon mumbled between bites, "this is glorious."

The warm, pillowy bread and the hot, juicy meat were the best things Silver had ever tasted in her life. She almost wanted to cry. Instead, she took another bite. Then another. When she'd finished her second and Brajon was licking his fingers after his third, they both settled back against the wall, hands on their bellies.

"I feel like a new person," Brajon said, smacking his lips. "I'll admit that Calidian food is almost as good as my mother's. I'm so full I could probably nap right here."

He closed his eyes, but Silver tugged at his hand and got to her feet.

"Come on!" She laughed. With her energy renewed and

the light fading quickly, she knew they needed to start looking for Arkilah. Besides, she wanted to see the rest of Calidia.

They rejoined the throngs. Just like in Jaspaton, people came out in droves at evening, when the heat of the midday sun had faded and the city was releasing its warmth back into the sky. She saw a scarf vendor and paused to consider one in a luminous shade of orange, and one stamped with big green flat-backed water dragons.

"Orange," Silver finally said, reaching for her bag of coins. Better not to draw any connection to dragons for now.

She chose one patterned with black tears for Brajon. Despite everything they had to do in Calidia, and despite a sticky sort of remorse from selling her father's ring, Silver was having fun with the money. There was a great sense of freedom in spending coins on the royal city's endless treasures.

They didn't know where they were going, but the streets were mostly flat, sloping very gently toward the center of the city, and so walking didn't feel as tiresome as it did in Jaspaton. The farther into the Calidian labyrinth they got, the busier it was. The buildings were taller, the noises louder, the smells stronger. There were metal-and-glass structures alongside buildings made of sandstone. Multiple shades of granite, too, from the quarries Silver knew were far to the south.

And then the sandstone fell away, and there was only glass and metal and white granite, and the green of lush low-lying plants that Silver had never seen before, and the sparkle of wide, shallow pools of blue, blue water.

Silver gasped, jolting to a stop and throwing an arm across Brajon's chest.

They'd reached the palace.

Twenty-Three

A low white wall ringed the whole palace. At least, Silver assumed it went all the way around. The grounds were so big that she couldn't see the end of them. The center building was a huge rounded-edged rectangle, not quite a dome and not quite angular like all the other buildings in town, but something in between. It seemed to flow like water, sometimes straight across and sometimes curving. There were six white towers around it, three on either side. The Calidian royal flag, a circlet of gemstones on a black background, fluttered from a dome on the top of each. Gold and silver winked at them from all angles. The precious metals were used as decoration on the tower walls and ceiling, on the statues in the pools, and around the doors and windows, like the tiles in the outer Calidian ring.

"Listen. Hear that?" Silver said to her cousin.

"I don't hear anything," Brajon said.

"Exactly. It's so quiet here. There aren't as many people. And they're not in a hurry."

As they approached the pools, Silver looked more closely

at the statues that rose from the water. They were all water dragons. Species Silver thought she recognized from trader stories, and others that were unfamiliar to her. A thin rod rose from the center of each statue, and bells hung down the side of the rods. When a sudden wind danced over their skin, the bells rang gently, eliciting a calming music.

"Oh, look," Silver squealed. She hopped over a low fence and dashed toward one of the pools, pointing at a small creature swimming slow laps around the circle.

But as soon as the creature saw her coming, it raised its long horn-shaped snout and let loose a shrill alarm.

"You!" An angry voice sailed across the palace grounds. "Get back from there before I arrest you!"

A man dressed in head-to-toe white ran toward her. Silver hadn't noticed him standing against the wall, since his clothes blended in perfectly with the palace, but now that she saw him, she realized there were many guards on the palace grounds, all dressed in white, all pressed against the wall. How many other guards throughout the city had they missed? The hairs on Silver's neck stood on end. They would have to be more careful.

Silver hastily backed away. "I'm sorry."

"You can't come in here. It's treason to trespass on the queen's property."

"I . . ." Silver pointed at the small creature who'd continued its turns around the pool. Its gray-and-black-striped tail and the black tufts on top of its head wiggled side to side as it swam. "It's just that I've never seen one before."

Suddenly, the guard smiled, his mustache bouncing with mirth at the ends, and his whole face became friendly. "Never seen an Abruq? Not from Calidia, then. Fine little water dragons. Can sound an alarm loud enough to wake the dead. Very useful."

"They're so cute."

"About the right size to cuddle in your arms, aren't they?" The guard shook his head. "Much too restless to stay still, though. And, like I said, noisy. They don't make good pets. People who attempt to keep them always find their homes in shambles after the first day. To be fair, I can't think of a single water dragon that would be a good pet. Even the mild-mannered ones need lots of food and water and—"

"Do you know all about water dragons?" Silver asked. She hoped he would have an idea where the dragons were kept.

"Some, and I could talk about them all day if I wasn't busy with my guard duties. But it's time for you to move off the queen's lawns now, sorry to say. Go on."

Silver dipped her head politely as she backed all the way to the fence and stepped over to the road. The guard lifted his chin to her in farewell and drifted back to his place against the wall.

"Wait," Silver called. "Can you tell us where the Maze Market is?"

The guard pointed to a shadowy alley over Silver's shoulder. "The entrance is there, but they close up at twilight. No one wants to work during the social hours."

Silver squinted to get a better look at the market entrance, but Brajon shook his head.

"Come on," he said. He tugged on Silver's arm. "Let's find somewhere to sleep, and try in the morning."

But a sense of urgency clicked in Silver's mind. "We don't have time to sleep. We don't even know how long we have until the races begin. We need to find Arkilah soon, or else Kirja . . ." Silver couldn't say the terrible thought out loud.

"We'll find her. We battled a cave monster to get to her!" Brajon looked left to right, then at the white walls of the palace. "Excuse me," he called to the guard. "Did we miss the qualifying races?"

"You're just in time," the guard called back. "Registration opens tomorrow morning, and the races begin in the evening."

"See," Brajon said, facing Silver again. "We have time, and we're not going to find Nebekker's friend tonight. People shouldn't wander around in the dark in unfamiliar cities."

Silver opened her mouth to argue that the cover of darkness could be good for their search.

A commotion made them spin away from the market. Down the road, a cart was rattling toward them so quickly Silver was sure the wheels would pop off at any moment.

"Run, you beast!" the driver roared, snapping a whip over the herd animal's head.

A yelling mob chased after the cart, kicking up more dust and pebbles.

"Stop him!" someone called. Others raised their own shouts. Even the Abruqs in the little palace pools tipped their noses up and raised alarms. The guards rushed to assess the situation.

Silver caught a flash of glittering purple and silver in the back of the cart, combined with a desperate whimper that she was sure only she heard. A water dragon!

Theft runs rampant before big races. Nebekker's words rang in Silver's ears.

She imagined it was Hiyyan in the runaway cart and did the only thing she possibly could. She stepped into the middle of the road, directly in the cart's path.

"Stop your cart," Silver shouted, flinging up her hands.

"Whoa, girl! Move your hide," the cart driver screamed, yanking on the reins.

Time seemed to slow as the cart hurtled toward Silver. People in the crowd screamed when they realized there was a girl standing in the middle of the road. A guard in white leaped over the palace railing.

Silver knew there was no way the driver could turn the herd animal fast enough to get around her, even if he wanted to. But the driver didn't try; he lowered his head, snarled at Silver, and kept his course.

Still, she stood her ground.

Until the guard slammed into her side, throwing her out of harm's way. Silver's breath rushed out of her as she landed hard on her back. The shouts died down as the crowd ran past, and, slowly, the dust did, too.

"Silver!" Brajon fell to his knees beside her. "Are you okay, cousin?"

"She's not," the guard said. It was the same guard who she'd talked to a short time ago. "She's out of her mind! What in the desert were you thinking, girl?"

"Thief," Silver said, weakly sputtering with dirt in her mouth. "I couldn't let him steal a water dragon."

"Your life is worth less to that thief than the dragon," the guard scolded.

Silver sat up and looked around. The cart had overturned, and the mob was descending on the driver.

"They stopped him!" she cried. "How?"

"This cousin of yours threw his bag at the herd animal," the guard said. "Spooked it enough to send them all crashing."

Silver threw her arms around Brajon and pulled back to give him an admiring look. "Good thinking."

"Unlike yours," he retorted. "You could have been killed!"

"I imagined what it would be like to"—Silver glanced at the guard and lowered her voice to a whisper—"lose *mine*, and knew I had to."

The guard looked curiously from Silver to Brajon and back, but then a man from the crowd, dressed all in dark blue, pulled on his shoulder.

"Arrest that man!" His eyes blazed as he pointed to the cart driver. "He attempted to steal my master's water dragon!"

"Try to stay out of trouble," the guard said to Silver as he went to address the theft.

"Silver," Brajon said, perfectly mimicking Rami Batal's voice. "Is it possible for you to stay out of trouble?"

Silver giggled at her cousin.

"Come on," Brajon said. "We don't need any more attention on us."

Silver wanted to stay and see what kind of water dragon would be released from the cart, but Brajon pulled her arm insistently and she let her cousin lead her away. Still, she looked back over her shoulder every few steps.

The sun was melting into the horizon, and the palace was going through a transition, day to night. Lights came on in the upper-floor windows. Lanterns throughout the garden were lit, though Silver never saw a person doing the lighting. The gold trim shimmered and sparkled, challenging the beauty of the stars. The striped tails of the Abruqs glistened where moonlight doused them.

Then an upper window was flung open, and there she was.

Queen Imea.

Twenty-Four

Silver stopped and stared at the monarch. The queen didn't look down but, instead, looked out over all of Calidia, like the vast desert beyond the city was drawing her gaze. Then, just as quickly as she appeared, she spun away from the window, her hair flinging over her shoulder.

Even from a distance, Silver could tell the queen was agitated. There was something about the sharpness of her movements. Another woman, draped with colorful fringed scarves, appeared, closing the windows, then she disappeared as well. The light went out in the room.

"Come on. Stop dawdling!" Brajon dragged Silver around a corner, and she lost sight of the palace. "I know I saw an inn back this way. Somewhere . . . Where was it?"

The streets that had been so easy to follow during the day were a maze after dark. They turned down one road, realized their mistake, and went back. Confusion dashed excitement away and tiredness took its place. They struggled to keep walking.

Silver's fingers fluttered over Nebekker's cool pendant. She worried about Hiyyan. She worried they were never going to find Arkilah. She worried that they had only one day to rescue Kirja. She couldn't fail. Nebekker was depending on her.

At the thought of the old woman, a circle of warmth touched her chest. Silver pressed her hand hard over the pendant. Did that mean Kirja was near? Silver turned in a slow circle, but other than the little pools, there was no sign of anywhere an Aquinder could hide. The pendant went cold again.

Silver's shoulders slumped. If they didn't find an inn soon, they'd have to settle for sleeping in a doorway.

As she scanned the roads, she spotted a group of people, two men and a boy who looked about her age, dressed head to toe in fitted dark-blue clothes. She recognized one of the men from the crowd chasing the cart, the one who'd told the guard his master's dragon had been stolen. The three entered a building.

"There! I see an inn!" she said. She and Brajon dashed across the road and followed the trio in.

When they entered, the room was full of people seated around tables, drinking from crystal goblets and talking over one another. The boy in dark blue turned around and gazed at Silver. She tried to defiantly hold his gaze, but when that became uncomfortable, she focused on a girl about her age, who was cleaning on the other side of the room. The girl looked them over carefully, then went back to her work.

Brajon stepped forward. "We'd like a room, please."

The innkeeper pressed a palm to his nose. "We have nothing for filthy dock children like you. Get out!"

"But we can pay," Silver said, reaching into her pack for the money.

The man dragged the cousins into the street. As the door was slamming shut, Silver heard the innkeeper's voice go as sweet as rose syrup as he helped the group of three.

Silver frowned. "But we asked for a room first."

"Yes, but they don't look like they, well, crawled out of a cave," Brajon said. "A doorway it is."

"Hey!" A fierce whisper came their way from an upper window of the inn. The cleaning girl stuck her head out and waved down at them. She looked over her shoulder, then back at them. She pointed to the end of the road. "Meet me there."

Silver started walking, but Brajon stayed behind.

"I don't think we should trust her," he said.

"We don't have a choice," Silver said.

"What if she tells the innkeeper we're standing there so he can come out and give us a proper beating?" Brajon folded his arms across his chest. "I've never met such mean people as Calidians. I can't wait to go home. Let's find a place to safely wait out the night. We can find Arkilah at first light, grab Kirja, and get out of here."

Silver hesitated, chewing on her bottom lip.

"Think about Hiyyan waiting back at the river caves," Brajon said. "He probably misses you. If he's still even there."

"Don't say that," Silver cried. Then she lowered her voice so passersby wouldn't overhear. "Even if our plan goes as easily as you just laid it out, we can't leave before the afternoon. If I don't race Hiyyan . . . if I don't claim him, he could be as easily stolen as Kirja was."

"Race him? No way. Why can't he hide? Kirja was in hiding for years."

"But Kirja was found. And now that Sagittaria knows that Aquinder exist, it'll only be a matter of time before Hiyyan is discovered. I have to do everything I can to protect him."

"Our focus is to rescue Kirja," Brajon said as he threw up his hands. "Not for you to go off and race water dragons for a thrill!"

"It's not about the thrill!" Silver shook her head. "You don't understand. I know that what's best for my water dragon is to make sure he can never be stolen. If you want to go, then go. I can find Arkilah myself. Maybe I'll ask the cleaning girl for help."

"That's it?" he said. "You want me to just go?" Brajon's face was turning pink. "After everything I've done. You couldn't have gotten this far without me. You would have been run down by that cart if not for me. You would have been torn to shreds by that cave monster and sucked alive by the worms and—"

"If not for you, I could have swum Hiyyan through the cave river, arrived a day ago, rescued Kirja, and gotten back to Jaspaton by now!"

"Then take that creature and fly to the other side of the world. Maybe there, you'd find people who actually like you."

Silver sucked in a pained breath. Brajon had never spoken to her that way.

"I'd rather have a Flying Black-Eyed Scorpion help me than a two-faced Dwakka like—"

"Be quiet, you two!" There was that fierce whisper again. The cleaning girl had appeared out of nowhere and was glaring at them both. "Follow me."

She darted to the end of the road and turned the corner.

Behind the buildings, a narrow alley bathed in shadows stretched farther than Silver could see. The girl disappeared into it.

"Come on," she said over her shoulder.

Silver avoided her cousin's gaze as she went into the alley. Brajon followed behind her, but only after sighing loudly to let her know how irritated he was.

"Here," the girl said. She waited for them, holding a plain door open.

Silver stepped inside. It was a tiny room with only a single small square window to let in what little light from the Calidian lanterns could find its way there. When Silver's eyes adjusted, she saw a mat with a blanket on one side of the wall, a small ceramic bowl, and a pitcher filled with steaming water. There was also a small pile of clothes, neatly folded, in one corner.

"Where are we?" Silver asked.

"In my room. This is the back of the inn. Well, a little cubby in the back of the inn."

"This is your home?" The cleaning girl's face closed off at Silver's tone of disbelief. Silver's cheeks flushed. She hadn't meant to upset the girl, but she was taken aback. The girl didn't have books or pictures or cushions or anything that made it seem like it was hers. "What I meant was that we can't stay in your home. It's too generous."

"I'm not offering it out of charity. You said you could pay." The girl rolled her eyes and held out her hand.

"Oh." Silver reached for her coins, counted out enough to fit in a circle in her palm, and passed them to the girl, who scrutinized them.

"I was hoping for more, but this will do," the girl said,

tucking the coins into her apron. "Since you're a friend to water dragons."

"What do you mean?" Silver asked.

"I overheard one of the men in blue talking about a street urchin with badly cut hair who stopped the theft of their dragon. I assume that was you." The girl pinched her nose. "Not too many people in this area fit that description."

"We're not street urchins," Brajon said. "We've just been traveling a long ti—Ow!" Silver was grinding her heel into Brajon's toes.

"We helped a water dragon, yes," she said.

The girl nodded. "A friend of water dragons is welcome here."

"But where will *you* sleep?" Silver looked around the tiny room.

"In the kitchen," the girl said. "I sleep there half the time anyway. The cook loves to give me tasks in the middle of the night and she doesn't want to come all the way back here to wake me up." She put on a defiant face, but Silver saw her exhaustion.

The girl pointed to the basin. "I brought you hot water for cleaning."

"We got the message from the owner of the inn. We smell," Brajon said drily.

"Mr. Homm would never let dirty kids like you in there. Besides, we're full until the dragon races are over, at least. Better get down to the seawall early tomorrow if you want a spot to watch. People start heading there before sunrise."

Silver bit her lip. They had to find Arkilah and get Kirja *soon*. "And where do we find the seawall?"

The girl shot her a quizzical look. "Don't you know

anything? It's the wall that meets the ocean, of course. First through third are south of the docks. I'm going to try to watch some of them. If Mr. Homm lets me. There are more than a hundred dragons in Calidia right now trying to qualify. Or just be registered."

"You know a lot about these races for a cleaning girl," Brajon said.

The girl glared at him. "You don't know anything about me," she said, but then turned away and swallowed hard. She seemed to pick her next words carefully. "I know how to listen. No one thinks much of someone like me, so they talk freely. I know more gossip than anyone in this city. You should see all the racers and squires sitting around, boasting about their dragons. They're all sure they're going to qualify here and then win the final cup at the Spring Festival. The deals, the treachery, the amount of money that exchanges hands as bets . . ." The girl shook her head. "I could start my own kingdom with it. Anyway, I have to get back to work, or Mr. Homm will come looking for me and we'll all be sleeping down at the docks tonight."

"Wait," Silver said. "What's your name?"

"Mele," the girl called over her shoulder. Then she disappeared around the corner, and Silver and Brajon were left alone in the tiny room.

Twenty-Five

Silver sighed with happiness as she lowered her hands into the washbasin. Brajon had offered to wait outside to let Silver wash up first: his way of apologizing for their argument. There was a small piece of soap in the basin, so Silver wet her new scarf and lathered it up, then wiped down her skin. When she finished, she tried to wring the dirt out of the scarf, but it was stained. So much for that pretty orange color she'd loved.

She poured some water over her head, watching gunk and suds rinse out of her hair. The water in the basin was now black. She could hardly blame Mr. Homm for turning them away. Especially when there were guests as smartly dressed as those men in blue they had followed into the inn. She wondered where they were from and what kind of water dragon someone had tried to steal from them.

Brajon rapped on the door. "Are you done yet?"

Silver shook droplets of water from her hair and traded places with her cousin. As she waited outside, she thought about the next day's plan. First thing tomorrow, they would go to the seawall.

She knew the most important thing was to find Kirja, but also . . . her chance to prove herself as a racer was here and now. If she signed up for one of the races and won, Sagittaria Wonder couldn't ignore her. And, if she claimed Hiyyan as hers, he would be safe.

The trouble was, how could Silver sign up for a qualifying race without exposing Hiyyan to danger?

Silver shook her head. No, they had to focus on finding Arkilah first. Nebekker had told them that Arkilah could help them rescue Kirja from Sagittaria.

Silver paced up and down the alley. Her heart ached. She missed Jaspaton, just a little, and she *really* missed Hiyyan.

Hiyyan. Maybe he could help her figure out what to do. Silver closed her eyes and pictured the Aquinder in her mind. A feeling of peace swept over her.

She thought his name. *Can you hear me from this far away? I have an idea, and I need your—*

"What are you doing?"

Silver's eyes flew open. Mele was standing in front of her, squinting curiously. She held a small package wrapped in cloth.

"Nothing," Silver said. "Just waiting for Brajon to finish cleaning up."

Mele stared at her. "You were thinking really hard."

"There's more than sand between my ears," Silver said, and grinned.

Mele arched an eyebrow but didn't press. "I brought you this." She unwrapped the cloth and pulled the lid off a small ceramic pot.

"Persimmon pudding," Silver exclaimed. Her mouth watered. "You didn't have to do that. You're very kind!"

Mele scowled and pushed the crockery at Silver. "It's not kindness—just leftovers from one of the rich racers. Guess he found the taste too common."

"It's a good thing I'm more common than sand. His loss, my gain."

For the first time, an almost-smile cracked Mele's face. But as soon as it almost appeared, it vanished. "Well, you need it. You're the skinniest girl I've ever seen."

"We didn't exactly have time to eat while fight—" Silver bit her tongue. Mele was right; it was easy to be loose-tongued around her. For all she knew, Mele could be one of Sagittaria's spies. Silver feebly finished with: "while in the desert."

"People who don't understand the ways of the desert shouldn't go into the desert," Mele huffed.

Silver hid a smile. Imagine a Calidian girl talking to *her* about the desert!

Mele turned to go.

"Wait," Silver said. She didn't trust the cleaning girl, but her gut told her Mele knew some things Silver didn't. "You know the desert, then? So you're not from Calidia."

"That's none of your business." Mele's eyes darkened, and for the first time, Silver realized they were more green than brown.

"I was just wondering how you ended up here, cleaning up after people who don't even like persimmon pudding."

"You're one to talk. You can't even clean up after yourself. I earned this job, and this is a good position for a girl like me."

Silver raised her eyebrows. "A girl with something to hide?"

"No!" Flustered, Mele clenched her fists. Her voice

lowered. "This is the closest work I could find to the water dragons. I have to stay. I just *have* to."

Mele's eyes shone with tears, but before Silver could say anything more, Brajon opened the door, scrubbed clean of dirt. Mele took the opportunity to run around the corner. Silver let out a slow breath. Trying to get secrets out of Mele was harder than climbing dunes.

Silver pushed herself into the room and collapsed in exhaustion on the mat. She offered up the pudding to Brajon. "I'm going to share this with you even though you say horrible things to me."

The cousins licked the bowl of every last morsel.

With the night bathing the room in inky darkness, Silver stretched out and closed her eyes for one last effort before sleep.

She pictured her beautiful Aquinder. His glorious blue-and-white coloring, the mane that was growing longer by the day, his bright eyes and quick, goofy grin. *Are you all right?* she asked him.

Silver's belly filled with a lazy kind of warmth, and she smiled.

Sweet dreams, Hiyyan.

Twenty-Six

Despite the tiny size of the window, morning light soaked into Silver on the sleeping mat. She blinked a few times against the strength of the sun and rolled over with a smile. She knew exactly what she had to do to rescue Kirja.

Brajon lay on the floor, happily snoring away like a herd animal.

"Brajon, wake up!"

"No, thank you," he mumbled.

Silver reached her foot over and nudged his side. Hard.

Brajon shot up. "Ow!" He rubbed his ribs. "What was that for?"

"Come on. I have a race to win!"

Brajon blinked at his cousin. "What? I thought we decided you weren't racing. We have to find Arkilah and save Kirja."

"We're going to do both." Silver gathered her things. She counted her coins and nodded, pleased enough with the amount of money they had left.

"There's no way. Unless you're planning to show a baby Aquinder to all of Calidia and put a target on his back!"

"He's not a baby anymore." Silver rubbed her thumb over her water dragon burn. "I have a plan. It's safer for Hiyyan to be claimed. Look what happened to Kirja."

"Nebekker had good reason to never race her," Brajon said.

Silver raised her hand to tuck her hair behind her ears, then lowered it when she realized there wasn't much hair left. "She did what she thought was best for her bond with Kirja. I just think a different way is better."

"Have you thought about how Calidia will react when Sagittaria rides in on Kirja? And then sees Hiyyan?"

"I don't think Sagittaria is going to ride Kirja," Silver said. "Not in the qualifiers."

Queen Imea's voice echoed in Silver's head. *It never does to show all our secrets right away, now does it? Oh, I love when the final card is played on the table.*

"No," Silver said slowly, "the queen is going to hold Kirja back until the very last race."

"You meet Queen Imea one time, and now you know all her deepest secrets?" he said.

"I don't. But just in case, we'll head to the market first. Arkilah will help us find Kirja, and you'll sneak her out of the city during the qualifiers. I won't be far behind."

"Not far behind? You mean you'll be *with us*."

Silver shook her head. "I have to race, Brajon."

Brajon shuffled his feet. "I don't know about this plan . . ."

"Do you have a better one?" Silver raised her eyebrows, but her cousin didn't say anything else. "Right," she said. "Because there isn't another plan. Don't worry—I'll have Hiyyan, and he can fly, remember? There's no way any of them can catch up to us."

"And how will you race him in front of the biggest crowds in Calidia without revealing that he's an Aquinder?"

"I'll smear camouin on his wings," Silver lifted her chin, prepared to defy Brajon. "There was enough from just brushing against that cave beast to cover my hands. We'll go back and"—Silver wrinkled her nose—"harvest the rest."

"You're being reckless," Brajon said, shaking his head. "Get caught with camouin and you could be put to death. And have you even asked Hiyyan if he wants to race?" At Silver's silence, Brajon pushed on. "Plus, you haven't resolved the biggest question of your plan."

"Which is?"

"We don't know where Kirja's being kept."

There was a knock at the door. Silver grinned. "Right on time." She threw the door open.

Mele stood in the alleyway, still wiping sleep from her eyes, holding a small plate of herby eggs.

"Good morning, Mele," Silver said. "Brajon and I have some questions for the girl who hears everything in this city."

Twenty-Seven

Mele's eyes widened and she turned to run, but Silver grabbed her by the arm. She pulled the girl into the room, then slammed the door shut.

"Ow," Mele said. "You're strong for someone so small." She glared at the cousins and rubbed her arm.

"I need you to help us," Silver said. "Since we're both friends of water dragons, of course. We need you to take us to the woman called Arkilah. She reads the stars in the Maze Market."

"The Maze Market is three levels and many streets deep. You think I know where one woman is in that labyrinth?" Mele said. But Silver saw the way Mele's eyes darted to the door.

Silver folded her arms across her chest and moved to block Mele from escape. "Last night you said you hear everything—"

"Everything about the *races*," Mele said. "But there are hundreds of thousands of people in this city. I don't know the whereabouts of one!"

Silver nibbled her bottom lip. Mele definitely had

information Silver wanted, but how to get it out of her? She reached into her bag and pulled out a silver coin.

Mele's face went dark. "You think you can bribe me?"

Silver hesitated, but she held out the coin anyway. "Think of it as a token of appreciation. You also said last night that this was the closest place to the water dragons."

Mele took the coin, dropped it in her apron pocket, and shrugged. "It's closest to the palace, and everyone knows the dragons are near the palace. That doesn't mean just anyone gets access to the Royal Pools."

"But you also said you couldn't leave. *Couldn't.* Not that you don't want to leave. Why do you *have* to stay close to the water dragons?"

"None of your business," Mele said. "I shouldn't have helped you two. I thought you were a friend to—"

"I *am* a friend to water dragons."

Silver took a deep breath. This was the riskiest part of her plan. What if she was wrong about Mele? She continued talking, more softly now. She had to be right. "But I know what I heard in your voice last night. I know how you feel, because that's the same way I feel. I know what it's like to be bonded to a water dragon. To an Aquinder."

Mele gasped, and her eyes sparkled dangerously.

Silver rushed on, the words tumbling out. "I know what it looks like. And I see it in you."

Mele froze, and her expression went blank. Silver's heart thumped in the too-long silence, and she became convinced that she had been wrong to reveal her secrets. She glanced at Brajon, prepared to run for it.

But then Mele's chin quivered. "You don't know what you're talking about."

"I know because—"

Mele whipped around. "No! You don't know what they'll do to us if they find out about the bond."

"Then tell me," Silver cried. "What will they do?"

Mele's eyes went wild, and her fingers clenched and unclenched. "I can't tell you anything. I don't know everything anyway. But I do know one thing: I'm safe here, and my water dragon is safe where she is. I can feel it. That's the best we can hope for right now. Probably ever. Maybe someday if I earn enough money, I can buy—"

"Her freedom?" Silver said. "Why should you have to when you belong together? Mele, help us. If we can only find Kirja, the Aquinder I'm looking for, we can make a plan to rescue her. You can release your dragon, too. We'll all flee together."

Mele licked her lips. "An Aquinder?" She laughed quietly. "I didn't think they existed."

"No one knows. Please don't tell."

"I won't," Mele said.

"Thank you. Now, if you can help us find Arkilah, she'll help us get Kirja out of Calidia before the races start."

Mele shook her head. "Sorry. I can't risk everything for a couple of strangers who actually believe Aquinder exist. For all I know, the desert might have muddled your brains."

The old Mele was back. Right when Silver was starting to like the girl.

Mele sighed. "I can tell you two things, but after that, I'm done with you, and with the races. Leave me out of it. Deal?"

Silver shared a look with Brajon, but she knew all the treats in the world couldn't coax a desert fox if it was too skittish. And Mele was certainly skittish.

"All right," Silver said. "Tell us what you can, and after that we'll never bother you again."

"There's an unofficial prize for the winners of the Autumn Festival semifinals. Have you heard of the Winners' Audience?"

When Silver shook her head, Mele's expression went smug. "Well, you hardly know anything about the races, so I'm not surprised."

"Get on with it," Silver groaned.

"If you're one of the five qualifiers, you earn an invitation for a dinner and an audience with the queen in the palace that night. She allows each winner to ask her for one favor . . . Within reason, of course," Mele said. "Most of the time, racers ask for money. It's so common that I've heard there's a little table set up next to her throne in advance with a line of boxes filled with coins."

Mele leaned in conspiratorially. "One year, a racer asked for his greatest rival to be killed."

"Killed?" Brajon looked nervously at Silver.

"Don't worry. Queen Imea laughed in his face and dismissed him from the palace. Rivals have been killed before, but not as official royal protocol."

Silver winced. Dragon theft . . . huge bets . . . murder . . . Water dragon racing was turning out to be more dangerous than she'd anticipated. But none of it changed her mind. Silver rubbed the water dragon mark on her wrist again. Racing was what she was made for.

"We don't want anyone killed," Silver said.

"No, but if you're one of the five finalists, you get to ask Queen Imea for a favor, and—"

"Kirja," Silver breathed. "I could ask for her freedom. How do I become a finalist?"

"You start at the bottom," Mele said. "The top two from each semiqualifier move on to the five qualifying races. Then, it's win at all costs."

Brajon opened his mouth as if to protest, but nothing came out. Silver was filled with triumph. Finally, things were going her way.

"Thank you for this information," she said. "Now, we need to find Arkilah. That's our first plan. I also need to get down to the seawall and get registered to race, just in case Arkilah doesn't work out. Winning will be our backup plan."

Silver tossed her bag over her shoulder and got ready to leave, but she paused when Brajon spoke up.

"Wait! Mele had two things to tell us, remember? What's the second thing?"

"Oh, that." Mele shrugged. "Only that the woman you seek, Arkilah, is very likely dead."

Silver's mouth dropped open. "No!"

"Arkilah was famous around here," Mele said. "She used to take most of her evening meals at the inn. One day, she told us she'd been invited to the palace. She went in, and that was the last anyone has seen or heard of her. That was three years ago. Most people think she told someone a bad fortune and was disposed of."

Silver watched Brajon swallow slowly. *"Disposed of?"* he said. "That seems to happen a lot in Calidia."

Mele shrugged again.

Despite the worry making her skin tingle, Silver threw her shoulders back. "Brajon, there's no backup plan anymore. There's only one plan. I have to race Hiyyan, and I have to win!"

Twenty-Eight

The only place the sea—and therefore the docks and the seawall south of them—could be was on the other side of the palace. Silver could see the rest of the city stretching out in a semicircle around her, and it was full of roads and buildings. No water to be seen, other than the shallow palace pools the Abruqs paddled in, which weren't big enough to be the Royal Pools, where the racing dragons were kept.

She closed her eyes and breathed through her nose. Arkilah. Nebekker's friend. Dead. How was Silver going to tell the old woman the news? Her heart grieved for Nebekker, who didn't have many friends as it was. Silver circled the pendant with her finger.

Fortunately, the Winners' Audience meant the way was still open for Silver to get Kirja out of Calidia, even without Nebekker's friend.

Silver opened her eyes. The morning throngs brought immense energy to the city. Calidians and tourists alike swept along the lane that circled the palace. People like the three inn guests in dark blue.

Silver saw the two men and the boy laughing and slapping one another on the backs as they left the inn. One of the men must be a racer, she thought, and the boy, his squire. Suddenly, as if hearing her thoughts, the boy looked over his shoulder and spotted her lurking behind them. He winked at her, then slowed to a stop and motioned for his companions to go on without him.

Silver's face burned. He had a lot of nerve thinking she would go right up to him . . . which she would.

"We're going to need a good breakfast today," she said, passing a few coins to Brajon and pointing to a food vendor with a long line.

While her cousin eagerly took the money and got in line, Silver walked up to the boy in blue.

"You clean up decently well," the boy said. "I can only smell a tiny bit of that stench from last night on you."

Silver's mouth fell open. The boy laughed.

"I'm teasing. A big part of my culture, but I apologize if you're not used to it."

"No, we tease, too," Silver huffed. "Just not so much with strangers."

"I'm Ferdi. Not a stranger to you anymore. And anyone who would save a water dragon isn't a stranger to me. She's a hero."

Despite the boy's bravado—when Brajon talked like that, Silver rolled her eyes—she found herself smiling back. "My name's Silver."

"Silver." The boy grinned. "You're here for the races, I

assume. I was on my way to check on my water dragon. Want to meet her?"

"The water dragon that almost got stolen is yours?" Silver's heart leaped, but she calmed it down quickly. "I would love to, but I'm short on time."

"Come on, Silver. It's just at the guest pools near the seawall. It'll only take a moment." Ferdi waved off her hesitation. "Your friend will be in that line longer than it'll take us. Look how busy it is. Besides, she's the best water dragon you've ever seen—promise you that."

Ferdi puffed out his chest. Silver liked how proud the boy was of his water dragon, even though she knew that *Hiyyan* was the best dragon she would ever see in her life.

"Show me, then."

They walked the wide avenue circling the palace, and as they got closer to the sea, Silver gaped at all the people waving flags. The colorful strips of fabric were emblazoned with the emblems of the world's greatest water dragon racers: the yellow horn on a white background for Honoria Messum, who rode the trumpet-nosed Calypto; the red, pink, and black stripes of the Bebisor riding dynasty, wherein every rider takes a blood oath to win—or die trying; and the Desert Nations flag imposed over a background of sea blue for Sagittaria Wonder, who rode for the queen herself.

As though he'd seen it all before, Ferdi continued rambling on about his water dragon.

"I got her for my fifth birthday, but my father wouldn't let me ride her until I was eight. Three long years of training. You have no idea how much I wanted to disobey my father. But no one disobeys my father. He is very strict."

"I know what you mean," Silver said quietly.

"I couldn't believe it when he gave me permission to come to these races alone! Well, not so much alone." Ferdi pointed his thumb over his shoulder.

When Silver looked, she discovered that one of the men she'd seen with him at the inn was trailing them.

"You have guards?"

"More like babysitters."

As the swarm of people grew larger, Silver realized more than one person had stopped to glance at them or was making a concerted effort to move out of their path.

Silver drew her eyebrows together. "And who's your father?"

But Ferdi pointed to something in the distance. "There she is! Isn't she a magnificent beast?"

The change in the air hit Silver swiftly. Salt and brine, like the juices from the crocks of pickled sea vegetables traders often brought to Jaspaton, lingered under her nose. She stood on her tiptoes to try to see over the heads in front of her.

"Oh, she dipped down again," Ferdi said. "Glitherns do that, you know."

"Glitherns?" Silver racked her brain. "I've never heard of them."

Ferdi nodded. "Lots of people haven't. They're so rare they're practically mythical."

"I know something about that, at least," Silver said.

But Ferdi wasn't done. He talked faster as he grew more excited. "They're the only water dragons who can live their entire lives underwater. All water dragons have gills to help them breathe underwater, of course. But none have ones as big and efficient as a Glithern's. Other breeds might stay under for several hours—and a lot less than that if they're racing—but my dragon? Never has to come up for air! When we race, she stays under the surface the whole time. Makes her one of the fastest water dragons in the racing world. And the hardest to find."

"Except—oof!" A large man's elbow dug into Silver's side.

"My apologies," he said, turning to them. It was the palace guard from the day before, dressed in his immaculate white uniform. He smiled at Silver, then looked at Ferdi. The color drained from his cheeks.

"Truly! I . . . I didn't mean," he stammered.

"Not a problem. It's crowded here," Ferdi said quickly, pulling Silver along by her arm.

"What was that all about?" Silver said. Inside, though, she was shaking herself for almost giving Hiyyan away. It was hard not to brag about her own water dragon when Ferdi took so much delight in his Glithern.

Ferdi shrugged and looked down, letting his hair fall over his face. "Nothing. Just a friendly stranger."

Silver knew there was more to it than that, but it was better not to ask questions, so that he wouldn't start asking questions of his own.

"Only a desert fox could get through here," she muttered as they jostled through the crowds.

Ferdi looked amused. "I've never seen a desert fox. But oh, look over there!"

This time, when Silver looked where Ferdi pointed, she saw the dark-blue-and-brilliant-orange head of a water dragon break the surface of the pool. The dragon looked around in a slow circle, then paused once she caught sight of Ferdi. The sun striking her skin reflected millions of rainbows. Silver had to shade her eyes against the brilliance.

"So bright! And so many colors," Silver said. "She looked purple in the cart."

"She's every color, depending on the light. That's the other reason she races underwater. Otherwise, I could temporarily blind my opponents with her dazzle."

"That's the rule for Glitherns, then—that they have to stay underwater during races?" Silver asked.

"No. There are no rules against the dragon's special features. I just think it's fairer to race that way. I win on my own merit. Because I'm the best racer."

He waved to his Glithern. The water dragon's narrowed eyes and sharp snout softened, her jaw fell open in a huge grin, and her tongue drooped out. Silver had to giggle.

Water dragons were all the same.

The Glithern splashed her tail against the water and dove under again.

"She's beautiful," Silver said.

"Her name's Hoonazoor. Do you want to meet her?"

Yes, every cell inside Silver screamed. But Brajon would be wondering where she was soon. "I can't," she said. "I have to be somewhere right now. Thank you for showing me your Glithern."

Silver started back through the crowd, sneaking one last glimpse at the stunning water dragon.

"Races start at six," Ferdi called after her. "Don't forget to watch me. I'll be the one winning!"

Twenty-Nine

Six o'clock was too soon for Silver's comfort. She needed to figure out how to get Hiyyan registered for the races, and then how to get back to the cave to gather the camouin.

Luckily, the kind palace guard was straight ahead, buying a box of sweet jellies from a vendor. Brajon was probably still in line at the breakfast cart. There was time for a detour.

"Hello again," Silver said, pausing at his side.

"You again! Lemon jelly?" the guard asked, holding the box to her.

"No, thank you. I was wondering if you know where the water dragons get registered."

"You couldn't ask your friend there? He knows."

"He's not my . . . He had to run. But I thought that since you see everything that goes on around the palace . . ."

The guard gave his mustache a twirl and leaned in conspiratorially. His eyes twinkled. "I *do* see everything. Even things I'm not supposed to."

"Well, I just need to know one thing," Silver said

impatiently. The sun had risen high enough in the sky that the royal city's streets were beginning to bake.

The guard shrugged and stood upright again.

"You're a squire, and your rider sent you along to register, yes? I thought about becoming a water dragon squire when I was about your age. But it's too competitive here in Calidia. Hundreds—no, thousands of kids try to get picked, and only a handful make it." The guard popped a pink jelly into his mouth. "It's all right, now. I like the guardship. An easy job most days. Even when the seawall gets crowded like this, it's not too bad. Especially with little squires like you to keep me amused. Follow me. I'll take you right to registration." The guard headed toward the seawall, and Silver gratefully fell into step with him.

"Who are you signing up?" the guard asked between bites of jellies. "Where are you from?"

Silver squirmed. Lying was necessary, but she still felt awful doing it.

"Kolghan," she said. It was the name of a desert town far to the west of Jaspaton. She didn't know much about it, only that it was renowned for its shell jewelry.

"That's some distance," the guard said. His cheeks took on a rosy hue as he talked to her. "I didn't think you had a water dragon there anymore. Not since your last Vaprozy retired and your town decided to use the river for shellfish farming instead of dragon training."

"It's a new one," Silver said, fibbing again. "A young . . . Vaprozy."

"Bred for racing, I'd guess. That's an exciting thing for you to be part of. The breeding program here in Calidia is the second largest in the world," the guard said, boasting. "Biggest one after Runesque, which is out there in deep sea, of course. But you'll know all about that."

"Yes." Silver nodded, but her insides were twisting like a ball of yarn. *Runesque?* She'd never heard of it.

"How many races has your young Vaprozy won?"

"None. I mean, today will be his first." She stood up straighter.

"That's the spirit!" The guard patted her on the shoulder. "Although I have to say, I can't help but have a bit of a laugh when I see the Vaprozys racing. Haven't seen one in action since before your old girl retired, but I thought I saw one training out in the sea yesterday. Must have been yours, eh?"

Silver nodded along, but she had no idea what the guard was talking about. What could be so amusing about racing?

"People might make fun, but you just ignore them and be proud of how well you've trained him up," the guard said. He smiled.

"I will. I am. I mean, we all are." If Silver's insides were to twist any more, they would wring her as dry as the desert.

"Good. Ah, here we are. See those folks sitting on that platform? Sign up with them. And all the best to you. I'm a lucky one. Don't have to work today, so I can come down to the festivities before the races begin. I'll be looking out for your Vaprozy and cheering him on. Oh, and speaking of looking out, look there. Famous folks all around this morning!"

The crowd noise built. Silver's stomach lurched when she spotted Sagittaria Wonder. The racer had appeared near the seawall and was gazing over the water. When the water dragon racer turned, her eyes swept the throngs, and her fierce gaze seemed to catch on Silver and the guard—or was that only Silver's imagination?

Sagittaria set her jaw and walked in the direction of the palace, the people spreading apart to create a path for her. Silver breathed a sigh of relief. Against her skin, Nebekker's stone pendant warmed. Silver looked around. Did that mean Kirja was near?

Silver waved good-bye to the guard and headed for the short set of stairs to the platform, citing squire duties. She swallowed and looked over her shoulder as she climbed. No Sagittaria Wonder in sight. A man with pale hair flowing to his waist was finishing his registration as Silver walked up. Parchment was strewn all over, and three of the four people sitting behind the table were furiously making notes with feathered quills.

"Can I help you?" said a tall, narrow woman who wore a hat in the shape of a flower. The petals bobbed as she looked Silver up and down. She sniffed.

"I'm here to register a dragon for my racer," Silver said.

"We explicitly said in the registration materials not to send squires." The woman rolled her eyes and sighed. "I'll take your information. But tell your racer that I'm not amused. Name?"

Silver smiled. This part had come to her in her dream last night.

"Desert Fox."

"Age of dragon?"

"One year," Silver said. A trader had told her that was the age water dragons began to hit peak form.

The woman nodded. "Place of training?"

"The deep desert," Silver said without thinking, then hesitated. "I mean, a river near the desert."

The woman looked up at Silver. "Really? How interesting. What body of water?"

One of the men behind the table spoke up. He was so old his skin looked like paper. "No time for chitchat, Keppleroo. Just register the dragon."

From beneath her bobbing petals, Keppleroo glared at the ancient man before turning her attention back to Silver. "Preferred racing time? We can't guarantee a time, of course, unless you're registering a Daknyan."

Silver thought back to the collection of water dragon facts tacked to her bedroom walls. *Daknyan. Light-sensitive eyes. Can't race while the sun's up.*

"Can you tell me which race Sagittaria Wonder is in?"

The woman's mouth twitched. "Oh, child. Everyone wants to test themselves against Sagittaria Wonder. But it's the easiest way to ensure that you won't move on to the finals."

"I'll . . . I mean, *my rider* will take that challenge," Silver said firmly. That would wipe the smug expression off Sagittaria's face.

"Well, you don't have the option. The races are sorted randomly after registration closes. No one will know who or what they're up against. Too much knowledge lends itself to cheating."

"And there's already plenty of that," the old man put in. "You're not a cheater, are you?"

"No." Silver held her head up high. To save Kirja, Silver had become a lot of things she wasn't proud of: a disappointment, a thief, a liar. But she wasn't a cheater.

The woman finished making a note on the parchment and gave Silver a numbered tag from a pile on the table. "Here's your assignment. Place it on the back of your rider's uniform. The race schedule will be posted on the seawall just below us at noon, so check back then to match your number to your race."

"So I won't know who I'm up against—"

"Until you're at the starting line. Correct. The first races test speed. If you move through to the semifinals, you'll be tested on speed and agility. Next!"

The person registering next to her jostled her as she turned away from the table.

"Oh, hello. You look familiar." The man in dark blue—one of Ferdi's companions—raised his eyebrows at her. "What are you doing up here?"

"Registering for my rider." Silver hastily tucked her number in her coin pouch.

The man looked suspicious. He reached over as though he were going to dig through her bag. Silver pulled back, right into a sturdy figure. The other man in blue.

"I think this whelp has something to hide," he said over Silver's head. "There's more to her than just a street urchin, I think."

"I'm not a street urchin," Silver said.

"Of course not. You're a hero, too! Saving water dragons from theft." The men laughed. "Ahrid, what shall we do with her?"

The first man snatched her tag. "Number one hundred fifteen. That's a lot of water dragons. Cam, do you really think there are one hundred fifteen dragons in Calidia right now? That's . . . why, that's an *army* full, isn't it?"

A shudder went down Silver's spine. There was something about the man's words and his smile and the way his friend gripped her shoulder that reminded her of Sagittaria Wonder.

But Silver raised her chin and sniffed derisively. "There can't be that many. Where would they be kept? They would fill up the guest pool."

Ahrid chuckled. "They would, if everyone here were a special guest of the queen. But they're not. Most dragons are over there."

The man pointed over Silver's shoulder. Cam spun her around.

Silver's eyebrows shot up, and her mouth dropped open. The seawall cut across the palace grounds, creating a private lawn and beach for the royals, before continuing on the other side of the palace. There, where there were no docks or grand ships bearing exotic goods from around the world, the open seas churned with white-capped waves. Water dragons. Maybe not hundreds of them, but a lot. Dozens. More than Silver ever thought she would see in her lifetime.

Some of the dragons swam, darting to and fro as their racers put them through their exercises. Some floated along lazily, soaking up the sun's rays. Others formed groups, playing and talking. Silver strained her ears.

"They're singing," she whispered to herself in wonder. Could Hiyyan sing, too?

Silver recognized some of the breeds from the drawings that were on her bedroom walls, but others were new to her. And still others were so far away that even when she squinted she couldn't quite tell them apart.

It was magical. A dream come true. She felt like she could lift off the platform and float right over to the water dragons.

"If only you had a scarf to wipe away your drool," Ahrid said. He smirked, still holding her tag. "Bet a street urchin like you dreams of being close enough to a water dragon to touch them. I don't believe you have a rider."

"I do too." Silver glared. "And a water dragon."

"No rider would let you near their precious beast, no matter how many times you step in front of a cart. Dragons are worth more than silks, more than jewels."

"More than kingdoms, in some cases," Cam said.

"It's none of your business," Silver snapped.

"It's not? I make it my job to assess Ferdi's potential opponents. And you *are* up here registering, after all."

"For my rider," Silver said. "And you don't need to worry about Ferdi. His father thinks he's good enough to be here, and that's all that matters."

The two men shared a shadowed look.

"You know more about Ferdi than you should."

"Aw, don't listen to her." Cam grabbed the tag and pressed it into Silver's palm. "You can lie to the folks at the table, but you're boring me with your stories. Go on. Get lost." Cam shoved Silver off the platform.

Fighting the urge to shove the man back, Silver gritted her teeth and melted into the crowd. Better that the man believed she was a liar. She wanted to keep her secret a bit longer. Needed to if, as Ahrid said, they took a special interest in Ferdi's opponents. But as she looked back at the platform one last time, she saw Cam still standing there, a curious look on his face.

Thirty

Silver shoved the man's suspicious expression out of her mind. She needed to focus on finding camouin and another way to disguise Hiyyan and herself before the race. There might be enough camouin to hide Hiyyan's wings, but his face—and hers—needed a different kind of disguise. Too bad her Aquinder couldn't stay underwater the entire race like Ferdi's dragon did.

At her side, Silver's fingers worked back and forth as she thought, her bedraggled scarf rubbing against her skin. The fabric was smooth, the weave tight, and Silver wondered what it was made of. Cotton? Silk? Not Jaspatonian wool, and definitely not Aquinder fur. Both so useful. *There are thousands of ways yarnwork is useful and wonderful,* her mother had once said to her, when Silver had complained about learning it.

Silver had an idea.

There wasn't much time to collect everything she needed to make her plan work, but to do that, she had to find Brajon. She darted down the road, back to the breakfast stand, but when she got there, he was nowhere to be found.

"You would disappear," she muttered. Never mind that she was the one who took off first. She craned her neck left and right but caught no sight of her cousin.

What she did catch sight of were two guards posting a new notice on a wall near the palace. Most people paid little mind—there were many colorful flyers promoting merchants or festival events—but Silver crept closer. The wind shifted so that the delicately briny breeze became something harsh and cold, something with a touch of a warning.

There, on that poster, was her face.

WANTED: JEWELRY THIEF. REWARD OFFERED.

Silver's breath flew from her. Fortunately, her hair was still long, and it was a rough enough sketch that the resemblance wasn't immediately obvious. But Silver was certain it was meant to be her. Sagittaria had seen Silver moments before. How had she spread the notices so quickly? All of a sudden, her presence in Calidia was more dangerous than ever. The thief notices would spread over the city soon enough.

"No," she said under her breath. "You're the real thief, Sagittaria Wonder!"

Silver melted backward, her head down. She used her peripheral vision to try to spot Brajon, but he stubbornly remained missing. There wasn't time to track him down. She would have to go about her tasks and hope to run into him along the way. He couldn't have gone far from the seawall.

Silver pushed through the festival crowds in and out of the center of Calidia, hoping to get to the shops she needed before the flyers did. She bought a new scarf and wrapped it around the bottom half of her face. Dull, inconspicuous brown this time. And she ducked into a cosmetics shop to pick up a kohl pencil, rubbing it against the back of her hand. It left a dark, oily black mark.

As Silver counted out the coins, she asked the shop owner, "Do you know where I can find a fibers shop?"

The shopkeeper gave Silver directions, and she set off again, tucking the kohl pencil into her bag and keeping her head low. Occasionally, racers were walking their water dragons in town, drawing admiring crowds. Energy and anticipation were thick in the air. Silver wanted to be in those crowds, but she pressed on, hoping that people would be more interested in the water dragons than the notices on the walls. After all, didn't thieves run rampant here? But like the man who had bought her father's ring had said, guards did, too.

Silver inhaled deeply. Food vendors were cooking festival breads stuffed with farmer cheese—some savory with a thick layer of herbs on top, and some sweet and drizzled with honey—for midmorning treats. Hunger and homesickness rained over her so hard Silver had to put her hand against a blue-and-white-tiled door to steady herself.

She bought a round of bread and some fruit on her way to the fibers shop, eating quickly as she walked. People in Jaspaton sat down for their meals, but it seemed that here in Calidia, everyone enjoyed street food.

When her eye caught a glimpse of another poster with her face, Silver broke into a jog until she reached the fibers shop. Upon entering, she was overwhelmed with all the types and colors of wool on the shelves.

"What's this?" she asked a stock boy. Her fingers ran across a pale-blue fabric as slinky and smooth as water.

"Sea-crystal silk," he said, swatting her juice-dotted hands away. "Don't touch it. You'll leave fingerprints."

"Sorry." Silver could imagine Queen Imea sweeping through her palace in a gown made from the luscious sea-crystal silk. Someday, maybe she would be as famous and loved as Sagittaria Wonder and would need sea-crystal silk gowns for all her visits to the palace parties and fancy dinners. She went to the purchase counter.

"I'd like thin wool yarn, please. In orange and white and brown. I'm in a hurry."

The boy behind the counter—a taller and older version of the boy stocking the shelves—pulled down several balls of yarn. The counter boy squinted at her, as though trying to make out her features under her scarf.

"These will do." Silver didn't even inspect the yarn. She paid quickly, thanked the boy, and left.

As Silver blended back into the crowd, she noticed that the streets in midcity were a bit quieter. Perhaps everyone was already down at the seawall to watch the preparation for the races. With several hours before the first races began, she needed to find a safe and quiet space. And she needed to find her cousin.

"Why didn't you just wait for me at the breakfast vendor?" Silver groaned out loud. Brajon was still nowhere to be seen, and they were running out of time. If only she could contact him just by thinking her thoughts at him.

Her head shot up. "Maybe Hiyyan can help."

Silver tucked herself into a side street, pressed against a shaded wall, and closed her eyes to the streams of people flowing by. *Hiyyan, can you hear me?*

Instantly, that warm, comforting feeling filled her. Despite her worry, she couldn't keep back a smile. Her Aquinder, her bond.

I've lost Brajon. Is there any way you can sniff him out?

Silver knew it was unlikely—Hiyyan was still some distance from the city, and there were so many people. The water dragon's responding emotion was full of doubt.

Please try.

It felt strange to be part of Hiyyan's sensory sweep of the city. Sort of like riding a dune board with her eyes closed. The smells came to her in a dizzying tumble: clay and dirt, bread and sweets, body odor and perfumes, animals of all sorts, and, strongest of all, the sea. But even Hiyyan couldn't find the unique scent that was Brajon.

Silver gnawed her lip. She couldn't leave her cousin lost in the city, but she couldn't stay, either. She had a lot to get done before the races, and time wouldn't stop while she searched for him—especially while people were searching for her. With one last glance around, she made up her mind.

"I hope you think to come back to the cave entrance, Brajon," she whispered before pushing off the wall and away from the rings of midcity.

The roads zigzagged into the outer rings. Silver memorized the buildings she passed so that she could easily find her way back again.

"Tailor," she murmured. "Sweetshop. Kite vendor." She couldn't keep herself from stopping to marvel at the kites. They were as tall as she was. Intricate cuts in the paper gave them a lacy look.

"Dragon kites for the celebrations," the vendor said merrily.

She ducked her head and ran on. It had taken her and Brajon an entire day to cross the city when they'd arrived, but Silver didn't have that long.

A boy was just finishing unloading a cart of fruit at a shop. He climbed up on his cycling contraption and put his feet on the pedals, ready to head off again.

"Wait," Silver called. "Are you going back out to the orchards?"

"I am. Hopefully for my last delivery. I want to get down to the seawall!"

"Can I ride with you? I can pay."

The boy gave a sideways grin. "Climb in. You don't have to pay. I like the idea of carting a pretty girl around. It'll make my friends jealous."

Silver blinked, then shook her head. A pretty girl? He was just saying that. Probably the type to flirt with anyone, if it meant he could get his way. Just like Brajon.

Silver waved off his remark and climbed in the back as the boy braced himself and pushed. They flew through the city roads, swerving so hard that Silver gripped the sides of the cart until her knuckles were white. They passed a green-and-white-speckled dragon, which lunged toward them snarling, its trainers holding its chains as tightly as they could.

The boy laughed, but Silver's stomach lurched with a combination of pity for the imprisoned Hop-Slawn and motion sickness. How could she ride Hiyyan through the air one day, soaring up and down and side to side and even spinning upside down without a problem, when one ride in a cart almost made her lose her breakfast?

The boy pedaled all the way to the outer circle of the city and beyond. He stopped at a smattering of low clay buildings. Silver hopped out.

"Are you sure I can't pay you for the ride?" she said.

"No, but—"

The boy's eyes narrowed, and in a flash like lightning, Silver realized her scarf had fallen down around her neck.

Silver didn't wait around for the boy to finish what he wanted to say. She hastily pulled up the fabric and ran for the trees.

"I thought so!" he yelled. "You're the thief!" The boy grabbed for her, but Silver twisted away from his reaching fingers and kept running.

Thirty-One

The orchards felt like a different world. So quiet without all the noise of thousands of people moving and yelling. Just her swift footfalls, and the boy breathing down her neck. Silver was quick and nimble, but the boy, with his long stride, was just as swift, keeping up easily.

Keep running, keep runn—oof!

The boy tackled Silver to the ground. He sat on her back, pinning her down.

"Get off me!"

The boy laughed. He wrenched away Silver's bag and dumped the contents on the ground.

"Useless, useless," he muttered. Silver saw her balls of yarn and kohl pencil roll away. "Aha!"

Although Silver was still pressed to the ground, a jingling sound told Silver the boy had found her money and the jewelry. The boy shifted, and then a piece of paper was shoved in Silver's face.

"See that? It says 'reward.' I wonder if the queen's reward

is worth as much as these jewels. Tell me what they're worth, and I'll think about letting you go."

Silver spat at the sketch of her face.

"Have it your way. I'll keep both."

He hauled Silver to her feet. She struggled, but he was much bigger than she was—even taller than Brajon—and he had a firm grip. She leaned back to spit in his smug face, too, but in one surprising movement, he spun her so her back was to his front and pinned her arms together, then unwound her scarf from her neck.

"Let me go!" The more she struggled, the more her arms screamed with pain, until she was certain the bones were about to snap. The boy dragged her backward, and even though Silver dug her heels into the soft orchard soil, he succeeded in slamming her to the ground and against a tree. The boy wrestled her wrists around the trunk and knotted them together with her scarf.

He stood before her, admiring his handiwork.

Silver glared. "You don't know what you're doing. I'm not a thief. You are. Those jewels belong to my family."

"Wrong. They belong to me. And soon you'll belong to the queen. Don't go anywhere." With that, the boy sprinted back in the direction of his cart.

Silver struggled against the knots and banged her head against the tree in frustration. She could almost hear Sagittaria Wonder's bitter laughter ringing through the orchard. *You're nothing but a talentless child.* How many times had Silver proved her right?

A heavier scent of the desert filled her nose, with the salty sea air far back behind her. Silver stopped struggling against her bonds and fought back tears. Even though she and Brajon had been in Calidia only one day and one night, she missed the simplicity of the desert. What had she gotten herself into? She'd come here to rescue Kirja, only to get caught herself.

Silver reached her mind to Hiyyan's again, still waiting at the river cave. It was easy to make a connection with him, and as soon as she did, she felt his burst of excitement. He knew how close she was. A mad, low giggle bubbled up in her throat despite everything.

Hello, she said in her mind. *I have failed Kirja. And I'm a bit tied up at the moment.*

She conjured up an image of her bound hands and sent it toward Hiyyan. He responded with alarm, then an image of a dragon talon slicing neatly through the bonds.

I don't have one of those! She sensed Hiyyan rustle and bit back a wave of panic. *No, don't come here! Sagittaria might be on her way, and I couldn't bear if she found out about you, too.*

Silver looked around. Her bag's contents were strewn everywhere. Where one ball of yarn was half unwound, she saw the tip of her dagger sticking out. The boy hadn't noticed it when he'd tossed the yarn aside. If she could just reach it . . .

She wriggled and stretched her toes as far as she could. It was close. More maneuvering bought her another inch.

Something in the soil shuffled, and Silver froze. A desert scorpion peered out of its hiding place to see what was disturbing its home. But not just any scorpion: a Flying Black-Eyed Scorpion. They attacked as fast as lightning and, since they only had one sting in them, they flew straight for their adversary's eyes. The Flying Black-Eyeds weren't named for their own eye color, but how they permanently blinded whomever they stung.

Silver breathed slowly and silently, facing off with the scorpion in a game of Don't Move.

The scorpion raised its tail, glistening black. Sweat dripped down Silver's palms to her fingers, watering the orchard tree. Her dagger was just to the right of the scorpion.

Silver bit back a whimper, then steeled herself. There was only one way of dealing with an attacking Black-Eyed Scorpion: Get it to sting anywhere but the eyes.

With her eyes closed, she took in a deep breath. Then she flung her left foot out.

The pain as the scorpion sank its stinger into her foot was dazzling. Silver yelped and let a single sob escape, but then she bit her lip against the building throbs in her foot and opened her eyes. She knew it would hurt but the damage would pass. The scorpion, stinger lost, skittered away.

Her right foot reached for the trailing yarn, dragging it closer inch by inch. When it was close enough, Silver twisted her body around the tree trunk. Her fingers grabbed the dagger and after a few moments of scrabbling, she was able to unsheathe it and work the blade haphazardly through her scarf.

Silver got to her feet and limped in a circle, collecting the rest of her things before the horrible boy came back.

"Who knew I'd go through so many scarves," she muttered.

The sound of a group approaching in the distance reached her. Silver dragged herself toward the outer road and her Aquinder. She still wasn't completely sure how their mental communication was working, especially when singing seemed to be the natural water dragon language, but it felt right. Silver continued thinking her words as though she were speaking to Hiyyan, perhaps rubbing his furry belly. She needed to keep her mind off her aching foot.

It'll be our first race soon. We're registered and everything. Isn't that amazing? You and me, cutting through the water, becoming the greatest racers of all time. Well, maybe not this first race, but it will happen! It's my dream coming true. Only two races, and when we win them both, I'll be able to ask Queen Imea for your mother back.

Silver waited for some kind of response. Not words, but a feeling. Something that told her he either approved or rejected her ideas.

The feeling never came.

Instead, Hiyyan did.

Thirty-Two

When Silver saw the deep blue of his body against the pale-blue sky, she rushed forward, meeting him just on the other side of the road into Calidia.

Hiyyan landed, knocking Silver off her feet, and wiggled on the ground with glee, obviously happy that they were together again. Silver doubled over, her laughter and sobs combining until her belly ached.

Hiyyan paused, his back on the ground, his feet in the air, and his tongue lolling out the side of his mouth in a dopey grin.

"I'm happy to see you, too," Silver said, wrapping her arms around his neck and trying to ignore the throbbing pain in her foot. "Hopefully, after this, we won't have to be separated ever again." She dug her hands into Hiyyan's soft mane and laid her head on his side, then started walking to the hole in the ground.

"But now I have to go back into the cave to get the camouin," she said. "And you'll need to keep a lookout—or a listen-out—for anyone coming. There are people looking for me, and if they get close, we have to run. Unless it's Brajon."

An image of Brajon skulking around the cave came to her mind, and Silver nodded. "Right. He needs to come back and meet us here."

"Hugggrrr." Hiyyan's low grumblings were tinged with frustration.

Silver carefully lowered herself partway into the cave opening. Her swollen foot thrummed inside her boot, so she took it off to relieve the pressure. She tiptoed to the remains of the white cave beast. In the light of the larger opening, the pile of bones seemed less threatening than before. Still, Silver moved slowly, her heart racing as though expecting it to come back to life and attack her. But as she scooped camouin off the bones, the creature didn't move.

"There's much less here than I thought there would be," Silver said, tucking the small amount in her bag. She glanced at Hiyyan's wings and did some mental calculations.

It had to be enough. There was no going back now.

She returned to the entrance and sat. Hiyyan settled in next to her, ears perked. Every few seconds, he turned them, as though he were scanning the whole desert for sounds. Silver knew that if she focused on Hiyyan, she could probably hear what he was hearing, too, but she had other things to focus on.

She pulled the yarn from her bag. An image of a desert fox danced in her mind. She tried to turn the animal's coloration into a pattern her fingers could follow. She began with the brown wool, weaving the thin yarn around and between her hook and fingers, just as Nebekker had taught her. It took a few tries of weaving, then unraveling, then trying again, but eventually she figured out how to adapt the scale pattern with her own image of a desert fox.

Once that was figured out, her fingers flew so fast they were a blur. She added the orange wool, then the white. Back to the orange, then to the brown. She fashioned the ears separately, then attached them to the top of the mask, using her dagger to cut the ends of the yarn. When she was finished, she started on Hiyyan's disguise.

Silver worked the wool and let her mind drift into a scene. She and her Aquinder, being showered with medals and gold and adoration. Walking the halls of the Calidian palace, Sagittaria Wonder relegated to the corners. Silver smirked at the idea.

"We'll be wearing sea-crystal silk, too," she said to Hiyyan absently.

And still, she worked the wool until it was a large piece of fabric. The sun was high in the sky, indicating midday.

"Let's give this a try," Silver said. She draped the wool over Hiyyan's back. "Hold still," she said. But when she attempted to tuck his wings under, the water dragon balked.

"Mrrph." Hiyyan shook his head and scuttled out of the cave entrance, dragging bits of wool in the sand.

"Hiyyan! There isn't enough camouin to cover your wings."

"Mrrrawww!"

"Come here!"

The Aquinder shook his head, then ducked his neck down and backed right out of the fabric disguise. Silver scrambled out, limped to the wool, and gathered it in her arms. It was heavy, but Hiyyan was big and strong. It probably felt like nothing to him.

"Sagittaria Wonder knows I'm here, but she doesn't know

all the reasons why. If people know what kind of dragon you are, there's going to be trouble." Silver sent Hiyyan an image of the crowds in Calidia. "They'll go wild, and then how will we get to the Winners' Audience and ask for your mother back?"

Hiyyan flopped on his belly and looked away from her.

Silver dropped the wool on the ground and went to her water dragon, sitting beside him and putting her arms around his neck.

"It's not just Kirja. If we don't race, they'll try to kidnap you, too. Those are the rules."

Hiyyan's skin went cold. Silver got his message loud and clear: *Those aren't the rules in* my *world.*

"We're not in your world," she said.

Silver thought back to what Nebekker had said about never racing Kirja. A bond wasn't the same as claiming. Silver understood that, but she had seen other things, too. Like the green-and-white dragon she'd passed during her cart ride. It was contained by several lengths of chain, wrapped around its body and head, with three men keeping it from running off. At first, she'd thought its face was angry, but perhaps it was sad . . . or desperate.

Hiyyan absorbed the image, then turned his head to her, searching her face with his big, dark eyes.

"On the other hand," Silver said, "there were those adorable Abruqs in the pools. They seemed happy enough to be where they were."

Hiyyan nudged her and showed his teeth.

"No, I don't want to trade you for an Abruq. Knock that off."

"Mrruggrr." Hiyyan stuck his chin in the air.

Silver's voice softened. "I don't want to lose you at all, Hiyyan. Ever. We'll show up and cross that finish line, and that's it. One Aquinder safe. We can be together without fear in *any* world. We'll be free. Your wings will never be bound again. Then all we'll have to do is get your mother back."

Hiyyan sighed, blowing a ball of sand into the air. He tucked his muzzle into Silver's palm.

"Let's practice. Without the disguise. You can get your first taste of the sea."

Hiyyan's eyes flashed, and his grin was as big as the desert.

Thirty-Three

Silver poked her head out of the cave entrance and looked around. A desert beetle marched in front of her, but all else was quiet. Were there still guards among the trees, scouring the orchard for any sign of her? Was the boy going to come back?

There should be a way to access the sea without going through Calidia, she thought. The city was a semicircle, with the sea making a border along the edges. That meant the city tucked around the water, like there was an inlet. But the shoreline must continue past the city in at least one direction.

Hiyyan stood and shook the sand out of his wings impatiently.

"We can't fly," Silver said. "Someone might see us."

The water dragon let out a whoosh of air that sounded almost like a sigh.

"But we don't have time for anything else."

Hiyyan flapped his wings so hard with joy that he lifted off the ground and churned dirt all over Silver. She spit gravel out of her mouth.

"Thanks for that." She laughed.

Hiyyan landed and bent his leg for her to climb up. Silver's heart beat so fast and hard she thought her chest would burst.

It was finally happening. She was going to fly.

She dug her fingers into Hiyyan's ever-growing mane and hoisted herself up, swinging her still-painful foot over his back and landing square in the middle, her face pressed against his lizardlike skin.

Hiyyan straightened his legs and rose, unfurling his wings to their massive span. He began to run.

Silver wasn't ready. Her hands clutched at his mane again, but she couldn't hold on. She toppled off the water dragon and landed with a crunching thud.

"Hey!" she said.

Hiyyan looked at Silver sheepishly.

"Let's try again," she said. "This time, give me a warning before sprinting off."

Hiyyan crouched. Silver raised herself up. Once she was centered on her water dragon's back, he craned his head at her, a silent question in his eyes.

"Okay. I'm ready." Silver lowered her body so that only her head was up. She held onto his mane for dear life.

Hiyyan's wings stretched again, the beautiful violets, blues, and pinks that, Silver had read, were reserved for the male Aquinder on full display. He took a few steps toward the road, sending waves of warmth back to Silver, to check in on her.

She tightened her grip until her knuckles went white. Then she nodded.

Hiyyan burst into a run.

Silver bounced on his back, clenching her thigh muscles and digging her feet in, determined not to be thrown off again.

Her eyes squinted against the sting of rushing air. She anticipated what it'd feel like to fly, and her thoughts went back to the feeling of soaring down the sand dunes on Brajon's dune board.

It will be freedom, she thought to Hiyyan. *It will be* everything.

When they had gained enough speed that the orchard trees blurred together, Hiyyan gave one great thrust of his wings. Silver's stomach dropped to the desert floor as they darted into the air.

She sucked in her first breath of sapphire-blue sky and let out a sound of pure wonder.

The air was crystal clear and cool. As Hiyyan flapped his wings, he radiated happiness, and his emotion seeped into Silver's bones. She loosened her grip and slowly, carefully sat up higher and higher. Her hair whipped behind her, snapping at the ends. The wind bit at her lips and ears.

The feeling of flying was hard to describe. She felt unstoppable, and exhilarated to her very core. Everything she'd ever wanted, and everything she wanted for Hiyyan, was coming alive in that moment.

"We did it, Hiyyan!" Silver said. She laughed and laughed as they soared across the desert. "Woooooo!"

Her shrieks must have startled desert foxes back into their underground burrows and made sleepy desert beetles roll over on their backs. Hiyyan honked, too, his joy echoing over the sands.

Silver never would have predicted how natural it felt to be on Hiyyan's back. How smooth and graceful they both were. Especially for two creatures who flopped and tripped whenever they went about on their own two, or four, feet.

In the distance, Silver saw the indigo of the sea.

"Let's go this way." She tugged gently on the left side of Hiyyan's mane.

As he turned, his body was all muscle and power. Silver held on tight again so she wouldn't slip down his side. Her feet tucked into the nooks where his wings met his body.

Every turn and swoop felt huge. Like they were carving the sky into pieces. Eventually, Silver got comfortable enough to sit up fully, her back tall, and close her eyes to just feel the world rush past her.

"We have to fly as far from Calidia as we can," she said. "The clouds will help camouflage us, and I don't think there will be very many people looking up when they're distracted by the races, but just in case, we have to be careful."

Silver looked back at Calidia. The palace towers pushed into the sky above all else. From up this high, she could even see the sea. The great cargo ships that waited at the docks looked like children's toys. She wished she could see Kirja from here.

Silver craned her neck farther over her shoulder. Deep in the orchards, a smattering of specks roved among the trees. One of those specks stopped moving and seemed to be looking up. She quickly looked forward again. Had any of them seen her?

There was nothing to do but move forward with her plans. She still had her disguise to count on. With her arm outstretched toward the water, Silver sent her thoughts to Hiyyan. *See that cliff? Let's enter the sea on the other side of it. We'll be out of view of Calidia there.*

Hiyyan grunted his response, and Silver grinned. When Kirja had been rescued and this was all over, Silver would test the limits of their communication, moving farther and farther away from Hiyyan to see if he could still hear her. It had worked when she was in the orchard and he was near the river cave. Maybe there was no limit to how far apart they could be.

They flew over the cliff, and as soon as the dragon cleared the rock, he dove toward the water. Silver's mouth opened in a silent scream. Salty sea air rushed past her ears so loud it sounded like rampaging herd animals. Her stomach wasn't near her feet anymore; it had lurched up and got stuck in her throat.

"Hiyyan!" Silver's eyes teared up. She could see nothing but water.

And then, Hiyyan hit the sea with a monumental splash. Silver had time to suck in one last breath before they dove under the waves. She squeezed her legs and clutched her fists around the dragon's mane. Silver's lungs began to burn, but before she started to really panic, they burst back up and bobbed on the surface of the sea.

"I can't swim—you know that!" she sputtered. Her clothes were soaked, but at least her bag, made of soft but tough leather, repelled the water.

Hiyyan snorted and paddled his legs.

"Oh, you would have saved me if I'd fallen off?" Silver coughed up seawater. "I think a better idea is that we get you fitted for a saddle."

This time, her Aquinder growled.

"Just learn to swim? That's easy for you to say. I don't have webbed toes like you do."

The Aquinder huffed two short breaths. Silver glared and squeezed seawater out of her hair. Hiyyan laughed.

"Since we're bonded," she said, "what do you think would happen to you if I drowned?"

She laughed as Hiyyan's jaw dropped open.

"Enough teasing. Time to be serious. The race is in a few hours, and you've never even swum in an open ocean. So . . . swim."

Hiyyan didn't have to be told twice.

Thirty-Four

The dragon pulled his wings close to his body and paddled harder with his legs. They picked up some speed, but Silver knew it wasn't nearly fast enough to win any races.

"Use your tail, too," she suggested.

He swished his tail side to side—slowly at first, then more quickly as he established an easy rhythm. That definitely helped them gain speed. Hiyyan sank lower into the water, and Silver followed his lead until her head just barely reached over the top of Hiyyan's, letting her see what was ahead of them.

"Now your wings," Silver said.

The Aquinder unfurled his wings over the water, skimming the surface with their tips. He dipped them under, pushed them back, lifted them, and dipped again. Each time he dipped, Silver thought she was going to slip off his back. But after a few rows, she got the hang of the rhythm.

"Okay," she said. "Faster now."

Hiyyan followed her instruction, rowing his wings quickly.

His movements were rough at first. It took a few attempts, but it wasn't long until he seemed to figure out the best height to lift his wings, and how deep to put them in the water to gain the most speed as quickly as possible.

Good, Silver thought. *Keep it up.*

He responded with an image of them flying away from Calidia with Kirja in tow.

Exactly, Silver thought. *For Kirja. And for us.*

She wished she'd stayed longer near the seawall and watched the other water dragons practicing. She had no idea what kinds of water dragon abilities they might be up against. She didn't even know the length of the races. Was it a sprint, or a longer distance? Would they have to surge forward quickly, or was there time to build up their speed?

Silver swallowed. She wasn't well prepared for the races. She wasn't well prepared for any of the things she was doing. But she was going to succeed. There was no other option.

"On the count of three, turn and go back the way we came," she told her Aquinder. "One, two, three!"

Hiyyan was a natural at turning. He dipped one wing into the water and spun them around, then propelled them forward in a straight line again.

"Nice! Let's do it again."

They practiced turning, building up speed, turning, and sprinting some more. At first, Hiyyan got better and faster with every pass, but after about an hour of practicing, he began to slow down and his breathing came heavier.

Silver patted him on the side. "Okay. You're tired. Let's take a break." She looked at the drooping sun. "We're going to need to head back to Calidia soon anyway. The races are about to start."

Silver changed out of her wet clothing on a cove beach as Hiyyan bobbed in the water, ducking his head under every few minutes to catch a fish. She had begun shivering, but at least the cold had numbed the pain in her foot. When she slid on the racing suit Nebekker had made her, she warmed right through to her bones. She pulled her tunic back over her racing suit and forced her boots back on her feet.

An image of Kirja found her again, and then a particular scent, and Silver realized Hiyyan could smell his mother in the riding suit, her fur woven into the fibers. Silver wished she had something like that . . . some way to feel close to her mother right then.

She shook away thoughts of Sersha Batal. There wasn't time to be sentimental. She walked around the cove until she spotted a small hole in a stone wall, high enough up a sheer cliff that no human could see or reach it.

Hiyyan, she thought. *Can you hide my things up in that hole, please?*

The water dragon took her sack and lifted it up to the hole. Then he came back for her, a questioning look in his eyes.

"Yes, I'm sorry. It's time to get you dressed, too."

Hiyyan pulled his body onto the beach and held still as Silver draped the fabric over his back. She tried to be gentle as she tucked his wings in, but when she accidentally hit a tender spot in his joint, she felt it in her shoulders, too.

The final touch was to pull the hood over Hiyyan's head: It was fashioned to look like a fox, just like hers. She took a step back and tilted her head to the side. Hiyyan's wings were mostly hidden, but Silver was going to spread the little bit of camouin she had over the exposed parts once they got closer to the city. Then he would look mottled, rather than blue, sort of like the green-and-white dragon in Calidia. His mane still poked out here and there, but that actually added furry authenticity to the disguise. It had to be enough.

"I hope there's nothing in the rules against these uniforms," she said. Her belly began to hurt again. Nerves were making her sick. But she pressed her face against Hiyyan's, soaking in his calmness, and nodded.

"Ready to win?" she asked.

Her Aquinder grinned, and Silver did, too.

"Let's go."

Thirty-Five

They hugged the shoreline as they paddled toward Calidia. Silver had been mulling over how to enter the city so that they could save the surprise of their presence for the race. She still had to check the lineups at the seawall to find out what time she was scheduled to race. And she needed to find Brajon. If it were even possible to find him in the crowds.

Hiyyan breathed heavily, pulling Silver out of her thoughts.

"You're tired already?"

Silver looked down one of Hiyyan's flanks and saw that his woven disguise was now sodden with seawater. There was no way he could win a race dragging all that heavy, wet wool.

Silver frowned. "This is not Jaspatonian-quality wool."

She racked her brain, but first, she needed to know how much time she had to come up with a new plan. As they moved closer to the docks, she patted Hiyyan's side.

"Let me off by that big ship right there. The one with the red flags. It looks empty. I'll climb onto the dock and run over to see what time our race is. Hide behind the ship until I get back."

Hiyyan pulled in next to the dock, and Silver felt a change come over him. He mewled softly as he ducked his head down close to the water.

Silver followed the line of his gaze. Just around the tip of another ship, she could see the very edge of the water dragon warm-up area. Hiyyan watched the other dragons with curiosity, but there was another emotion there, too: uncertainty.

Silver felt a pang of sorrow. Hiyyan had grown up all alone in the desert.

"I'm sorry you can't go over to those dragons right now," she told him. "After we win, I'll take you to meet all the dragons in the world."

Hiyyan turned his face away and batted his eyes closed.

Silver pulled her mask on, climbed onto the dock, and dashed to the seawall. The crowds were shoulder to shoulder. Even someone as small as she was had trouble moving between everyone.

"Excuse me. Please, let me through."

"Back in your place," a large man with a gravelly voice said, shoving her. Silver fell on her backside.

"How rude," a woman said, helping Silver to her feet, then tapping the man on the shoulder. "Did you push this little girl?"

The man turned and crossed his arms over his chest. "If she wanted a better spot, she should have gotten here earlier."

"Well . . ."

While the two adults argued, Silver darted past and shoved her way to the front rows. That's when she realized why the crowds were so dense and so loud. The races had started already.

"Oh no." Silver stood on her tiptoes, straining to see the schedule. What if her number had already been called? But before she could find out, she saw something even better. There, standing on top of the wall near the registration platform, was her cousin. Relief so overwhelmed Silver that she almost fell over again.

"Brajon!" She waved to him, pulling her mask up slightly so he'd get a quick peek at her face. "Excuse me," she said. "That's my cousin. I have to get to him." She climbed past a group draped in team flags and reached for Brajon's hand.

In the sea, water dragons were battling for the finish line. Silver desperately wanted to stay and watch. Especially when she saw Ferdi riding . . . nothing? The boy skimmed across the top of the water, legs crossed, his hands holding reins that disappeared under the surface. His Glithern stayed under the whole time, even after they crossed the finish line in first place. Fascinating!

"Where have you been?" Brajon's face was a desert storm cloud. "You just walked off!"

"Shh," Silver hissed. "I'm sorry—I had to get away from people."

Brajon lowered his voice. "I thought you were kidnapped. I thought you were dead! If not for Mele, I would be pounding Queen Imea's door down right now, looking for you. Have you seen the posters?"

"Yes, that's why I had to get out of here. But what about Mele?" As they talked, Silver peered over her cousin's shoulder for her number. "My race starts at six thirty."

"Six thirty?" Brajon said. "That's in ten minutes."

"Ten?" Silver squeaked. "Help, Brajon. The disguise I made for Hiyyan isn't going to work. It's soaked with seawater."

"There isn't anything else." Her cousin looked down, refusing to meet Silver's eyes. "You don't have to win to claim him. Go slowly, and cross the finish line in your own time. Protect Hiyyan."

"The wool is pulling, though. What if part of his wing pokes through? I can already see patches of blue through the fabric. If someone looks close enough, they'll start asking questions. Think, Brajon. We only have ten minutes!"

Brajon sighed deeply. Determination took over the set of his jaw and the glint in his eye. He pulled Silver by the arm down the seawall and away from the crowds.

He reached into his pack and handed her a small bag. "I went back for this after I couldn't find you."

Silver peeked inside and gasped. Suddenly, the image Hiyyan had sent her of Brajon at the cave entrance made sense. They must have just missed each other. "But you said—"

"I know what I said. And it's true!" Brajon smiled sheepishly. "So be careful, Silver. I mean it. Use only what you absolutely need, and get it off Hiyyan as soon as possible."

"Brajon, thank you."

"I guess even I have some dreams of glory." He shrugged. "The first miner in hundreds of years to find camouin! I understand now how easy it is to get caught up in wanting to stand out."

"You've always stood out, cousin," Silver said.

Brajon's cheeks flushed, but he shook his head, smiling, and continued talking.

"It's liquid now, but remember, heat activates the camouflage and solidifies the metal, too. Go claim Hiyyan," he said, breaking into a run. "I have an idea for how to find Kirja. Mele showed me how to get to the royal training grounds earlier—"

Silver dashed to catch up with her cousin. "She *has* to be there! If you can get her out while I'm racing, we don't have to worry about appearing before the queen!"

"But—"

"You'll have to fly. North. To the cliff that looks like a snub-beaked bird. I'll meet you there as soon as I can."

"Wait—"

But Silver couldn't wait. She broke off from her cousin and sprinted down the seawall, calling with her mind.

Hiyyan, it's time.

Thirty-Six

Hiyyan peeked from behind the ship. Silver yanked off her tunic and threw it into the ocean, her thoughts swirling with visions of winning. This race, and then the semifinal.

And then to the Island Nations Spring Festival, for the glorious final.

When Silver reached Hiyyan, she combined her camouin with Brajon's and smeared a thin layer over the Aquinder's wings. His skin was still warm from swimming and flying, so the camouin activated slightly, though not as much as Silver had hoped. More important, though, Hiyyan's wings disappeared.

"Your body will heat up even more when we race, so that'll help keep the camouin in place," she said. "Hopefully," she added as the edges of the smeared metal oozed slowly down Hiyyan's sides. "It only has to hold until we cross the finish line."

She kept some of the wool to sit on, and made sure it hung slightly over the camouin so that it didn't look like there was a hole in Hiyyan's body. Then she used her knife to cut the rest of the fiber away from Hiyyan's hood, keeping the disguise in place over his face.

Hiyyan's wings struggled against the camouin, and he let out a small cry of distress.

"Just one race, my friend," Silver said, trying to soothe him. "And only to claim you."

She slid onto Hiyyan's back, affixed the race number to her clothing, pulled Hiyyan's mane, and rushed him to the starting line. She barely had time to glance left and right at the other dragons, taking in a multitude of colors and shapes, before the horn sounded and the race began.

Hiyyan surged forward so quickly it left Silver breathless. She slipped backward but caught herself before sliding all the way down her Aquinder's tail and into the sea. The rider to her left laughed. She almost screamed at Hiyyan to slow down, but she bit her tongue, her dreams of glory so near she could taste them. Hiyyan was holding his own in the race.

Silver pulled herself up until she was settled just behind Hiyyan's mane again.

"Go," she screamed. "Faster!"

The finish line flags fluttered far ahead. Mere dots on the horizon. They had time to pass everyone if Hiyyan could keep his pace. Silver clutched Hiyyan's mane, lowered her body, and clenched her teeth. She looked left and right again, assessing her opponents through curtains of splashing water.

She recognized the dragon with the laughing rider. She had a picture of a Floatillion on her bedroom wall back home. The water dragon was so huge and round that it seemed impossible it could swim with any real speed. But it was easily keeping up with Hiyyan, moving its massive bulk with what Silver assumed were huge, muscular legs beneath the surface of the water.

On her other side, an Umbrillo used the fanlike fins around its neck to help gain speed, opening and closing them with little bursts of air. Hiyyan had almost caught up to the Umbrillo.

Past the finned dragon were two more water dragons, including a Vaprozy. Finally, Silver understood why the guard thought that was such a funny racing breed. She'd known that it sucked air in through its mouth, then released it out its backside with a gust of speed. But now she discovered the stench that came with it.

But the water dragon Silver was most worried about was in the last lane. The Shorsa, glittering lavender and sage, was known for its speed. It zipped ahead of everyone, churning water with its tail, upright.

That's who we have to catch up with, Silver thought to Hiyyan. *If the Shorsa gets too far ahead, we have no chance. Faster!*

Hiyyan sent back an array of confusion that seemed to say, *Faster?*

Silver knew she was there only to claim Hiyyan, but the farther they got along the racecourse, the more some other desire bubbled up in her. It threatened to burst from her like fireworks. She wanted more than to own a dragon by law: She wanted to win.

That was her destiny.

Her wrist burn throbbed as she clenched her fists tighter in Hiyyan's mane.

"Go, Hiyyan!"

Silver couldn't tell if the mask-muffled roar in her ears was the cheering crowd or the churning sea. She hooked her feet into the joints where Hiyyan's wings met his body. He squirmed, and she knew he must feel trapped under the camouin. But even if he could spread his wings, there wasn't room. The lanes were too narrow, and her opponents were too close—especially the Floatillion, who took up every bit of space in its lane plus a little in hers.

Silver pulled her body as close to Hiyyan as she could, to minimize wind resistance. The wet and cold of the sea flicked off her riding suit, and she silently thanked Nebekker for her nimble work. In a race as tight as this one, being lightweight and dry would make a difference. The Umbrillo rider was soaked, hit with water from his own dragon, and also from the Vaprozy to his right.

Silver's blood rushed through her body. Her knuckles turned even whiter. She licked her lips, tasting a layer of salt.

Visions of Aquinder in ancient battles flitted through her mind. Those riders swept and soared over the deserts, directing their dragons with tightly gripped reins. Silver could almost taste the glory of the olden days. She wanted it.

"*Swim*, Hiyyan!" she yelled.

There was a roar, then a screech. The Umbrillo had jumped lanes with a fierce cry, whipping its tail at the Vaprozy. The Vaprozy bucked, its rider flinging into the air and landing in the sea far outside the racecourse. The Umbrillo returned to its lane and bared its teeth at Hiyyan.

Were attacks like that legal in water dragon racing?

Silver's heart thudded as she faced forward again. The attack had left the Umbrillo behind Hiyyan slightly. But not enough for Silver to feel comfortable about their chances to advance.

The racecourse wasn't a straight line, and Silver saw there

was a curve coming up. How could they take advantage of the curve? She closed her eyes and sent her water dragon a scene: Hiyyan, nearly sideways, pushing around the curve with one wing in the water and one wing partly outstretched, guiding them like an airborne rudder.

Silver didn't trust that the camouin would still hide all of Hiyyan's wings if he spread them fully. But one wing, halfway stretched, should still be camouflaged enough, and could be useful.

Silver sucked in a deep breath and used her foot to scrape away some of the camouin down Hiyyan's left side. They were almost to the curve. But Hiyyan's breathing was heavy behind his disguise. She could tell he wanted to slow down.

"Almost, Hiyyan," Silver said. She pictured a ferocious ball of energy and sent it to him. "We're so close! Use your wing."

Hiyyan tipped onto his side. Silver closed her eyes and dug her legs into his sides as hard as she could, so that she wouldn't end up in the sea. Her fists were so tight her nails cut into the skin of her palms. She clenched her teeth.

"Arrgghhh," she groaned. Her limbs were wound until bursting, her muscles straining in her arms and thighs. And still, she was slipping.

She dug down to the dark depths of her strength and put everything she had into holding on, but her left hand lost its grip on Hiyyan's mane. Her body rolled. The greedy sea grabbed at her, desperate to pull her into its black lifelessness.

She shifted her weight to her right leg, still hooked over Hiyyan's back, and held on. She had to stay on his back. For the win. For Kirja. To stay alive.

Silver screamed into the water. Her muscles burned. Not just hers, but Hiyyan's, too. They both wanted to give up.

No! Hold on.

Hiyyan righted himself, pulling Silver away from the sea. With one more burst of strength, she forced herself upright once more. Gasping for breath, she looked around. The Floatillion was far behind, wheezing as it tried to catch up. They'd passed the Umbrillo. The only dragon that was beating them was the Shorsa.

The flags grew larger. They were almost at the end of the race. They had a shot at qualifying!

"Go," Silver shouted. She did the only thing she could think of: She sent Hiyyan an image of Queen Imea handing Kirja over to Silver. "For your mother!"

Hiyyan tucked his wing, and with one great push that created a massive wave behind them, he thrust them over the finish line.

Thirty-Seven

Silver threw her arms in the air.

"We did it!" she screamed. "Second place, but we qualified! And we'll do even better in the next race."

She hugged her Aquinder's neck and caught her breath. She couldn't keep a massive grin off her face.

But Hiyyan's body was icier than the seawater—so icy that the camouin began to slowly soften.

"How can you be cold after all that swimming?" Silver said, worried. "Stay warm or the camouin's going to drip into the sea."

The other water dragons and their riders swam away from the finish line. Some reached out to shake Silver's hand, congratulating her and patting Hiyyan on his masked nose. Silver's chest puffed out a little more with each well-wisher's comment. Other racers glared as they swam off, their festival aspirations dashed by the mysterious pair. And still others hovered, waiting to get a closer look at the odd-looking water dragon, unlike any breed they'd seen.

Silver gave Hiyyan a comforting rub, but his skin stayed cool under her fingertips.

"What's wrong?" Silver whispered, moving close to Hiyyan's left ear. Hiyyan turned his head in the opposite direction and gave her a low growl.

There wasn't time to probe further. Silver quickly scanned the horizon. No Brajon, no Kirja. And no chaos among the crowds, as she'd assumed there would be if an alarm had gone up indicating that intruders had taken Kirja. Had they made it out of Calidia? She had to get to the cliffs to meet them. They had to get as far away as possible.

"Congratulations, Desert Fox." The woman who'd registered Silver earlier in the day rode over on a pink-and-orange Droller. She'd taken off her flower hat, and she wore a blue jumpsuit made of some kind of shiny material that water rolled off of. It glistened as she looked down at the list she carried and made some notes.

The Droller, a massive water dragon able to carry twenty humans, greeted Hiyyan with a nuzzle rub. Silver recalled that Drollers were the most peaceful and calm of the water dragons.

The woman tossed a small purse to Silver, who caught it against her chest. "You have qualified for tomorrow's semifinals. You must be at the seawall at high noon to claim your spot."

Silver smiled, but the weight of the coins in the purse sat as heavy as the rock in the bottom of her stomach. She hoped Mele had helped Brajon find Kirja. She hoped she wouldn't have to face the queen. Or Sagittaria Wonder.

Silver pressed her heels into Hiyyan's side gently to get him to move past the woman and paddle past the docks.

Once they were behind the empty ships, she pulled his hood off.

"Hiyyan, I don't know what's wrong, but we have to go back to the cliffs. Kirja *has* to be there."

Hiyyan's mood immediately improved, and he let loose a mewl of excitement. With renewed energy, the Aquinder swam on. When they were out of sight of Calidia, Silver collected the softened camouin from his sides and put it into her bag, and Hiyyan opened his wings.

As they flew, Silver searched the shoreline for any sign of her cousin and Kirja. It all looked the same as before. When they got to the cliffs, Hiyyan hovered at the hole so Silver could retrieve her things. Everything was as she'd left it. But still no sign of the other Aquinder.

"Brajon!" she called. Her voice echoed off the walls and into the ocean. There was no reply.

They flew in circles for several minutes, hoping Kirja and Brajon would miraculously appear on the horizon. They never did. Silver's chest grew heavy with the truth.

Brajon and Kirja were still in Calidia.

"We have to go back for them," Silver told Hiyyan.

He let out a low growl, then stubbornly lowered himself to the ground.

"I'm sorry, but we can't rest now," Silver said urgently. "I know we still don't have your mother, but I need your help. I've done all of this for you: traveled this far, upset my family, made these disguises. People think I'm a thief! And I don't want to be face-to-face with Sagittaria Wonder again after she . . . she . . ." Silver's face lit with shame, and she shook her head, as though she could shake off that first meeting with the great water dragon racer.

The water dragon refused to even meet her eyes.

"Hiyyan, I used camouin," Silver cried. "If someone finds out about that, I don't even know what would happen to me. But you just want to sit here and mope?"

For a moment, Hiyyan was silent. Then, his lips pulled away from his teeth, he raised his face to the slowly darkening sky, and he let loose an earth-shaking roar that choked off with what sounded like a sob.

Then he stomped off.

Silver dropped to the sand, hands shaking. So maybe the race had been hard. Maybe they'd both had to work for a good position. But that's what it took to become a great water dragon racer! Hard work, struggle.

Nothing Silver had done so far on this journey was easy.

All to get Kirja back from Sagittaria Wonder.

All so *Hiyyan* could be happy.

Silver let out a breath and stared at the sea. If Hiyyan was happy, so was she. The reverse was true, too.

Behind her, Hiyyan crunched some pebbles as he moved closer. A vision filled Silver's mind.

Hundreds of Aquinder soaring over burning desert cities. Their human riders roared victoriously, their faces bloodthirsty. They yanked the chains they used to control their water dragons, the metal digging painfully into the Aquinder's mouths.

Hot tears rolled down Silver's face.

"Is that what you think of me?" she asked. "That I'm like them? Just because I pushed you during the race? I just wanted us to be our best. My father always made it clear I wasn't trying hard enough. Wasn't good enough."

She slowly wiped her cheeks. "But maybe you don't want

the same things I do. Maybe we're not meant to be—" It was too painful to finish the thought.

With every word Silver said, Hiyyan's head drooped lower and lower until, finally, his chin rested in the sand. Two huge, sad eyes gazed up at her.

"Forget it, Hiyyan. Just take me back to the docks so I can find Brajon."

Silently, the water dragon got into position and Silver climbed on his back. His skin was cold, and her limbs were stiff, and as he took to the sky, they both jostled and bounced, their movements completely at odds with each other. Silver gritted her teeth as a headache built behind her eyes.

When Hiyyan had flown as close to the docks as he safely could, he landed with an inelegant splash. With a gasp, Silver rolled off his back and into the sea.

Before she could panic, Hiyyan lifted her out of the water by the back of her racing suit and deposited her on the wood dock.

She wrapped the pieces of brown scarf around her head as best she could and walked with a limp through the archways of the harbor. But as she disappeared into the shade of the stone columns, one more vision came to her: Hiyyan, struggling in their first water dragon race. Silver was on his back, her face twisted with the desire to win at all costs. The Silver in the vision closed her eyes.

That was the moment Silver had manipulated Hiyyan to swim faster, with the promise of Kirja.

A chill raced down Silver's spine. She hadn't sent that vision because of Kirja; she'd sent it because she was desperate to win at any cost. Hiyyan knew the truth, and it was time for Silver to be honest with herself, too.

Thirty-Eight

As Silver held her scarf pieces over her face, scanning the crowds for Brajon, everything that had happened over the last several days piled up on her. She wanted to drop her bag and sleep it all away. Instead, she picked up the pace, her stomach gurgling. The morning bread and fruit seemed so long ago.

"Food," she croaked.

Silver's attention was fully on the first fried-dough vendor she could see, the smell of sugar and spices drawing her close, so when a hand reached out and grabbed her elbow, she easily stumbled into the alleyway. Her assailant pulled the mask out of her bag and held it up.

"I knew you were more than a street urchin, *Desert Fox*," Ferdi said. His eyes flashed, and his mouth turned up in amusement. "Heroes like you don't stop at rescuing stolen Glitherns, do they? I think there's more to your dragon, too. How about letting me in on your secret?"

"My secrets are none of your business. Let me go!" Silver

yanked her arm away, but Ferdi had a tight grip. Was he going to turn her in to the queen?

"I'm not your enemy." Ferdi's eyes swept the streets, studying the faces of the people walking to and fro. He pulled Silver farther away from the crowds, into the deep shadows, and lowered his voice. "You're playing a dangerous game. I don't think you realize what's going on here."

"What's going on is that I need to find my cousin and get out of Calidia." Silver forced her words out, but her voice shook and the hairs on her neck stood on end. How much did Ferdi know about Hiyyan? Or about Kirja?

"I can help you. I know how to get under the Royal Pools." Ferdi licked his lips as he chose his next words. "Hoonazoor does a lot of exploring under those waters, and no one but me knows about it."

Silver caught her breath. Was Ferdi bonded to his Glithern? "And she shows you what she sees?"

Ferdi wrinkled his brow. "Shows me?"

"Never mind," Silver said hastily.

Ferdi looked at her hard. "The first day I got to Calidia, Hoonazoor disappeared for longer than I'd expected. When she came back, we went for a practice ride and she took me to a whole different set of pools. I've seen where Queen Imea keeps her dragon stock." Ferdi's eyes turned brighter than normal again, and Silver began to back up.

"Have you seen the posters?"

Ferdi nodded. "And I don't care. Because I've also seen the Aq—"

"No," Silver said. "Don't say it out loud!" She looked around, but they were alone. Her palms went up. "Please, Ferdi. That dragon doesn't belong to the queen. She belongs with a friend of mine, and I'm trying to reunite them."

"The queen stole it? Thieves everywhere I look."

"Not exactly." Silver paused, and the air between them grew thick. Could she trust Ferdi with her story? It was dangerous to tell secrets to too many people.

After several beats, Ferdi sighed. "Of course you don't trust me. You don't even know who I am. And if you did, you'd trust me even less. I'm not going to turn you in. Go free. Find your friends. But before you do, tell me one thing I can do to help you. I'll do it—promise. Then maybe you'll decide you can trust me."

"Why?"

Ferdi looked over Silver's shoulder and nodded. "I'm hesitant to tell my story, too."

Silver saw the two companions who followed Ferdi everywhere lingering at the entrance to the alley, discussing something.

"I'm hoping I won't need your help," she said. "I plan to win my race tomorrow and ask Queen Imea for what I want."

"The Winners' Audience," he said, and let out a low whistle. "Disguise in place, I assume. Do you think that will work? No one's ever asked for one of her dragons."

Silver clutched Nebekker's pendant. "It's not hers!"

"Keep quiet!" Ferdi rubbed his thumb against his chin. "All eyes and ears will be on you when you approach the queen. Are you ready for the whole world to know your secret?"

"No, but if everyone's watching, the queen will have to act honorably."

At that, Ferdi looked a little hesitant but gave a quick nod.

"I don't know if I can help you win your race tomorrow, but if you do win, I'll do what I can to make the Winners' Audience easy for you." An impish smile lifted Ferdi's cheeks. "Create a diversion so the guards don't realize you're the same girl as on the posters? That could be fun. My father's anger would churn like a whirlpool to hear I caused chaos in the Calidian palace."

"Thanks for your help," Silver said. She smiled gratefully. "If that doesn't work, I might need you to show me how to get under those pools."

Ferdi's companions raised their voices and looked toward the shadows.

"Sounds like an adventure. One we'll have to continue in the morning." His companions were approaching. "Go this way." Ferdi pointed to a bend at the end of the alleyway. "It will let you out closer to the shops."

Silver pulled up her scarves and turned away, but Ferdi grabbed her arm again. His expression was compassionate.

"Good luck and be careful."

Thirty-Nine

Silver doubled back until she was near the seawall again and made a stop at the fried-dough vendor. Her winnings were substantial enough for many, many meals in Calidia—and certainly things finer than street-vendor food. But as she shoved eggs baked in tomatoes, plus the fried dough that should have been sweet, in her mouth as she dodged the crowds near the inn, she realized that after her fight with Hiyyan, everything tasted like sand. With a hard swallow and a look over her shoulder, she darted to the road behind Mr. Homm's inn and knocked on the little door to Mele's room.

"Brajon?" she whispered.

Her cousin flung open the door, yanked her inside, and slammed it shut behind him.

His grin was as bright as the desert sun. Even Mele looked happy for once.

"You got through!" Brajon said. "There's buzz all over the city about the fierce masked racer and who she is under the disguise. How does it feel, water dragon racer?"

Silver tried to force a smile, but her insides were shriveled. Everything she'd imagined about winning was different. Instead of triumph, she felt shame.

"Even better," Brajon went on, "now you can get one more race over with in the morning, march into the palace, demand Kirja back, and we can go home. By dinnertime, I'll be sitting down to my mother's warm spiced beans. Mmmmm."

"That's nice for you," Silver blurted. "What about me?"

Brajon exchanged a look with Mele. He leaned against the wall and closed his eyes.

"All right, Silver. Tell me. What about you?"

Silver dropped her pack and slid to the ground. The stone floor felt cool. She rubbed her wrist slowly, feeling the roughness of her healing scar. The one she was sure looked just like a coiled water dragon.

"I spend almost every waking moment wishing I was chasing glory, wanting to be on the water, enjoying the dust and noise and excitement of Calidia," Silver said. "This is where I belong, this is what I was made for. And I'm worried that I'm going to lose that somehow."

Silver thought of Hiyyan's growl and fought back tears. She shook her head. It was time to be honest.

"No, that's not it. I think I've lost Hiyyan. And lost sight of what matters, too. Something happened during the race earlier. If you thought I was driven to be a water dragon racer before . . . now it's even worse," she said. "I feel the pull so strongly that I'm sure I'll die if I don't listen. And listening to that made me get into a big fight with Hiyyan."

Silver licked her lips. Salt had dried them out, and they hurt. If she were home in Jaspaton, her mother would track down the most soothing ointment and apply it with the gentlest of touches. She missed her mother. Her father, too. But most of all, she felt guilty.

"We came here to save Kirja from Sagittaria, and to race Hiyyan so I could claim him and save him, too. But I abandoned you and Kirja when you needed me most, and I told Hiyyan I didn't care how he felt. All for the win. I've been so selfish."

Mele cleared her throat, then stepped forward to take Silver's hands.

"I understand that feeling," Mele said. "But with your bond, you're not the only one you have to think about. You and Hiyyan are a team. Nothing can change that—not even your dreams. Why do you think I work here, cleaning up after ungrateful guests? Bonds mean sacrifice."

"Your heart was in the right place," Brajon said. "You just got lost in the moment. But you probably shouldn't keep upsetting Hiyyan. He's big enough to gobble you in one bite."

Silver laughed quietly. "The best thing I can do for Hiyyan right now is get Kirja back, and that means we have to race again." Her eyes flicked to Mele. "Unless . . ."

"Oh no. Keep me out of this," Mele said.

"I've heard there are underground pools, but I don't know how to get to them," Silver said. "This boy I met—another racer—said he'd show me after the Winners' Audience. If we can even get that far." Silver shook her head. "I just don't know if Hiyyan's up to racing again. But if there's a local who has her own connection to the water dragons . . ."

Mele shook her head. "How many times do I have to tell you that I don't want to be involved? Everything you're doing is dangerous. You think the races are just a game, but I've heard things! I know the lengths people go to in order to win . . . I know the things they bet, the things they lose. Not just things. Lives! And those are the lesser racers. The royals' water dragons are a whole other game. One I don't want to touch."

"But the water dragon we're looking for isn't a royal dragon," Brajon said. "And we don't want to get involved, either. We just want to get what we came for and get out of here."

He'd looked pointedly at Silver when he said *we*, but Silver couldn't meet his eyes. She stared at the ground instead.

"I'm not going to get rid of you until I help you, am I?" Mele groaned, then narrowed her eyes. "Unless I turned you in. That would sort things out—and fill my pockets."

"Mele, please." Silver held her hands out, palms up. "We need your help. The dragons need your help."

"If you didn't know about my . . . situation with my water dragon, I probably would help. But I can't risk my secret, either." Mele sighed. "The Royal Pools are on the south side of the palace. They're most likely fed by the Sonflir River. There are underground springs, which probably connect to the river, in the caves. I suppose you could access them through the south orchards. I used to go down there all the time when I was little."

Silver and Brajon looked at each other with bright eyes. If there was anything they knew, it was underground river caves.

"I'm going to get Hiyyan," Silver said. "Mele, can you show Brajon how to access the Sonflir River? If I can win tomorrow and get a Winners' Audience while Ferdi creates a diversion and you two are approaching the Royal Pools from underground . . . we'll have the best chance to get Kirja out."

◊ ◊ ◊

AFTER BRAJON AND Mele left, Silver paced Mele's room, trying to decide the best thing to say to Hiyyan. *I'm sorry* seemed too small for what she'd done. How she'd taken advantage of him.

Even though she ached to see her water dragon immediately, she knew she had work to do first. Before she could even apologize and ask Hiyyan to race one more time, she had to do everything possible to make the race comfortable for him. He deserved that.

In Jaspaton, the communal bread oven was the center of the city's social world. It was also swelteringly hot, and busy enough that a girl her size could slip in and out of the area unnoticed. Surely, Calidia had a communal oven, too. What kind of desert city would it be without one?

Even though the sun had dipped past the horizon some time ago, the city glowed with light: ornate Calidian metal lanterns on every street corner and in the hands of many; sizzling sparkler wands carried by the children; and, over the harbor, fireworks blooming pink, blue, and green. Silver pressed her scarf over her face and kept to the shadows, always looking left, right, and over her shoulder for people who might be following her.

Silver wished Hiyyan were with her. His keen sense of smell would pick up the location of the ovens immediately. Instead, she sniffed alone. A few more steps, and there it was: the lingering scent of freshly baked bread.

She darted down lanes and around corners until she came upon the largest clay oven she'd ever seen. There were several wide openings to allow for many hundreds of loaves to be baked at once. Now, though, only a small section of the oven was being used.

Silver sat in a quiet, shadowy spot next to the oven

opening farthest from the road and pulled the remaining camouin and wool out of her bag. Just as Hiyyan needed Kirja, Silver was realizing that she also needed her parents, and the skills they'd taught her, too.

Silver pressed the camouin into small pins with holes on either end. Her first attempts were a mess—it was a difficult metal to work. But she thought back to what her father had taught her about observing the properties of different metals. This one needed heat to keep it stable. So she wove chains with the wool and wrapped the camouin around the chains. Then, when the bakers weren't looking, she pushed one end of wool into the oven fire, waited for the fiber to light, then pulled it out again. Heat traveled through the core of every camouin pin, solidifying them into hollow and lightweight, but strong, pieces of metal. In this manner, Silver created a sort of rough chain mail to drape over Hiyyan's flanks. The pins allowed for movement, so the chain mail would conceal his wings but not suffocate them. It would, hopefully, keep him comfortable while they raced. At least until they could safely reveal his true nature.

By the time she had finished, the road was empty and the bakers were scooping ash over their fires, putting the oven's heat to sleep until the next day. Silver packed up and pushed her way to the docks, her cheeks flushed and her heart racing. Would Hiyyan come for her?

First, she had to see if Hiyyan would even listen to her.

Silver cleared her thoughts and pictured the Aquinder. She imagined their first meeting. There had been a tickle of curiosity. What was that noise across the river? Then a rush of overwhelming emotion as Hiyyan raced to her. And finally, hugging him: when everything felt right in the world.

"If I could go back, I would," Silver said. *If I could be patient, knowing that we would meet someday, no matter what, I would wait.*

Silver then thought about the stolen moments walking underground in the river caves, on their way to Calidia, when she would absently put a hand out to touch Hiyyan's flank or look closely at his wings to make sure the delicate tissue there hadn't scratched against a wall. They'd bonded so quickly, Silver and her Aquinder, and their connection was strong.

Stronger than her desire to be a great water dragon racer.

She sent Hiyyan a vision of where she stood. *I'm here.*

There was movement at all hours on the docks, with ships being loaded and unloaded, rodents scurrying underfoot, and glistening strips of light on the surface of the water, swaying with the tide. It was much darker here than nearer the palace. Silver crouched behind a large crate and fixed her vision on a dark blob in the distance. Her chest warmed, and she sought Nebekker's pendant, but the jewelry was cool and still.

No, it was something else that was filling her with cozy happiness. Hiyyan was swimming toward her.

"You came," Silver said, wrapping her arms around her Aquinder's neck as he pulled up to the dock. She gazed into his eyes. There were so many words to say that it was impossible to speak out loud.

I'll give it up, if that's what you want, she thought. *You're worth more than a trophy. And I'll do better. I'll think about both of us, not just me. I understand that there's a part of me that's very human, that there's a hunger that could become dangerous. I will fight that, to keep you safe.*

Hiyyan sat back on his haunches, but he craned his neck forward, his face close enough to Silver's that she felt his breath on her skin. She placed her palms on either side of his head.

I'm sorry, Hiyyan.

Immediately, Silver's hands and feet warmed. Her shoulders lifted, and her chest opened to let her lungs take in more air. She breathed deeply and let the air out slowly, then smiled.

Girl and water dragon touched foreheads. Silver closed her eyes, the corners of her mouth turning up. This was how they were supposed to be.

A vision filled her mind: Hiyyan and Silver, gliding across a finish line, their opponents far behind them.

Startled, Silver pulled back.

You want *to race?*

In the vision, admirers gathered around them. Including Kirja.

"Mrowr," Hiyyan said softly.

Silver understood. Hiyyan wanted more than racing. He wanted true freedom to be himself in the world.

Just like she did.

She nodded and rubbed her face in his mane. Part of her wanted to say more, but another part knew there was nothing more to say. Their bond was everything.

She climbed onto Hiyyan's back, and together, dragon and rider paddled up the coast.

FORTY

They slept in the cove until the midmorning sun began burning the back of Silver's neck. She gently nudged Hiyyan awake and felt a current of shared excitement flow between them. Today was race day.

Silver showed Hiyyan the camouin disguise and helped him into it.

"Not a bad fit," she said. "How does it feel?"

Hiyyan tugged here and there so the draping metal settled where it felt best, and growled with appreciation. Silver smiled. There was a new feeling between the two of them. A quiet, steady determination to work together to meet their goals.

They rode back into Calidia to check the posted race schedule at the seawall. Desert Fox was listed in the third semifinal heat. Just beneath Ferdi's name. Silver shaded her eyes with her hand and peered up. The sun was just about dead center in the sky. Out on the racecourse, a handful of riders began moving their water dragons toward the starting line. The air at the seawall buzzed with a sudden energy.

"How much longer until the first semifinal race?" Silver asked a woman beside her through her scarf.

"Ten minutes until the first and best. Look!"

There was Sagittaria Wonder, astride a Dwakka, in the center lane. Silver's heart fluttered with hope. Kirja wasn't being claimed today. The Aquinder was still a secret.

She peered at the sea past the racecourse. In the distance, Ferdi seemed to float atop the water, his Glithern warming up for their race. Sweat beaded on Silver's temples as the minutes counted down.

Sagittaria's race began with a wail of the horn.

The crowd roared with delight, waving banners and Desert Nations flags. A man sitting on a tall stool shouted race progress over the noise as people exchanged coins with a fevered frenzy.

"Where are your colors, girl?" the woman asked. "Who do you support?"

Silver thought about her desert fox mask, safely hidden in her bag. "My favorite racers are later," she said.

Despite everything, the way Sagittaria Wonder raced took Silver's breath away. She kept tight control of her Dwakka around bends, over obstacles, and as they dipped into the sea and out of sight before rising to the surface again. She seemed relaxed, even as her opponents screamed at their water dragons. She radiated the confidence that she would win, no matter what. She was that good.

The flame that burned in Silver grew to a roaring fire. Would she ever become that kind of racer, too?

With a flick of the reins from Sagittaria Wonder, the Dwakka deftly avoided the grasping eel-like tentacles of the dull-gray Decodro one lane over. The crowd roared with laughter and cheered at her maneuver, but Sagittaria's calm expression didn't change. She was as cool as seawater.

As the race grew tighter, the challengers became desperate, using any means possible to take their opponents out. A field of eight narrowed to six, then five and four, as two water dragons were injured and two more fell so far behind they had no hope of catching up. One failed challenger was bucked off his water dragon but still attached by a line, so that he was dragged through the churning waters. But Sagittaria held a comfortable lead, making it all look easy.

When she and her Dwakka crossed the finish line in first place, the crowd went wild. Silver cheered just as loudly. It felt like she was experiencing a once-in-a-lifetime event.

The woman beside her chuckled. "As to be expected! Our queen's racer is the best in the world."

Sagittaria Wonder took one winner's lap, waving to her adoring fans and pausing to bow her head to Queen Imea, who watched from a palace balcony, before moving into the warm-up area.

Ferdi crossed paths with Sagittaria as he and his Glithern left the warm-up area. She said something that made him laugh, and Silver went cold. Were Sagittaria and Ferdi friends?

Silver quickly left the seawall and collected Hiyyan at the docks, adjusting their disguises to cover as much as possible. They paddled slowly to the warm-up area as the second race was off. Then, it was their turn to line up.

The seas churned with water dragons moving to the starting line for their heat. She looked warily all around—no Sagittaria, no guards, no Abruqs. Did they know who Desert Fox was under the mask? With a deep breath, she steered Hiyyan to the flag of Calidia marking the beginning of the course. Her hands tingled under fistfuls of mane. Her eyes trailed down to the camouin that she'd carefully wrapped around Hiyyan's wings. He pressed against the metal instinctively, but he didn't complain.

They were in lane two. On their left, closest to the seawall, was a Dwakka. This one was somewhat smaller than Sagittaria Wonder's, but its two heads seemed just as observant, always swerving side to side. On their right, a familiar face snarled. It was the green-and-white Hop-Slawn from earlier, and it looked like it had never stopped being angry. Even now, the rider held tight to chains that attached in six different places on the water dragon's faceplate, headpiece, and collar.

Hiyyan could be a touch reluctant about racing, but this dragon obviously hated it. Despite fearing the Hop-Slawn a bit, Silver felt horribly sorry for it.

Ferdi was silent, two dragons away, but his body was hunched over and his knuckles, wrapped around Hoonazoor's reins, were white. Did Silver have any hope of beating him and his Glithern?

"Desert Fox!" A cry reached Silver from the seawall. She leaned forward to peer between the dragons around her.

What she saw made her body tingle as though festival fireworks had been set off in her belly. A group of people pressed against the wall, each of them wearing a rough facsimile of Silver's fox mask. The tallest of them, standing in the back, waved a dark-brown flag with a desert-fox face in the center. They all cheered. It was a small group and their flag was unpolished, made up of scraps of fabric cut roughly, but that didn't matter to Silver.

They were cheering for her. They wanted Hiyyan to win. They were there to support them.

She and Hiyyan had fans.

Silver swallowed an unexpected lump. She realized she was grinning so big her cheeks were beginning to hurt.

Look, Hiyyan. They're here for us.

Silver forced her face muscles to relax, and lifted her hand in a wave. The group went wild, jumping up and down, whooping and hollering. The Dwakka rider, to her left, moved into her line of vision, blocking the desert-fox fans.

"You must be young if that group of dune beetles excites you," the Hop-Slawn rider whispered to Silver. "You should quit racing while you're ahead. My master will pay you your weight in gold to lose."

Silver shot him a glare. "You couldn't afford my price."

"Name your price, then. My master's made his fortune in silks. He can meet it. That Dwakka rider took my offer."

Silver glanced at the Dwakka rider again. Her hair was gray, and her face, lined with years. Perhaps she was through with racing and wanted some rest. Silver hadn't truly begun yet.

She faced the Hop-Slawn rider again. "That cape is very fine silk. But it'll slow you down. Does your master force you to wear it? If so, he thinks more about his silks than about you."

"I'm sure it's the same for your master. Who owns your dragon?"

"No one owns him, and no one owns me."

"No one, perhaps, but this race will. Forget my offer. I'll wager your qualifying-race winnings that you don't make it past the first obstacle." The Hop-Slawn rider threw back his head and laughed. Even his water dragon snorted a few times.

Hiyyan sent ripples of warmth through his body to reassure Silver, but even he couldn't dismiss her troubled thoughts. She'd talked so often about the feats Sagittaria Wonder had accomplished. The speed and the whirlpools . . . but Silver hadn't let herself think about how she, too, would have to take on those same challenges.

Until now.

Silver pressed her lips together and narrowed her eyes. The starting bang sounded, and they were off.

Forty-One

Hiyyan lowered his head to a point aimed at the finish line in the far distance. Silver rounded her back, keeping close to him. As the Aquinder bolted forward, Silver was stunned to see that the landscape of the racecourse was shifting before her eyes. Challenges rose from the water, course markers moved, and pieces of the sea seemed to disappear completely into blackness.

It's changing, Silver thought to Hiyyan. She knew that the racemasters kept the details of the course shrouded in mystery to discourage cheating. Now, it seemed that they had come up with a constantly shifting course to make sure the riders couldn't anticipate challenges.

Had Silver been less terrified, she would have been impressed. But her fear was making her hands tremble more than when she tried to set tiny jewels into gold.

Hiyyan sent her pulses of warmth, and she clenched her fists until they stilled.

"You're right. Nowhere to go but forward," she said.

Her water dragon gave one great roar, and the crowd matched his volume. Blood rushed into Silver's cheeks.

Hiyyan's legs worked furiously below the surface while Silver hung on tightly and searched for a glimpse of the first obstacle.

Their heat was well matched. No water dragon shot out in front, and none were left behind. That both comforted and worried Silver. It would be a close race, which meant the racers would fight for any slight advantage. She watched her opponents out of the corners of her eyes, on high alert for any dodgy activity.

Two lanes away, Ferdi skimmed the water, his face determined. Then his eyes went wide, and Silver whipped forward.

From the depths of the sea, oval creatures trailing long, thin tails shot into the sky. They were the size of Jaspatonian flatbreads, and their glossy black fins moved back and forth a few times as they reached their peak height, then they curled toward the riders and zoomed straight for them.

"Watch out," Silver yelled.

Hiyyan deftly dodged the first attack just before a second creature shot at Silver. She leaned to her right, but the creature skimmed her arm with the sharp edge of its fin, opening a bloody line in her skin. She hissed and clapped her hand over the wound to suppress the bleeding as Hiyyan weaved side to side through the field of flying rays. When they reached the last wave of razor-finned sea creatures, the Aquinder pushed forward with all his might—thrusting them straight into the next obstacle.

Silver and Hiyyan dropped off the face of the earth.

At least, that's how it felt when they tipped into the swirling hole that had opened across the racecourse. Here, then, was one of the famed whirlpools Sagittaria could ride through with hardly any effort.

Silver, on the other hand, panicked.

"Hiyyan!" she managed to scream before the seawater smacked her in the face and drowned out her words. Her head spun one direction and her body another, until she was too dizzy to see clearly.

Water sloshed up Hiyyan's sides, the whirlpool emitting a high-pitched whistling sound. Something gripped her cut arm, and Silver screamed again.

"Stop fighting it!" Ferdi was next to her, somehow. "Look at me!"

But the water kept flinging, and Hiyyan kept spinning, and Silver couldn't breathe. Her hands slipped from Hiyyan's mane, and her hips slid across his back.

"Focus," Ferdi shouted.

"I can't," Silver sputtered as salt water burned her eyes and filled her nose.

The impossibility of the situation—a debut water dragon racer trying to win a big race—threatened to pull her under the water.

"You're Desert Fox. You can do this!" They were the last words Ferdi yelled to her as the whirlpool whisked him and his Glithern away.

She wiped her hand across her face, trying to ignore the sting. Her wounded arm had gone numb.

Ferdi slowly moved up the side of the whirlpool, closer and closer to the sea's surface with each lurch.

Silver's teeth chattered. "I won't . . . let a whirlpool . . . get in the way . . . of winning. Climb, Hiyyan. Like them. A little at a time."

Hiyyan pointed his snout to the sky and pushed with his hind legs. Silver pressed low against his back, turning her face away from the splashing water as best she could, and they moved upward bit by bit, as though leaping to different levels. Below, other racers were struggling with the whirlpool, too. But still more were out of Silver's sight, and she worried that they were far ahead of them in the race.

Beneath her, Hiyyan breathed heavily.

Keep it up, she told him. *You're doing great.*

When they finally broke free from the swirls and reached the surface again, dragon and rider both sucked in air.

Silver scanned the horizon. They had fallen behind four other dragons, including Ferdi's Glithern.

"We . . . can't . . . rest . . ." Silver said, her chest heaving with exertion. "Just keep moving."

For a while, the course led them in a straight line. There was one section with rivulets, where the water ran perpendicular to the sea's current, and here the Shorsa in the farthest lane tripped, falling back enough for Silver and Hiyyan to catch up. Still, as they began to find a speed and rhythm, Silver's worries grew. She knew that some new obstacle must be coming up, and soon.

Hard snorts pierced the air. There was little distance between most racers, with only two left far behind, including the racer who had accepted the bribe to lose. Ferdi glanced over and nodded once to Silver. She gritted her teeth and blinked salt water from her eyes.

The sky shifted.

No, it wasn't the sky, but the blue sea—rising into a mountain with a dangerously steep slope. The Shorsa reached the foot of the mountain first and began a slow and steady climb. The Hop-Slawn rider grunted.

"Everyone goes over," he snarled. Then he dug his heels into his water dragon, and they both vanished into the side of the water mountain.

Like the Shorsa, Ferdi climbed, and Silver would, too. This mountain was no greater challenge than the dunes back home.

"I know we're almost there, Hiyyan."

The Aquinder pushed up the rushing mountain waters, straining his muscles to gain each tiny bit of height. His wings struggled against the camouin cage, and she couldn't help thinking how he could have so easily flown. She felt his effort in her own limbs, and she struggled not to slip off his back.

A mixture of seawater and sweat flowed from her temples. Her hot, clammy hands kept sliding over Hiyyan's fur. But she could see the top of the mountain, and when she chanced a peek behind her, she realized they'd already climbed more than halfway. Ferdi was falling behind, and even the Shorsa was only a head's length in front of them.

As she and Hiyyan crested the mountain, their heavy, thick pulse pounded as one. Then a burst of cold air met them.

Just ahead, the finish line flags glittered in the sun.

"Go, Hiyyan!"

Silver wished her water dragon could spread his wings and fly to the finish. Instead, they inelegantly tumbled down the back side of the mountain and met the mirror surface of the sea once more.

Hiyyan threw everything he had left into his effort, but the Shorsa was dashing ahead.

Silver peeked at the Hop-Slawn that had gone through the

wall instead of over as it gained on Hiyyan, too. It strained and snorted angrily. The rider screamed and slapped its flanks with a whip. Silver cringed.

His expression looked too much like how she'd felt in the first race.

And she would never do that to Hiyyan again.

Silver loosened her grip on Hiyyan's mane. She closed her eyes and breathed deeply, slowly, sinking into the rise and fall of her Aquinder's movements. Warmth slowly built in her legs, then her belly. She reached for and saw the things Hiyyan was seeing: the end of the race closing in, the life beyond with Kirja and the sea and . . . her.

Her thoughts went to Jaspaton, the great pale city carved into the desert cliffs. A steady thrum began in her chest; a slow but deep heartbeat to match the drum music that was played at festivals.

Thump . . . thump.

She envisioned meteors dancing across a dune-tipped sky. Her mother and father stood, looking out over the sands, hoping for a sign of Silver.

I am here, and I am safe. She imagined her words flowing toward her parents, as soft as a breeze, gently stirring their black hair.

And still, the Jaspaton drums beat.

Thump . . . thump.

They were waiting for her—her parents and Brajon and Kirja and all of Jaspaton and all of the deep desert. Waiting for Silver to prove herself, to touch her destiny.

Nebekker was waiting for her, and the legend of Gulad Nakim was waiting for her. A scrappy group of Desert Fox fans held their breath, and Silver felt strangely close to them.

She would pave the way for Aquinder to be safely revealed to the world again.

Thump . . . thump.

The drum sound soared across the sands and over the sea. Silver opened her eyes and came back to Hiyyan. She realized their heartbeats matched. Their skin was the same temperature. They breathed at the same pace. They were one. The air fought against them, but the sea urged them forward until they were a nose ahead of the pack, and then a neck, and then half a body's length.

Silver smiled. *Let go, Hiyyan. Relax. We'll do this together.*

Hiyyan gave a contented sigh. His legs pushed the water. His body settled into his natural racing form.

He relaxed and, with a triumphant cry, shot them across the finish line.

Forty-Two

You can't go anywhere looking like that," Mele said.

It had been an hour since Silver's winning race, and her body still buzzed. Hiyyan was hidden back in the cove, and Silver and Brajon hid in Mele's room. They listened to the cheers as the final races concluded, and then they heard music and singing start as the festivities continued. The pendant at Silver's throat pulsed gently. A constant reminder of why she'd come to Calidia and how close she was to rescuing Kirja.

"You're not the first one to tell me that," Silver said.

"Let me see your winnings." Mele held out her hand, and Silver dropped the purse in the girl's palm. Mele peeked inside, then nodded in satisfaction. "There's more than enough here to make us all presentable to Queen Imea."

"All?"

"I've wanted to see the inside of the palace since I came to Calidia. You wouldn't believe the stories I've heard! Sweeping granite arches, shimmering gold walls, tile ceilings. And," she said, her eyes sparkling, "I've heard streams run through every part of the palace, where the dragons can swim. There's no way I'm letting you go without me!"

"Can I dress in crystal-sea silk?"

Mele puffed out her cheeks. "You didn't win *that* much money."

"You're not going to wear the desert-fox mask, are you?" Brajon said.

Silver nodded. "I have to. I don't completely understand . . . I feel certain they know who I am! But until I'm sure, I can't give my identity away until the very last moment. Sagittaria might hide Kirja somewhere that we could never find her."

"Your soggy mask would look ridiculous with a gown. Trust me to sort it out," Mele said.

Silver tugged the ends of her ill-cropped hair. She nodded. "Make us worthy of the queen's audience, Mele, and in return, I'll bring you both as my squires."

Mele whooped and Brajon groaned at the same time.

Mele ducked away. Silver paced the little alleyway room, her hands clammy. She knew she was attempting the impossible.

But she couldn't back out now.

The cousins took turns cleaning up in the washbasin, and by the time they were both scrubbed, Mele had returned, her hands full of boxes. She set them on the ground and opened the first. Inside, a filmy orange gown, heavily beaded, winked at her. It slid over Silver's skin like water.

"The closest I could get to crystal-sea silk on our budget," Mele said.

In a smaller box, a matching veil was nestled in delicate paper, along with many strands of jewelry to be draped over Silver's hair and down her face. Silver touched the coppery metals and semiprecious stones and thought of her father. These items were simpler than anything Rami Batal would make—he would likely think them beneath him—but Silver still felt close to home as Mele attached the veil and jewels.

The last time she'd worn metals and gems like this, she'd felt ashamed, first by the task, and then by Sagittaria Wonder. Now, she would stand before her idol again, but this time, she would meet her triumphantly, winner to winner. Instinctively, her chin lifted.

Mele appraised her, then let out a short breath. "You look regal," she said. "I almost believe you can actually take on Queen Imea."

"Believe it, because I have to," Silver whispered.

But if Silver looked different in her Winners' Audience attire, it paled in comparison to the change that came over Mele once she stepped into her emerald-green gown and simple veil. It was as though a light, as subtle and warm as a spring desert sunrise, glowed from within her. Her beauty—and she was already very beautiful, with her wide eyes, straight nose, and thick hair—became the stuff of desert lore. Silver wondered if this inner light, this transformation, was what the ancient mystics looked for when they searched the entire nation for a new queen.

"You scrub off nicely," Brajon said, entering the room and looking at Mele with frank admiration. He turned to his cousin. "And you look about right for a desert fox. How about me?" Brajon put his arms out and turned in a slow circle. His blue tunic was shot through with strands of silver that sparkled as he moved.

"Very nice," Mele said.

"I've seen beetles with more polish," Silver teased. "But

it'll have to do. Hopefully, no one will throw you out of the palace."

Brajon clapped his hands. "Happy to have your approval, cousin."

Silver took a deep breath and pulled her shoulders back. Out the tiny window, twilight had settled over Calidia. "To the queen."

Forty-Three

If Silver had thought she could sneak into the palace, quietly ask Queen Imea for Kirja back, then fly away with no one taking notice, she was mistaken.

She, Brajon, and Mele made their way down the path toward the palace entrance. Calidian lanterns lit the way, and on either side of them, hundreds of revelers were tossing orange and pink flower petals, waving sparklers, cheering, and even flying paper dragon kites high overhead. The noise was deafening, and Silver was glad the veil hid her shock and uneasiness. Out of the corner of her eye, she saw the friendly guard in the throngs. Silver almost went to him to say hello, but she remembered that he thought she was a lowly squire. She shrank back, sad to be embroiled in so many lies. She couldn't wait for when she could just be Silver Batal again.

Silver snuck a look at Brajon and Mele, and saw that they were both as speechless as she was.

"Stand tall. Don't slump." A gentle hand took her elbow. Ferdi's warm eyes gazed down at Silver as he joined the group.

"What are you doing here? You—"

"Lost my race to an upstart with a mythical dragon?" The island boy's eyes danced in the lantern light, and he gave her a crooked grin. His long white brocade jacket glimmered over gold-threaded leggings. He looked like he belonged in a royal palace. "Fortunately, I didn't need to win to get an invitation tonight."

Silver thought back to his shared laugh with Sagittaria Wonder. "Because you're Sagittaria's friend? Then why should I trust you?"

"Because I haven't turned you over to the guards?" Ferdi made an exasperated sound. "You should be glad I'm here. I have chaos to create, remember?" He nodded at the crowds. "*You* don't have to do much to create chaos, though. Look at all those people whispering. They're desperate to know who the girl is behind the mysterious disguise."

"They'll be disappointed to discover she's a failed ele-jeweler from a nowhere city out in the scrubbiest corner of the desert."

"Or a great water dragon racing champion. Hmm . . ." Ferdi looked over Silver's head. "Am I walking with the wrong person? I've never heard Desert Fox say anything that wasn't a grand boast."

Silver surprised herself by laughing. She wasn't sure why he was being so mysterious, but he had, after all, been instrumental in helping her win the race. She didn't know how she would have gotten past the whirlpool without him.

"It's all just a little overwhelming," she said.

"If you think this is something, look there." Ferdi pointed straight ahead.

The foursome crossed a short white marble bridge over a stream and walked under a thick arch striped with gold. As the palace entrance opened up before them, Silver's breath caught in her throat.

Silver's and Mele's slippers softly *shush*ed over elaborate stone murals inlaid in the floor, depicting desert scenes. Ferdi's and Brajon's boots clicked on polished tile, each featuring a tiny painted water dragon. More tiles lined the walls—millions of colorful, glittering squares as small as the tip of a thumb—and Silver realized that the tiles weren't clay; they were precious stones. Swirls of lapis depicted the waves of the sea, while carnelian and agate formed the dunes of the desert. There were gardens whose flower petals were made of amethyst and garnet, and panels of well-known desert motifs separating each scene.

The ceilings soared overhead, rising and dipping in domes and arches, supported by intricate, lacy metalwork so fine Silver found herself growing dizzy as she tried to see it.

They passed under another archway and entered a plaza. Three sides of the square were bordered with waterways, while an orchard of miniature fruit trees and carved stone benches created a lush centerpiece. This time, when Silver looked up, it was the Calidian stars that winked back at her. People paused here, milling about with glasses of cordial and picking delicate pastries and finger foods off the trays that were being passed around by servers in all white. Music drifted over from some corner of the courtyard, while tiny gemstone lanterns, in the style of Jaspaton, cast a muted, colorful glow over everything.

"Don't stop now," Ferdi said. "The throne room is through there."

"You know a lot about this place," Brajon said, busy filling his hands with flaky meat pies and crunchy crystalized nuts.

Mele held a glass of cordial, which she sipped delicately, but Silver's stomach was so knotted she couldn't imagine eating or drinking.

"I make sure I always know my way around," Ferdi said. "Lucky for you, that means I can help."

A blast of brass instruments cut through the festivities. Talking died down as people turned to the throne room entrance. A series of guards in white came through, two by two, then split to create a walkway. Then the king regent appeared, paused on the steps that led from the throne room down to the courtyard, and fell to one knee.

"Queen Imea," Silver whispered. She caught a movement out of the corner of her eye, near the throne room entrance. Lingering in the shadows, a figure in all black watched Silver. Sagittaria Wonder.

Silver nudged Ferdi with her shoulder. "She knows I'm here."

"The queen?" He followed Silver's gaze. "Ah, the racing champion. I'll take care of her."

But before Ferdi could cross the room, the queen made her entrance. She was as lovely and composed as Silver remembered, but instead of wearing a traveling gown, Queen Imea was wrapped in layers and layers of fine, cream-colored silks, beaded with precious stones, and weighted down with gold and silver adornments worked so fine they looked like spun sugar.

"Good evening," the queen said. "And welcome to all guests, in particular my most honored guests: my race winners. Our long tradition of sending the very best of the desert to the Island Nations Spring Festival has been enhanced this year." Queen Imea's gaze swept the room, falling on Silver.

Silver's blood raced. What did she mean by enhanced? Nebekker's pendant flared to life and warmed against her skin. Silver quickly placed her hand over it. Could the queen see the glow of it under her gown?

Queen Imea shifted her eyes, then beamed as she scanned the room. "Enhanced by what I believe is the strongest and most talented field of racers we have ever sent to the islands. I feel—I *know*—that the Desert Nations will be victorious this year and claim the title of the best water dragon racer in the world!"

As the queen threw her glittering arms in the air, cheers erupted from the crowd.

"See you later," Ferdi whispered, and he slipped away in the commotion. Silver watched him thread through the fabric of the attendees smoothly until, finally, he arrived at Sagittaria's side. He spoke to her, and they both laughed.

Suspicion grew in Silver's belly again. Was Ferdi part of some plan to ambush her? No, he had proven himself her friend. It was only nerves telling her otherwise. Still, she moved closer to her cousin as the air in the plaza grew thick.

"Which racer will lead the desert to glory? I'm so enthralled with the mystery that I've asked a friend to attend the Winners' Audiences, too," Queen Imea said. "Arkilah will read the stars, and perhaps that cosmos will reveal great secrets to us!"

"Arkilah?" Silver and Brajon said at the same time.

This time, when Queen Imea threw out her arms, it was to draw all attention to a woman in the crowd, rising to stand from a bench behind a citrus tree in the center of the courtyard.

The woman was about Silver's mother's age and, compared to everyone else in the room, should have been easy to notice.

Instead of a glittering gown, she wore layers of roughly hewn nomadic linen, topped with a variety of belts and straps holding an even greater assortment of pouches, bottles, crystals, and artifacts. But what was most intriguing about Arkilah were the dark lines running all over her exposed skin, from fingertips to the top of her shaved head. She was completely tattooed with constellations of the ancient gods.

The cousins peeled their eyes away from the fascinating nomadic woman and looked pointedly at Mele, whose eyes were wider than ever over the brim of her glass.

"I thought she was dead," Silver whispered.

"I didn't know," Mele said. "My sources aren't perfect. She disappeared ages ago."

"Well, the more allies, the better," Brajon said, pushing his cousin toward the citrus trees. "Come on, Silver. Go make a new friend."

Forty-Four

Even though beads of sweat had gathered under her jeweled headpiece, Silver walked forward with her head held high. Here was her chance to get Kirja and get out of the palace without revealing her identity.

The peridot Jaspatonian-style lantern that hung just to the left of Arkilah's head cast a strange green glow over her face. When Arkilah glanced down, Silver saw that even her eyelids were marked with lines and stars. Silver finally reached the stone bench, where the nomadic woman was once again sitting, and perched on the very edge. Arkilah was stiff, making neither word nor motion of welcome.

Silver cleared her throat. "Nebekker sent me," she whispered. Nebekker, who would be happy to hear her friend was alive. Nebekker, who was waiting, frail and weak, for Silver to return with Kirja.

"She said you could help me find"—here, Silver's voice dipped even lower, and she flashed Nebekker's pendant briefly before tucking it securely away again—"Kirja."

Arkilah didn't answer, but a breeze picked up and rattled

two of the tiny vials hanging from one of her sashes. She fixed Silver with a look that didn't betray any emotion. Not recognition or surprise or confusion.

"Nebekker said you were a friend of . . . water dragons. I don't know why or how, but you're supposed to help me," Silver said as she drew closer.

When Arkilah stayed silent, Silver snuck a quick look around the room. She couldn't see the queen on the other side of the citrus trees, but she spotted Ferdi, still plying Sagittaria Wonder with tales of some sort, despite the growing impatience on the racing champion's face. But even if Sagittaria was distracted, other people were watching Silver and Arkilah curiously. Silver needed to hurry.

"Is it true you can tell the future?" she blurted in a desperate attempt.

This, finally, got a reaction out of Arkilah.

"If I could, I would have seen you coming," she said. Her voice was as gravelly as the ground surrounding Jaspaton and thick with a familiar deep-desert accent. "Desert Fox. Everyone wants to know the answers to the great mystery of who you are and where you came from. Not to mention what breed of dragon you're racing."

"You are a mystic," Silver breathed.

Arkilah scoffed. "Queen Imea thinks I know things because of some divine power of interpretation. But I know things because I spend my life studying . . . searching for answers. And there are many things I still want to know. Like how can Nebekker think that I would help you when she left me alone to die in a frozen wasteland so many years ago?"

Silver's eyes widened. Nebekker did *what*? It didn't seem possible Nebekker could harm anyone in that way.

"Ah," Arkilah said. "So that old crone didn't tell you. You should be questioning your friendship with her. Never trust people, Desert Fox. Unfettered truth is the only thing of any worth. And I believe you can lead me to some new truths, just as I led Sagittaria Wonder to Nebekker."

"So you were the one who told her?" Silver cried, her face flushing with anger.

"Who do you think showed Sagittaria Wonder the scale pattern? Nebekker always guarded her work, and for good reason, but she never knew how closely I watched her and learned her particular skills. This was all before she betrayed me."

"So you betrayed her in return," Silver said through gritted teeth.

Arkilah shrugged. "I anticipate the chance to study a water dragon bond from its near inception."

The nomadic woman rose, her baubles and artifacts clinking, and disappeared on the other side of the fruit trees. Silver stared after Arkilah, her pulse racing. *From its near inception.* Did the woman mean her and Hiyyan?

Silver rushed back to where Brajon and Mele were waiting.

"What did she say?" Brajon asked. "Is she going to help us?"

Silver shook her head. "She's not the person we thought she would be. She said Nebekker . . ." Silver swallowed thickly. Nebekker had shown she would do almost anything to protect Kirja. But leave someone to die? "They're not friends anymore."

"What are we supposed to do now?" Brajon groaned.

"What we always planned on doing. We have to go

through with the Winners' Audience. I have to get Kirja back on my own." Arkilah's words echoed in her head. "And then we have to get out of here."

"Easier said than done, cousin." Brajon drew his brows together. "Look around."

Silver glanced at the walls of the room. The number of guards backed against the tiles seemed to have grown exponentially in the last few minutes. But they weren't the only reason chills were crawling up Silver's spine. It seemed the entire room had its eyes on her. The crowd had formed a long circle around Silver and the entrance to the throne room.

"I told Brajon we should get out of here now," Mele said. "But he refused."

"You're free to go," Brajon countered crossly. "Aren't you just here to gawk?"

"Enough! It's not safe," Silver said. "Mele, they've seen you with us. I don't want you walking out of here alone."

"I knew I should've minded my own business," Mele said, crossing her arms over her chest.

The energy shifted as everyone turned to watch Queen Imea slowly climbing the steps into the throne room and disappearing inside with a flourish of silks. Arkilah followed, but she paused at the top of the steps and faced the crowd.

"Our five winning racers are now invited to their audience with the queen," she said. "May your desire be pure, and your favor granted."

Sagittaria Wonder strode up the steps like it was second nature, followed by the rider of the Shorsa from Silver's first race.

"Go," Brajon said. "I'll be waiting for you at the base of those steps. Scream if you need me."

"Desert foxes don't scream," Silver said. "They snarl."

Silver saw Ferdi sidle up next to Brajon and Mele, and having them there boosted her confidence. She could even feel Hiyyan tentatively paddling down the coastline, from the cove to Calidia, as the most important moment of her journey beckoned. She would get Kirja back.

Silver climbed the steps and entered Queen Imea's grand throne room.

Forty-Five

Queen Imea cut an imposing figure. Her throne was constructed of swirls of tall iron, upon which colorful embroidered cushions perched. It sat upon a raised dais made from thick glass. A stream flowed through the room and under the dais, and in that stream, two Abruqs circled lazily.

Each throne arm was an iron water dragon, and Queen Imea placed her palms over their two heads. Another dragon head, this one pure gold, hung from the ceiling, surrounded by dripping gemstone tassels. To the right of the queen's throne, five gilded wooden boxes sat on a small table. Each one contained, Silver assumed, a small fortune in coins. But it was the view behind the throne that caught her attention most.

Three ornately tiled arches led out to a stone balcony. Beyond that, the obsidian sky opened up over the sea. From there, Queen Imea could watch every water dragon race—and she probably had. The view stretched so far that Silver wondered if one could see all the way to the Island Nations. Now, though, Arkilah stood on that balcony, her back to the throne room, staring up at the stars. How much had Nebekker's once-friend told the queen about Silver? How much could the heavens reveal?

"Sagittaria Wonder," the king regent, standing to the left of the queen, announced, summoning her forth.

Silver watched as the queen's favorite water dragon racer stepped onto the dais. She bowed before Queen Imea and took the wooden box offered her without a single word passing between them. They had obviously done this many times before; Sagittaria looked almost bored with it all.

"She will bring the desert great glory," came Arkilah's prediction from the balcony.

Silver didn't miss the way Sagittaria clenched her jaw, almost like she was suppressing a grimace. Or was it laughter? Perhaps the water dragon racer and the nomad didn't get along, each vying for the queen's favor. But then again, it had been Arkilah who'd led Sagittaria Wonder to Kirja.

The other three winning racers were called up in turn, two of them requesting the contents of the wooden box, while another requested a gift of farmland for his extended family in the southern regions.

"What a thoughtful and selfless request," Queen Imea said. She smiled and doubled the amount of land the racer had initially asked for.

"The riches to come to your family will exceed all that stood upon the table," Arkilah said.

The southern water dragon racer grinned and bowed again. All requests had been granted with a warm smile from the queen, which gave Silver confidence.

"Desert Fox," the king regent announced. Silver lifted her

skirts and walked forward. She tried not to pay attention to the way Sagittaria Wonder noiselessly set her wooden box on the ground and folded her arms across her chest, or the way the other racers squinted to try to see under Silver's veil.

"Queen Imea," Silver said, bowing. When she rose again, she noticed that the queen had not reached for a wooden box like she had with the other racers. Instead, Queen Imea sat so still and blank of expression that she could have been carved from granite.

Silver swallowed. Had those guards, positioned along the arches in the back of the room, shuffled a few inches closer, or was that Silver's imagination? Was there more noise behind her, streaming in from the courtyard, or was that a trick of the room?

The way everyone watched her, waiting, was no trick. Silver's arms went cold, and her head went light. She could really use one of Ferdi's diversions right then.

I need you, Silver said to Hiyyan. Her body warmed. She could tell that her Aquinder was close to Calidia now.

Before Silver could make her request, Arkilah reentered the throne room, standing to the side of the dais. The queen pressed her hands on the iron water dragon heads impatiently and snapped at Silver: "Who are you?"

The question hit Silver with the force of a sand storm, bringing her to life.

"I am Desert Fox," Silver said.

The queen stayed silent, waiting expectantly.

With her blood pounding in her ears, Silver slowly pulled the veil off her face.

Sagittaria Wonder started forward, her mouth twisting in

a frown. "I know you. You're that annoying little ele-jeweler from Jaspaton."

Silver began to cringe, but then she stopped herself. She wasn't ashamed about where she came from. It was a jeweler who'd taught her to work metal, so that she could make bindings for Hiyyan's wings. It was a yarnslady who'd taught her to work wool, so that she could disguise herself for the races. It was a community of family and tradition that had taught her to be strong and resilient, that had sent her into the world with useful gifts and the desire for greatness.

Silver Batal had all those things, and more.

"I am Desert Fox," she repeated, her voice carrying through the throne room and into the courtyard. "I am the ele-jeweler. I am a yarnslady's daughter. I am a Jaspatonian."

Her voice grew even louder, pride swelling in her chest. A roar began in her ears, as though all the deep desert applauded her efforts. The healing wound on her wrist burned deliciously, like it was brand-new. Somewhere in the sea over that throne room balcony, Hiyyan was sending Silver feelings of strength.

Silver threw her shoulders back.

"I am Silver Batal, Aquinder racer!"

The noise in the courtyard grew once more. There was a commotion behind her, but Silver didn't have the courage to look away from the queen. Queen Imea smiled down, her lips pressed together. Those violet eyes flashed, and the light bounced off her platinum hair like molten metal.

"Yes, Arkilah has told me a bit about you. She has a keen interest in studying you, and I think I'll allow her." The queen tapped her fingers slowly back and forth. "Silver. That's one of the lesser metals, isn't it? I do believe your father had promised me gold. Disappointing."

Before, the remark would have crushed Silver, but as she held the queen's gaze, a sleeping little memory came to life.

"You were going to be named Ruby," Sersha Batal had whispered to Silver. "Your father's favorite gemstone. But the night you were born was the clearest I could remember. The moon was full, and you opened your eyes and stared at the silvery light for a long time. Then you smiled."

Silver's father had gathered her close. "You're still my favorite gemstone, but your mother was right to pick Silver instead. My wondering, mysterious girl. You will accomplish such great things in this life."

"I am no disappointment," Silver said.

"I don't care what you are," Queen Imea said, waving away Silver's words. "Bring me the Aquinder you raced."

"That Aquinder belongs to me," Silver said. "I raced him, so I've claimed him. But the other Aquinder, the one Sagittaria stole, belongs to someone else. And now, before you at the Winners' Audience, I demand her return!"

Queen Imea stood, her presence so commanding that two of the other racers quickly left the room, their wooden boxes tucked securely under their arms. Silver heard shouting and screams from the courtyard. Had Ferdi finally started his distraction?

"Ridiculous child," Queen Imea said. "Both Aquinder must be destroyed. That is part of ancient treaty. To allow them to live would mean war."

"Then you must pick which law to follow. I raced my Aquinder, so he's mine. You would steal from me? According to the law—"

"You fool," Sagittaria Wonder said. "The law does not apply to the queen!"

The Abruqs moved closer.

On the sea, so did Hiyyan.

Before Silver could react, a group of people burst into the throne room. It was Ferdi's companions and another man, the tallest Silver had ever seen, who threw back his cloak and released waves of thick white hair.

"Queen Imea!" he boomed. "The royals are servants of the law, not above it."

As the crowd around the man bowed their heads, the queen had the grace to look shocked. But she quickly wiped her expression and bowed her head.

"King A-Malusni. Your ambassadors sent your regrets some weeks ago and told me your son would appear at our festival in your place. Imagine my surprise at seeing you now."

Over her left shoulder, a shocked voice rose. "Father?"

Forty-Six

Ferdi stood at the entrance to the throne room, Brajon and Mele on either side of him.

Silver's mouth dropped open. "Ferdi? That's your father . . . You're a . . ."

The king of the Island Nations held up a hand. "The girl is in compliance with the law, no matter what breed of dragon she rides."

Queen Imea stroked the front of her silk gown and gave an acquiescent smile. "You are correct on that count, King A-Malushi. The matter of the Aquinder is a complicated one. Perhaps we can discuss the ancient and sacred words of the treaty in detail and come to an understanding between our nations." Her sweet smile fell, and her eyes blazed. "However, this girl used an illegal and highly dangerous substance in her race."

"What?" Silver yelped. *The queen's final card.*

"The possession of camouin is illegal, and you are under arrest. Guards, seize her!"

The room erupted in chaos. The queen's men pushed

toward Silver, but Ferdi's companions—King A-Malusni's men—cut them off. Arkilah rushed from the dais, and the two Abruqs met her in the middle. Most peculiar of all, strange figures dressed in huge water dragon costumes streamed into the room, dancing riotously.

With all the commotion, Sagittaria Wonder slipped past everyone and reached Silver first.

"Let's go," Sagittaria said, dragging her backward by her arm.

"Brajon, help," Silver yelled, but her voice was lost in the noise.

She stumbled down the throne room steps and into the courtyard, yanked along mercilessly by the queen's water dragon racer.

"Let go of her," Brajon yelled. He tried to follow but was held back by two guards. A third had his arms around Mele. More water dragon–masked dancers added to the chaos, like some kind of nightmarish desert festival.

"Move faster," Sagittaria Wonder said. "Do you *want* the guards to catch you?"

Sagittaria hauled Silver through the courtyard grove, swerving left to right around the orange trees.

"What do you mean?" Silver gasped. Was Sagittaria Wonder helping her escape? The pain from Sagittaria's grip rushed up her arm. Silver's gown wrapped around her legs, causing her to falter, but Sagittaria Wonder kept going. When they reached the palace entrance, Sagittaria quickly ducked between two guards, but Silver ran into the chest of a third.

"Please, help us," she whispered.

"I knew there was something special about you," the kind

guard said. He looked down sternly, then nonchalantly shoved two of his colleagues into the pools. "Run, Desert Fox."

"But my cousin!"

Sagittaria Wonder grunted and pulled Silver around a corner. She paused in a shadowed nook but didn't release Silver's arm. "You have strange friends," she said. "Guards, princes, cleaning girls—"

"What about you?" Silver said. "Why are you helping me now? Why didn't you turn me in before this?"

"Even if I had, the queen would have wanted to make this matter as private as possible. There will be chaos when news of the Aquinder spreads. I sent those posters out in the hope that someone would turn you in as a thief and I could convince you to leave before you got too far into this dangerous game. But you just won't hold back, will you?" A spark lit up Sagittaria's eyes as she appraised Silver. "You need to understand that I'm not your friend and never will be. But, Desert Fox—Silver Batal, Aquinder racer—your courage has impressed me. I see myself as a girl in you. You are a water dragon racer. You are a winner. And you should be allowed to bring glory to these desert lands through your racing."

Emotion swelled inside Silver like music. She didn't know what to say to Sagittaria Wonder, queen's racer . . . hero. The words that rang in her ears were the ones she'd wanted to hear her whole life. Her thumb pressed hard against her burn mark.

"You think I'm a winner?" Silver asked.

"Well, not at everything. Your fiber arts need a bit of work," she said. And here, Sagittaria Wonder actually laughed. "But your connection with your dragon is something special. Racer to racer, I would never cage that up. Nor cage *you* up. But

Arkilah is different, so you must run, desert girl. Get your Aquinder and get out of here."

"I can't run! My cousin's in there. And Kirja—"

"Listen to me! I didn't drag you out of there so you could sacrifice yourself for others. They'll let your cousin go soon enough."

"And Kirja?"

"Isn't yours to worry about! Save yourself. Save your Aquinder. The queen is lying about killing any Aquinder—they're too precious. You may one day know freedom, and when you do, you'll race again. Run!"

Hiyyan was cutting through the sea and getting close to the docks. Silver could feel his movements, and his uncertainty.

She could also feel his hope. That she, Silver Batal, water dragon racer recognized by the greatest water dragon racer of them all, had saved his mother. She had finally won Sagittaria's approval. But that wasn't the promise she'd made Hiyyan.

"I can't run. And Kirja isn't the queen's water dragon."

Silver darted from Sagittaria Wonder.

Forty-Seven

Silver yanked the jewelry from her face, hitched her gown up, and got to the docks as fast as she could. It was much quieter on the streets of Calidia than it was in the palace, and either the guards posted outside didn't know what was going on, or they were inside the palace looking for her. She ran past the inn, merry with late-night storytellers, then the dark vendor carts, hulking in the shadowed corners of the streets.

Finally, she made it to the docks, passing under the wooden arches and over the shimmering black waves lapping the pilings. At the end of one dock, Hiyyan waited.

Without a thought, Silver leaped onto his back and threw her arms around his neck. *My Hiyyan.* She pulled the camouin from his sides and tossed the metal into the depths of the sea.

"Too much trouble to be worth it," she said, hooking her slippers into Hiyyan's wing joints. "Okay, my friend, let's rescue your mother."

She led him to the open harbor, then to the seawall. But soon, dozens of dark blobs were closing in on them.

"Abruqs. Oh, there's Ferdi, too!"

Before the Abruqs could reach her, Ferdi and Hoonazoor sped to her side.

"How did you find me?" Silver called out.

"Never mind that. Follow me," Ferdi said, and pulled his reins to turn his water dragon around.

The Glithern's speed was remarkable. Even faster than had been revealed in any of the races. Ferdi became a blur, and Hiyyan had to spread his wings and take to the sky to keep up.

"You're a prince?" Silver shouted down at him. "Why didn't you tell me?"

"There was never a right time," he yelled back.

Hoonazoor disappeared into a narrow cut in the shore on the opposite side of the palace from the seawall. Hiyyan kept near, sweeping so close to the palace that Silver's heart rose up her throat. But the guards were on the ground, scrambling to get across the palace beach, their heavy boots sinking into the soft sand, and the little Abruqs couldn't possibly keep up with the larger, faster water dragons. Back at the seawall, harpoons were being loaded, but Hiyyan swept around the corner long before they were released.

As they soared around the palace towers, spurred on by renewed shouts from the crowds, Silver spotted a huge lake with several water dragons. The fabled Royal Pools of Calidia. Silver squinted to see better. Several dragons . . . but not Kirja. But for the first time, the pendant stone pulsed with heat, and an intensity that hammered Silver's chest. Kirja had to be near.

"Where is she?"

Hiyyan let out an excited sound and dove for the ground.

"Do you see your mother?" Silver peered over his shoulder.

She still didn't spot Kirja, but she did see a girl, waving her arms over her head. "It's Mele! Fly close to her."

Hiyyan swooped down and slowed.

"Where's my cousin?" Silver called to Mele.

"They let him go. But I showed him how to get underground earlier today like you asked," the girl said. "He should be down there somewhere. Hopefully, no one follows him."

"I wouldn't count on that. Be on the lookout," Silver said.

Hoonazoor turned a circle in the holding pools.

"We have to hurry," Ferdi said. "Follow me."

"Come with us," Silver said to Mele.

But Mele shook her head. Her gaze went to a Shorsa not far away. "I can't."

"Is that your dragon? Bring her and come with us," Silver said.

"I can't. That's stealing."

"It doesn't matter what some list says. You belong together. It's water dragon law."

Mele hesitated. "But not our law!"

"Please, Mele," Silver said. "Guards are coming. I can't leave you here to get in trouble for me."

"I don't know the way. Not through these pools."

"Ferdi's dragon does."

Shouts came from the other side of the lake.

"Mele, we have to hurry," Silver said. "Please!"

The pretty Shorsa watched them, swishing its tail slowly, like she was waiting for Mele to make a decision.

"Your water dragon wants to go," Silver said. "Close your eyes . . . Feel what she feels. Your Shorsa will tell you I'm right."

"We don't have time for this," Ferdi shouted.

The guards were closing in on them. It was now or never. Mele let out a shrill whistle, and the Shorsa dove toward her. Mele scrambled onto the water dragon's back.

"Follow me," Ferdi said. And then he disappeared under the lake, with Mele and her Shorsa close behind.

Hiyyan lifted into the sky. Silver took a deep breath. Then they turned and dove into the lake.

Silver kept her eyes open for Ferdi and Mele as they sliced through the water. But they were hard to see. The Shorsa was small and very quick, and Hoonazoor's glittering coloring went dark once underwater, blending into the shadows. But they also trailed bubbles behind them, which Nebekker's pendant lit with an eerie effervescence. Hiyyan followed those bubbles until they broke through the water and surfaced behind Mele.

Silver reached into her bag for her lantern before remembering it had smashed in the caves. Her hand brushed against her dagger, and she pulled it out, fastening it around her waist with a bit of scarf.

"Not far now." Ferdi's voice came just ahead of Mele's.

"Where are we?"

"Sonflir River caves," Mele said. "There are well openings for the fruit orchards farther down the river. That's how Brajon will get in. They'll provide us with some light, too."

"How do you know your way?"

"My family works in one of the orchards. It was down here that I first saw Luap," Mele said, patting her Shorsa's neck.

"That Shorsa wasn't meant for the Calidians," Ferdi said. "She was bred for another nation. Mine. See the marking on her tail?"

Silver and Mele both examined the spot: three diagonal lines and a sunburst.

"My father's crest," Ferdi said.

"Your father," Silver said. "I keep forgetting that you are *Prince* Ferdi."

Ferdi sighed. "A free prince, for once. Or so I'd thought."

"A special guest of the queen, and friend to Sagittaria," Silver said carefully.

"That first part is true," he said. "The second is not."

Silver gave a soft grunt. "That's why you weren't upset when I beat you today."

"You'll never let me live that down." Ferdi laughed. "Yes, I would've been at the Winners' Audience win or lose. As is my duty," he said. "Anyway, we have to hurry. The guards—and who knows who else—will be down here before we know it. The holding tanks aren't far."

"Swim faster," Mele said. "Brajon should be just ahead of us."

Mele put emphasis on *should*, which made Silver worry. Her cousin could be in real trouble.

The water dragons pushed on, fighting against the current. Hiyyan was strong, but after the race and all the flying he'd done earlier that day, Silver could feel his exhaustion in her bones. They were both spent.

"We just need to find your mother, then get far enough away that we can rest safely," she told her Aquinder. "It's almost over."

The cave opened suddenly, and they swam into a colossal room, bigger than any underground space Silver had seen before. Crystals glittered from the ceiling, bouncing light everywhere, and Silver had to look down to keep from getting dizzy. The lake was like a perfectly clear topaz, and it was ringed with a shoreline of glittering white sand.

When her head stopped twirling, Silver looked up again. The walls were a rainbow of colors, showing the history of the river cutting through the cavern. And in the middle of it all, huge glass cages held water dragons.

Most bobbed docilely. Some were even asleep. But a few paced back and forth anxiously, and one Decodro even rammed its head against its cage over and over again, trying to break free. Silver's heart squeezed at the sight.

"We have to let them all go," she said to Mele.

"We can't. And they're not all here against their will. Some are part of the regular royal kennel."

"Kennel?"

"What we call the water dragons belonging to the royals."

Silver urged Hiyyan forward, looking for Kirja. She kept sneaking glances at the water dragon ramming its head, until tears began to roll down her face.

"Ow," Silver suddenly cried. Nebekker's pendant glowed hot enough to sear Silver's skin before cooling once more. "There's Kirja!"

Hiyyan let out a happy roar, but the old Aquinder stayed still and snorted in their direction. A warning.

"Oh, you found us. I thought you might come here."

The haughty voice of Sagittaria Wonder rang out. Silver whipped her head around to see the other side of the cave. Sagittaria was weaving in and out of the water tanks on the back of her Dwakka. Her dragon's two heads were focused on Silver's companions: one on Ferdi, the other on Mele.

"How do you like my kennel?" Sagittaria asked. "I've spent

my whole life building this water dragon empire. I started young. How old are you, ele-jeweler?"

"Thirteen," Silver said, to keep her distracted. Silver quickly glanced around the cavern. Where was Brajon?

"I began working with water dragons when I was five and an orphan. My parents were traders who were killed on the road to Calidia. When my only other relative learned they were dead, she left me at the docks. Do you know what that means for a Calidian child?"

A flicker of movement caught Silver's attention. Probably Sagittaria's shadow on the crystals. But just in case, Silver kept her eyes fixed on Sagittaria. She didn't want her to suspect anything.

"The lucky ones scraped by as beggars, but other children were snatched up by sailors to toil on their ships, never to be seen again. Once they'd outlived their usefulness . . . let's just say the seas are vast."

Silver swallowed. Another flicker of movement. Silver chanced another glance into the crystals and nearly gave a shout. Peeking from behind a rock was her cousin. Brajon pressed his finger to his lips. Silver had to keep the great dragon racer occupied.

"But not you," Silver said loudly. "You weren't taken, and you weren't killed."

"No. I would survive to get revenge on my aunt."

"What do you mean?" Silver asked.

Suddenly, the Dwakka's heads twisted away from Ferdi and Mele, swaying to the left and right. Their stubby ears were perked, listening.

"I asked you a question," Silver shouted. Her voice echoed. Brajon needed more time.

Sagittaria Wonder raised her eyebrows. The Dwakka heads swiveled back to Silver, whatever they'd heard drowned out.

"A combative Dwakka hung around the docks." Sagittaria patted her water dragon. "And I was the only person who wasn't afraid of it, didn't want to hurt it, or steal it. Dwakkas can be a little *intense*. Only *I* could compel him to bend to my will."

Sagittaria Wonder smirked. Silver gulped as she looked at the Dwakka, which didn't even have one smiling head to offset the ferocious one. Both heads were scowling.

Sagittaria continued. "Despite befriending this dragon and gaining his loyalty, despite winning our first races, despite gaining the attention and favor of the royal court—an orphan!—there was always something I wanted more than anything else."

"Revenge on your aunt."

Sagittaria Wonder waved her hand. "Oh, that. No, I achieved that quickly. Did you know water dragons hate the taste of human flesh? But whatever I ask for, I get."

Sagittaria patted the Dwakka again, and Silver's stomach turned.

"No, what I wanted was to realize my dreams. Sound familiar, Desert Fox? I care nothing for the spats the royals have, or for money. But to be the greatest? To show the whole world what this unwanted, pathetic little dock girl was capable of? That drives me, Desert Fox. That drives *us*. And later, when I heard there was a water dragon breed no one had seen in centuries . . . I had to know. Could it be real? Could I, a nobody from nowhere, hold a legend in my hands?"

Sagittaria Wonder pivoted suddenly and gazed at Kirja. Brajon, halfway to Kirja, dropped to the ground, pressing his face into the sand. He almost blended in, his dark clothing a shadow on the shoreline, but all Sagittaria had to do was look past Kirja's tank and she would see him.

"You know how it feels, Silver Batal of Jaspaton," Sagittaria Wonder said softly, turning back to her. "You know how all of it feels."

This time, the regret on her face seemed genuine. "I care more for the fate of water dragons than just about anything else, but I still can't give Kirja back."

"But she's not yours," Ferdi exclaimed. "Let us take her and go."

"No, she's not mine. But you, of all people, *Prince*, know these games are more complex than any commoner can imagine." Sagittaria Wonder nearly snarled at Ferdi. "And you might not survive if you get involved."

"I don't care about games," Silver said. "Kirja and Nebekker belong together."

"I'm sorry," Sagittaria Wonder said. And she really did sound sorry.

The Dwakka moved slowly in Silver's direction, both heads focused on her. "Kirja belongs to the queen now. And you, ele-jeweler . . . I wish you had run when you had the chance."

The Dwakka shot at Silver, both mouths open wide and fangs dripping with anticipation.

Forty-Eight

Mele screamed. Her Shorsa reared up in surprise, throwing Mele off and into the lake. Before Silver could lunge for her, one huge Dwakka head descended on Hiyyan and clamped its fangs onto the Aquinder's neck. Hiyyan screeched and threw his head back.

"No, Hiyyan," Silver yelled. It took all of her strength to keep hold of his mane and stay on his back. The lake was deep. If she got thrown off, she would drown.

"Hold on," Ferdi called, rushing toward the Dwakka. His Glithern rammed the Dwakka's underbelly, and the other Dwakka head screamed.

Silver pulled her knife from her belt and stuck it between her teeth, a metallic taste filling her mouth. She crawled up Hiyyan's back until she was within arm's reach of the Dwakka head that still held on to Hiyyan. She raised her arm and brought the knife down across its face. The sharp blade sliced into its cheek. The first head screeched and let go, but she didn't see the second head coming. It slammed into her shoulder.

"Augh!" she yelled. There was a popping sound, and sharp waves of pain exploded down her arm. She dropped the knife into the lake.

The second head aimed for her again, but Hiyyan saw and spun them around, whipping his tail at the Dwakka. He missed the head, instead swatting at its neck. It was enough to put the two-headed water dragon off balance.

"Again," Sagittaria Wonder said to the injured Dwakka head.

Dark-blue blood dripped down the side of the cut on the Dwakka's face, and from its mouth. Silver couldn't tell if all the blood was the Dwakka's, or if Hiyyan's blood was mixed in. Her Aquinder's neck was bleeding badly, and her own neck throbbed with pain.

And now Silver didn't have a weapon.

Except for her body.

Silver pulled herself to her feet, standing on Hiyyan's back with shaky legs. This could be the most reckless thing she'd ever done. If she missed, she would land in the lake. So she couldn't miss. That was the only option.

When the Dwakka head sailed close to Hiyyan, Silver let loose a battle cry and launched herself into the air. Surprised, the Dwakka pulled back suddenly. Silver gasped as the gap between her and the fearsome dragon grew. She reached her one good arm out as far as she could and managed to catch her fingers in the Dwakka's neck fins. The sharp scales at the edges of the fins sliced into her hands, but she held on, gritting her teeth, until she could swing herself onto the Dwakka's neck.

"Aaaaiiieee," Silver cried.

The Dwakka flung its head side to side, trying to dislodge

her. She wrapped her arm around the neck and held on tight.

"Get off my dragon," Sagittaria Wonder yelled.

Ferdi held back as the Dwakka kept swinging Silver around. He must have known that if Hoonazoor rammed again, Silver would get flung off into the water. Silver closed her eyes and squeezed tighter. She just had to hold on until Kirja was free. Her head swam with so much dizziness she thought she was going to pass out. But she held on. *Just a little longer.* She opened her eyes. That's when she saw Brajon at Kirja's tank.

"It's locked," Brajon shouted.

Ferdi rushed over to help. Sagittaria grabbed Silver's ankle and pulled.

"Come here!" the great water dragon rider said as she yanked Silver down the Dwakka's neck.

Instead of fighting, Silver let go. She slid down so fast she surprised Sagittaria Wonder, knocking her sideways in her saddle. Silver placed her boot on the champion's side and shoved. Sagittaria slid until she was hanging from the saddle by one foot, her head skimming the surface of the lake.

"Hurry, Brajon," Silver yelled.

She snatched the Dwakka's reins and tugged its heads back. They fought her for control, tearing the leather ropes right through her hands, leaving burning red marks across her palms. They lurched for Hiyyan again.

"I'm trying," Brajon said. His teeth were clenched. The lock wouldn't give.

Back on her Shorsa, Mele pointed. "Help him, Luap!"

The smallest of the water dragons in the cavern sped past the Dwakka and smashed into Kirja's tank. The glass held.

"Keep it up," Silver yelled. A hand gripped her calf. Sagittaria Wonder was using Silver to pull herself up, and Silver now tipped to the side. Sagittaria's jaw was clenched, her eyes furious slits.

Silver reached for the reins again, but they were too far away. Sagittaria pulled her down, and Silver fell. Her fingers scrambled and wrapped around the saddle, trying to keep herself on the Dwakka as her body stretched under Sagittaria's weight. She kicked her legs, but Sagittaria held them tightly.

"You. Are. So. Annoying," Sagittaria Wonder said. She pulled.

Silver yelped. One of her hands slipped off the saddle, and she dangled over the lake.

"You can't swim," Sagittaria said, and she laughed. A terrible sound that bounced around the cavern. "What kind of dragon rider doesn't know how to *swim*? I take back everything I've said. You don't deserve that Aquinder. You're nothing but a dockyard rat."

Silver's face burned. Her whole body groaned with the strain of holding on. But she was no rat.

She was a desert fox. Quick, clever, and capable.

Silver caught Ferdi's eye and let go.

Forty-Nine

The water greeted Silver Batal and Sagittaria Wonder with a mighty splash. Sagittaria flashed a terrible smile. Silver let out a trail of bubbles as Sagittaria pushed her even further down with her boot. Silver sank as Sagittaria propelled herself back up to the surface.

Right as Silver was about to run out of air, Hoonazoor appeared. With relief, she grabbed the Glithern's tail, and they headed for Kirja's cage. As she got closer, she saw that the thing she'd suspected was true.

She'd realized, as she watched the poor Decodro bang against the glass, that there had to be some way to access the dragons without opening the cages fully; one swift move and a dragon could escape. But tunnels—like burrows—were useful. And every glass cage had a small tunnel below the water surface. Not big enough for the dragons to get through. Not even big enough for most adults. A place to deliver food, most likely.

And a place to deliver a small rescuer. The tunnel hole was

barely big enough for Silver to squeeze through, but once she was in the tank, Kirja helped her bob up to the surface.

"How did you swim in there?" Sagittaria said. She had fallen for it. "Get out!" The dragon racer furiously worked the puzzle on the lock, and the door clicked open.

Brajon sat on Hiyyan's back, waiting for the right moment. "Go, Kirja!" he yelled.

Kirja grabbed the back of Silver's riding suit in her teeth and shot out of the cage. Hiyyan and Luap joined forces, shoving Sagittaria and her Dwakka into the cage. Ferdi slammed the door behind them and secured the lock.

Water dripped off Silver as she sat on Kirja's back. She watched Sagittaria Wonder pound on the holding tank, her angry screams muffled by the thick glass. The dragon racer was too big to escape through the tunnel.

"I'm sorry," Silver said. She meant it. Sagittaria wasn't just the cold standoffish woman Silver had first met in Jaspaton, nor the loyal servant of the queen, nor a fellow racer. She was all of that, including Silver's hero.

But she was an ugly kind of champion, someone who'd let her drive consume her. Silver would never let glory change her or destroy what she loved. She thought back to Jaspaton, to her father. She had things to mend.

"If you had run, I would have fought for your freedom," Sagittaria said. "Now?" The great water dragon racer shrugged. "Good luck, little fox. You'll need it."

"Shc doesn't need luck. She has us," Brajon called out.

Silver grinned and turned toward her friends. For the first time, Brajon looked somewhat comfortable holding on to Hiyyan's mane. Mele sat astride Luap; Hoonazoor had collected Ferdi; and Kirja and Hiyyan were nuzzling each other affectionately.

"Mele," Silver said. "How do we get out of here? There are hundreds of guards at the palace."

"We can go upriver to the well openings. You can fly home from there."

Silver started. "Aren't you coming with us?"

"My place is here, near Luap." Mele shook her head. "I won't leave her, and I won't steal her. I'm not a criminal."

"Like me?" Silver pressed her palm against Hiyyan's neck. The bond they shared was greater than some human-made law.

"We have to hurry," Brajon said. "Look!"

He pointed to the opening that led back to the palace. Shadows flitted about in the river. More water dragons. Coming for them.

"That's my cue to head back," Ferdi said. "Unlike Mele, I don't have a choice over whether to stay or go. But I promise I'll delay them as much as I can. And I won't tell them where you've gone. When you hear a story someday about how Prince Ferdi tried to capture the traitor Silver Batal, know that I had to lie about my involvement. Think of me instead as the one who arranged for dozens of dancing men in water dragon masks to infiltrate the Winners' Audience. That's the me I like best."

Silver reached a hand out to him. "Thank you, Ferdi," she said, but the words didn't feel enough for everything he'd done. The island prince nodded and flashed her one last smile before turning back the way they'd all come.

"Mele, let's go," Silver said firmly.

"But my Shorsa can't fly. How—"

"Leave that to me," Silver said. "Now come on!"

The three water dragons and their riders fled against the river current. They swam for an hour, at least, glancing over their shoulders regularly. The river caves were dark, except when they passed a well. Then, a weak light pricked the blackness. Still, they didn't stop. They passed more than a dozen wells before they felt safe enough to venture toward the surface.

"Try this one," Mele said as they came upon an opening in a sidewall of the river cave. Through it, a small stream poured into the main cave, joining the river on its way to the royal city.

"I'll make sure it's clear," Brajon said.

He got off Hiyyan and crept to the opening, then disappeared. Silver held her breath. It was possible the royal guards had been sent to the orchards to hunt them down. She strained to hear something. A yell, signs of a struggle. But then Brajon popped his head back into the cave and grinned.

"It's clear."

Silver released her breath. The water dragons pushed forward, out of the opening, and they were greeted by the night's friendly moon and a sky freckled with stars.

FIFTY

Silver tightened one last knot on Kirja's wing joint. "Does this hurt?" she asked the old water dragon.

Kirja moved her wing in a slow circle, then grunted softly. Silver glanced at Mele. They all hurt, at least a little bit. Brajon had popped Silver's dislocated shoulder back into place, but she was still nursing her sliced arm, plus numerous cuts, bumps, and bruises.

Still, they were alive. And they had Kirja.

"Let's give it a try, then," Silver said.

Mele looked at the hammock skeptically. "Are you sure it's going to hold?"

"Nebekker taught me this scale weave," Silver said proudly. "And this racing suit fabric is strong. As long as Luap doesn't fall out, it'll work. I promise."

Silver had made many promises on her journey, and they each still meant something to her. Once they'd reached the Jaspaton oasis and returned Kirja to Nebekker, she'd have made good on all of them, too.

"I wish we had time to test it," Silver said, "but Sagittaria will be sending guards to Jaspaton as we speak. We have to get there before they do. Climb on."

Despite her confident words, she chewed her lip as she watched Luap slither into the wool hammock. The Shorsa was one of the smallest breeds she knew of, but Luap was still several heads taller than Silver and many, many pounds heavier. As Silver climbed on Hiyyan's back and looked over at Brajon and Mele on Kirja's back, she pushed doubt away.

With her hands curled around Hiyyan's mane and the stars winking at her as if they shared a secret, Silver merged her thoughts with Hiyyan's. *Let's fly.*

The earth fell away as they joined the night sky. Wind rushed through Silver's short waves. She closed her eyes, the smell of the vast desert overwhelming her until her throat was choked with tears. She was finally going home.

Between them, Luap was indeed well supported by the hammock. Hiyyan and Kirja took turns beating their wings in the space between, so that they wouldn't hit each other. Silver could almost reach out to touch Brajon and Mele.

"How did it feel to win today, cousin?" Brajon asked. "We haven't had time to celebrate."

"You won with confidence," Mele said before Silver could reply. "You both looked like champions out there. Left poor Prince Ferdi and Hoonazoor in the dust."

"Thank you, Mele." Silver felt her cheeks go pink. "Did you watch all the races?"

Mele shook her head. "As many as I could. My way of saying good-bye. I wasn't planning on meeting back up with you." She shrugged. "Then again, I wasn't planning on ever leaving Calidia on the back of an Aquinder, with Luap beside me. It's strange wondering what will come next."

Silver understood Mele's words keenly.

"I don't know what's going to happen next, either," Silver admitted. "I hope Nebekker has a plan."

Silver took stock of their injuries. Kirja had a battered wing, and a lump was growing on Brajon's forehead. Hiyyan's neck still oozed shiny blood and, for the first time, Silver noticed a strange discoloration in his wing, right where the cave beast had ripped a tear. He hadn't complained. He hadn't complained about his injuries, but she felt whispers of his pain.

Brajon gave her his big, lopsided grin. "I'm really proud of you. You're a natural. Destined for this life."

Silver touched her water dragon burn. Destiny. And dreams. Two things that had carried her this far. But how long could they last, when Sagittaria Wonder and the queen and all the unimaginable forces at their fingertips were after her and Hiyyan and Kirja? Where would she go? Was there anywhere in the entire vast desert she could hide? Nebekker had tried to hide, and Sagittaria had flushed her out like a desert hawk seeking prey.

A face flashed in Silver's mind. An island boy who had turned out to be a prince. He had helped them once. Perhaps there was a place for them somewhere in the Island Nations.

"You've changed," Brajon said to her.

Silver knew it was true. She'd grown stronger and more graceful. Hiyyan had changed, too. He was bigger than Kirja, and still growing. His awkward baby-dragon flopping had grown into a gracefulness of his own. But there was still so much more for them to learn. Silver wanted to know the limits of her communication with her Aquinder. She wanted them to practice racing and flying. And to explore the world together.

First, she had to figure out how to make the world accept Aquinder.

"Look!" Brajon pointed to a spot in the distance.

Silver squinted. Far ahead, a vertical light challenged the luster of the stars.

Home.

"That's Jaspaton," Brajon told Mele. "Where we're from."

Mele, her arms securely around Brajon's waist, craned her neck. "It's so tall. Taller than Calidia. I didn't know there was a city bigger than that in the desert."

"It's not bigger. It's much smaller," Silver said. "It's just carved into the side of a cliff, so all its residents can look out over the desert and marvel at its beauty." A pang of homesickness stabbed her in the chest.

As they got closer, she could make out the different levels of homes and shops. She could see the lanterns at the stairs, lit for those moving up and down the city. She could see the Jaspatonian flags fluttering from the politicians' homes at the very top of the cliff.

She'd missed Jaspaton so much; she could hardly wait to step foot in her home city.

But first, they had to visit Nebekker.

It was as though the old woman, hiding far underground, were a beacon. When they got close to the oasis, Kirja became frantic. She roared into the night, her tail swishing back and forth mightily.

"Kirja," Silver said, trying to soothe her. "We're almost there." She pointed down. "The oasis."

Landing with a flustered Kirja, and Luap in a hammock,

was awkward. Once they hit the ground, Kirja tugged at the hammock on her side, desperate to run to Nebekker. She pulled so hard that she tipped Brajon and Mele off. They tumbled to the sand, bouncing on top of each other.

"Ow, just what I needed." Brajon sat up and rubbed his forehead. "It already feels like the inside of a mine in my brain. Hammers and all."

"I always figured you had rocks for brains," Silver said. "But maybe they're really jewels."

"Ha ha," Brajon mumbled.

Silver slid smoothly to the desert floor. She smiled at the familiar feeling of her boots sinking into the sand. She was home.

Mele helped Silver untie the hammock. The instant Kirja was free, she dashed into the dark and disappeared from sight with a mighty splash. Silver smiled, thinking about the water dragon's reunion with Nebekker. Both old creatures would be so happy.

"You can enter the river caves through the oasis lake with Luap," Silver told Mele. "Brajon, do you want to ride in with me, or walk through the cave entrance?"

Brajon fiddled with the hem of his tunic. "Actually, I'm going to go home."

Silver stared at him in shock. "I thought we were going to stick together! You're just going to go back *there* after all we've been through?"

"*There* is where I belong, cousin. I like Jaspaton. I like my life there. I belong. Flying and racing on the seas . . . that's not meant for me."

"But you're a hero now! I don't know what I would've done

without you, and I don't know if I can do whatever comes next without you, either." Silver swallowed. "I don't have that many favorite cousins, you know."

Tears filled her eyes. *You're not just my cousin. You're my best friend,* she wanted to say. But she knew if she opened her mouth, she would sob.

"I know. You're my best friend, too." Brajon smiled. Not his usual big, joking grin, but something softer. "I know I wasn't the nicest to Hiyyan at first. He always represented the beginning of something new for you. And the end of our old life together in Jaspaton—like when I used to call up to you from two streets below and you'd race down to eat my mother's feasts. That's been hard for me. But I will always watch you from afar. I will always ask traders for news of your victories. And when you're more famous than Sagittaria Wonder, I hope you'll come back to our little desert city and say hello sometimes. Don't get too big for us, all right?"

"I won't," Silver said, smiling through her tears. She never would. Jaspaton would always be the most beautiful place in the world to her. And her family would always hold her heart.

"I do have one more favor to ask," Brajon said. "Uh, it's kind of a long walk home, and I'm pretty tired. Do you think Hiyyan would give me one last ride?"

Silver laughed. She looked at her Aquinder and silently communicated with him. Hiyyan walked to Brajon, nuzzled his hair with his snout as if to say, *It's okay. I know you love me even though you're a ridiculous desert beetle,* and lowered himself so Brajon could climb on.

When Brajon was seated on the water dragon's back, he waved at his cousin. "Try to stay out of trouble, if you even can."

Then, he did flash that teasing Brajon grin. Hiyyan lifted off, favoring his healthy wing, and they disappeared into the night sky.

Silver sighed. Her heart ached, and so did her body. But there was still an annoying voice in the back of her mind that said she didn't have a lot of time to nurse her wounds or her heart. Sagittaria Wonder would be coming for Hiyyan.

And Silver was a criminal.

Fifty-One

Silver walked past the palm trees to the hidden cave entrance next to the lake as Mele and Luap dove into the oasis pool. She picked carefully down the wet path, descending until she turned the last corner and the cavern opened before her. Luap was dabbling in the river, Mele still on her back.

Kirja lay sprawled on the riverbank, her head in Nebekker's lap.

The old woman was tiny and frail. Hardly more than bones. Her eyes were closed, and she looked so much older and more worn than when Silver had last seen her.

But when Silver nudged a pebble and sent it rolling into the river, the old woman opened her eyes.

"You've returned. And you brought me my Kirja." Nebekker's voice was small. Hardly even a whisper.

"I promised I would," Silver said. "I keep my promises. But I was worried I'd been too selfish. That I'd—"

"Taken too long? Lost Kirja?" Nebekker nodded and closed her eyes again.

Silver nodded. "I'm worried about Kirja and Hiyyan, too. They have so many wounds."

"Not to worry. I have a dragon heartstone, assuming you haven't lost it."

"A *what?*"

"My pendant," Nebekker said.

"It's right here." Silver pulled out the jewelry. "What does that mean . . . *heartstone*? How does—"

A sound behind Silver made her stomach coil. She whipped around to look into the darkness. *Sagittaria Wonder?*

"Hello?"

No. That was not the voice of the legendary dragon racer. That was . . .

"Mother!" Silver's beautiful mother stepped into the light, dashing away all thoughts of Nebekker's pendant. When Sersha Batal saw Silver, she dropped the baskets she was carrying. Silver launched herself at her mother, throwing her arms around Sersha's neck. She hadn't realized just how much she'd ached for her mother until she saw her standing there. It felt like a missing piece of Silver had fallen back into place.

"My girl," Silver's mother said into her daughter's hair. "You're home."

Silver pulled away from the hug and helped her mother carry the baskets down to Nebekker.

"You found my letter," Silver said.

"I found it," Sersha said. "And I've experienced every possible emotion since I read it. Anger, worry, fear, pain, and even pride."

Silver wiped her eyes with the back of her hand.

"I've come down here twice," Sersha said. "To bring supplies and get news about you. But there hasn't been any news.

Until now." Her eyes shone with unshed tears. "You're finally back. Safe."

"Your mother's very trustworthy," Nebekker said. "I've known that for a very long time."

"How?" Silver said.

Her mother shrugged. "When Nebekker arrived in Jaspaton, she was an outcast. A foreigner," Sersha said. "Someone who didn't have family. She wouldn't even tell us where she'd come from. People said she was a spy from the Island Nations. Said she didn't belong here. I didn't believe them. So your aunt Yidla and I befriended her. Nebekker was cold, but after a time—many years, in fact—she began to thaw out. She told me about her life as a girl. About Kirja. I promised her that she would find safety here. I promised I would help take care of her."

"Nebekker, why didn't you tell me?" Silver said.

She thought about what Arkilah had said, her claim that Nebekker had left her to die in a frozen wasteland. Was it possible Arkilah had been telling the truth?

"I'm sure there are many stories she hasn't told you," Sersha said. "It took many years before she'd tell me what I now know . . . and I'm sure that's not all of it."

She put her hands on her daughter's shoulders. "I thought I'd be able to send you to Calidia someday, convince your father to let you go, so you could train to race dragons. It is a powerful thing to see such strong dreams in one's child.

"But then Sagittaria Wonder came, and she wasn't the person we thought she would be. Not only that, but a special thing happened to you."

"Hiyyan," Silver said.

"Yes. Oh, and this must be Kirja. I've heard so much."

Sersha hung back, not sure how to approach the water dragon. All the marvels of seeing an Aquinder for the first time played across her face.

"We can't stay long," Silver said. She quickly told Nebekker and her mother what had happened in Calidia, leaving out any unimportant parts . . . like the fact she had used an illegal metal. When she got to the end, she tucked her short hair behind her ears. "So, you see, we can't stay here. We have to hide until we figure out what to do next."

"No, Silver. You'll stay," Sersha said. "We'll figure something out."

"Sagittaria knows this oasis is here," Silver said. "And there isn't anywhere else to hide in Jaspaton. But I'm hoping Nebekker and I can work it all out quickly. I made a friend who isn't from the desert, and he might be able to help. Laws can be changed."

Sersha was silent for a long time, then she nodded once. There was a muffled splash in the distance. A few seconds later, Hiyyan dropped into the river and swam straight for Silver.

Silver smiled. "This is Hiyyan, my Aquinder."

Sersha Batal went to the water dragon and put her face right up to his. "I expect you to take care of my girl," she said very seriously. "And to be back very quickly. I will be waiting for word, and I expect that word to come often." Hiyyan licked Silver's mother, then let his tongue loll out the side of his mouth in a goofy grin.

Sersha turned to Nebekker. "When the time is right," she told the old woman, "I'll be ready to rally our politicians."

Silver threw herself into her mother's arms again, pulling away only when she heard Mele joining them on the riverbank.

"And this is Mele. We couldn't have rescued Kirja without her." As she and Mele began repacking their bags with fresh supplies, Silver told Nebekker and her mother about how Mele had helped her and Brajon in Calidia.

"Where will we go?" Mele asked, her cheeks turning pink as Silver showered her with praise.

Nebekker shakily got to her feet. She was growing stronger by the moment. She nodded in the opposite direction from the oasis lake. "Upriver. Past Jaspaton and into the mountains. There are places up there to hide. Winter will set in soon, and the passes will be unreachable by outsiders. Most humans would be trapped, but we have these two overgrown birds to keep us mobile. It's the safest option. At least until we can give our Aquinder another safe option."

Silver's eyes sparkled. First, the mountains, then a whole world to explore. Someday, she and Hiyyan would have all the freedom they'd ever craved. A whole new life for her and her water dragon.

She was ready to race toward that adventure.

THE END